CHILL WATERS

After her failed marriage, Rachael Warren retreats to the old beachhouse in Jenny's Cove, where as a young girl she lived with her grandmother. It is the one place where she had always felt safe and loved. But now, all these years later, there is no comfort to be had in Jenny's Cove. Instead of the haven she so desperately seeks, Rachael becomes a target for a vicious predator whose own dark and twisted past forms a deadly bond between them — and sets her on a collision course with a crazed killer.

Books by Joan Hall Hovey
Published by The House of Ulverscroft:

LISTEN TO THE SHADOWS
NOWHERE TO HIDE

As well as penning suspense novels, Joan Hall Hovey's articles and short stories have appeared in such diverse publications as *The Reader*, *Atlantic Advocate*, *The Toronto Star*, *Mystery Scene*, *True Confessions*, *Home Life magazine*, *Seek* and various other magazines and newspapers. Her short story, *Dark Reunion* was selected for the Anthology, *Investigating Women*.

Visit Joan at her web site:

http://www.joanhallhovey.com

JOAN HALL HOVEY

CHILL WATERS

Complete and Unabridged

ULVERSCROFT
Leicester

First published in 2003 in the
United States of America

First Large Print Edition
published 2004

The moral right of the author has been asserted

Names, characters and incidents depicted in this
book are products of the author's imagination or are
used fictitiously. Any resemblance to actual events,
locales, organizations, or persons, living or dead,
.is entirely coincidental and beyond the intent
of the author or the publisher.

British Library CIP Data

Hovey, Joan Hall
    Chill waters.—Large print ed.—
    Ulverscroft large print series: suspense
    1. Suspense fiction
    2. Large type books
    I. Title
    823.9′14 [F]

    ISBN 1–84395–508–3

Published by
F. A. Thorpe (Publishing)
Anstey, Leicestershire

Set by Words & Graphics Ltd.
Anstey, Leicestershire
Printed and bound in Great Britain by
T. J. International Ltd., Padstow, Cornwall

This book is printed on acid-free paper

For Marsha Zed
With Love

It's like a lion at the door;
And when the door begins to crack,
It's like a stick across your back;
And when your back begins to smart,
It's like a penknife in your heart;
And when your heart begins to bleed
You're dead, and dead, and dead, indeed.

Anonymous; Nursery Rhyme

1

He stood near the ancient gnarled apple tree, which for years now had produced only sour wizened apples, waiting for her. The hot thick air hummed with the chirping of crickets. Behind him, an occasional fat June bug bumped against the screen door, drawn by the night-light. Now and then a car passed by, seeming only to emphasize his sense of aloneness. Not much traffic on Elder Avenue since they built the thruway.

Three houses down, Nealey's old black lab set to barking excitedly at something — a raccoon scavenging in a garbage can most likely, but it could just as well be shadows. The mutt had a game leg and was as deaf as his mother's turquoise plastic crucifix that hung on the wall above the TV. The old man oughta have him done away with, put the damn thing out of its misery. Maybe I'll do it for him one of these days, he thought, a grin playing at one corner of his cruel mouth. As he retrieved the pack of cigarettes from his jacket pocket, he heard Nealey's door open, heard the old man's low, gravelly voice call the dog inside.

He gazed up at the starry sky, grin fading as he envisioned Marie and that hotshot kid in the fruity white blazer slow dancing under these very stars. Bodies molded together, the kid's hands moving over her, groping . . . his breath hot in her ear . . .

With a muttered curse, he shook his head as if to banish the image, checked an impulse to crush the pack of cigarettes in his hand. Instead, he struck a match against the tree, but his hand was unsteady and it took a few tries before he managed to get it lit. Leaning his back against the tree he closed his eyes. The rough bark of the tree stabbed like jagged stone through his thin nylon jacket. He sucked smoke into his lungs, exhaled slowly, trying to calm himself.

He wasn't usually a heavy smoker, but four hours later, when he finally heard the car drive up, a small mound of butts had accumulated beside him on the ground. With slow deliberation, he mashed this latest one out too, and rose to his feet. Although stiff from sitting, at the same time a power born of rage surged through his veins like electricity.

Music drifted through the open car window — a soppy Manilow ballad about a girl named Mandy. Above the music, her laugh floated to him, high and lilting as wind chimes. Mocking him. The flirtatious note in her laugh made his throat tighten, his hands curl into fists at his sides. But it was the maddeningly long silence that followed, while the music went on playing, that made him want to fly at them, yank them both out of the car and beat that scummy kid with her until he had to crawl home through his own blood. He wanted to do it. He saw himself doing it.

It took all his will to remain where he was.

At last she got out of the car. He could see the pale flare of her skirt through the leaves.

'Night, Ricky. I had a really nice time.'

'Yeah, me too. Okay if I call you tomorrow?'

'Sure.'

'You wanna go to a movie? *Christine* is playing at the Capital.'

'Sounds great.'

The car door closed with a solid *thunk*. The kid's old man was a dentist; the car was a graduation present.

As Marie turned away and started up the path toward him, the kid gunned the motor and drove off, taillights glowing like twin rockets, swiftly disappearing into the night.

Now the only sounds were the crickets and the soft click of her shoes on the cement walk. Yet she looked to be almost floating toward him, her white, strapless dress blue in the moonlight.

When she left the house tonight, her black glossy hair had been swept up into a satiny swirl, a few wispy curls trailing down past her ears, now it was messed up. The muscle in his jaw ticked as he moved deeper into the shadows.

Her pearl drop earrings swayed lightly above her bare shoulders as she walked. He knew how smooth those shoulders would feel beneath his hands because he'd touched them before. He had touched her. Had tasted the warm, throbbing hollow of her traitorous throat, crushed her mouth beneath his own, sometimes to silence her crying. Even now, he could taste her salty tears on his tongue.

As she drew nearer to where he stood in the clot of darkness, she touched her fingertips to her mouth, a small secret smile on her lips like the goddamn Mona Lisa. Face all soft and dreamy — all of it for someone else — never for him.

He waited until she was directly parallel to him then stepped out of the shadows. He enjoyed hearing her gasp of shock, in seeing her hand leap to her breast in fright, the smile vanish as she stumbled on the walkway, nearly falling.

'Damn you! You scared me half to death.

What's wrong with you? Why are you always sneaking around? Always watching me. Can't I have one normal — '

His hand clamped hard and sudden over her mouth, cutting off her words. It made him feel good to see those lovely eyes widen with shock, then fear. Fear that turned swiftly to terror, then to pleading. But it was too late for that. Too late. The beast had risen up in him.

'It's midnight, Cinderella,' he whispered.

2

It was past noon and Rachael had to admit to herself that she was lost. She'd either missed the road leading down to Jenny's Cove or hadn't come to it yet.

Her shoulders ached with tension and she was sweating in the heavy bulky sweater. Chilly when she left this morning, the day now hung around her like a steam bath. The eight-year-old Cavalier, among its other problems, had no air-conditioning. Resentment stabbed her as she pictured Greg's red Mustang in the drive. *No, that's Greg's car; I'd rather have heatstroke.* Raking damp hair from the nape of her neck, tugging at the prickly wool sweater glued to her skin, it seemed she just might.

She considered stopping somewhere and changing into a cotton blouse, but everything was packed up, either in the bags on the back seat, or in boxes in the trunk. Anyway, Jenny's Cove had to be somewhere around here, didn't it? It couldn't just have disappeared into thin air.

'Happy birthday, Rachael,' she said aloud. 'Maybe you'll spend your forty-fifth year trying to find out where the hell you are.' The irony was not lost on her.

She massaged tired, burning eyes with the heel of her hand. Didn't get much sleep last night. She'd lain awake listening for Greg's car in the drive. Habit. The green numbers on the clock glowed 3:12 when she finally heard it. He came upstairs, walked past their door and went into Jeff's old room where he'd been sleeping for the past three weeks. Except there was a difference now — now that she knew. A defiant guilt maybe.

A silo sprang up in her rearview mirror and she eased up on the gas. Further on, she passed an old farmhouse with a scattering of outbuildings. Brown and white Guernsey cows languished in a field, some stood still as statues beneath a spreading elm tree, trying to find relief from the heat.

A small boy in overalls and a striped tee shirt waved to her as she drove past, the thumb of his free hand propped in his mouth. She thought of stopping to warn him of inherent dangers, but a semi bellowed impatiently behind her, then roared passed, a blast of wind buffeting her car.

Glancing in her rearview mirror, she was relieved to see a woman with a baby in her arms, hurrying down the driveway toward the little boy.

7

Rachael refocused her attention on the vaguely familiar landscape, sure that once this had been all farmland — fields stretching like patchwork quilts. Barns and silos. Now it wasn't so different from the suburbia she had left behind, with its streets winding up through fashionable developments.

As she drove on, her thoughts drifted back to Greg, the needle slipping easily into the raw groove of her soul, to the very moment when life as she'd known it, had stopped. And that was the reason she was on this road, trying to find a house she hadn't seen — made no effort to see — since she was sixteen years old.

Three weeks ago Tuesday, he'd called to say that he'd be working late again. Dinner was on the table; she'd cooked all his favorites. Swallowing her hurt, she snuffed the candles, cleared the food away. No use complaining. It only made him angry and defensive. She told herself she needed to be more understanding. Greg was under a lot of pressure with the new job. He wasn't used to being tied to a desk. He liked being on the road.

She would surprise him; take him out to dinner — someplace dimly lit, soft music playing in the background. It had been a while since they'd enjoyed a romantic evening together. Been a while since there'd been anything between them but the arguments and the silences.

Filled with new resolve, wearing her slate-blue dress and matching shoes, she dabbed Chanel No. 5 behind her ears and drove downtown to Greg's office building.

She had the car door open, had stepped one blue-shoed foot onto the sunny pavement when she saw them coming out of the building. She'd never set eyes on Administrative Assistant Lisa Richard, part of the package that came with Greg's new title of Sales Manager, but she knew. Rachael took in the model slim figure in the cream-colored suit, the honey-blonde hair that swayed seductively as the two descended the stone steps together. Greg's hand was possessively at her waist, Lisa smiling up at him.

Rachael didn't realize that she too was smiling, until she felt it set like a fool's mask on her face. Feeling suddenly old and ridiculous in the matching dress and shoes, she retreated inside the car and sped off, panicked that they would see her shame at catching them.

Only a few nights before, she'd summoned the courage to ask him if there was someone else. He denied it, told her she was *crazy*, that she needed to see a shrink. Then he slammed out of the house, an excuse, she knew now, to run to Lisa.

A horn blared, jarring Rachael back to the present. A yellow jeep filled with teenagers, hair flying in the wind, roared past.

Keep your mind on your driving, Rachael.

Up ahead, a store with a gas pump out front, and a Coca-Cola sign above the door lured her with the promise of a cold drink and a washroom. She flipped on her left signal light, waited as a truckload of precariously swaying logs rumbled past, then pulled off the road into the small parking lot, gravel crunching under her wheels.

After a visit to the washroom, she entered the store. The bell above the door tinkled airily, evoking a memory of penny candy and black licorice. Inside, it was cool and smelled faintly of apples.

The tall woman behind the counter made a final swipe at the display case then set the rag aside. With her Germanic features, iron-grey hair cut in a blunt style, ending just below her ears, she reminded Rachael of some aging movie star — Garbo, perhaps. Or Dietrich.

Classical music floated from the small radio on the counter. 'May I help you?'

'I hope so.' Rachael's own effort at a smile made her feel as if her facial muscles had atrophied. But it was a relief to stretch her limbs, to luxuriate in the pleasant coolness of the shop. 'I seem to be lost. I've been trying to find Bay Road without much success. It leads — or at least it used to lead — down to Jenny's Cove. I visited there as a girl. It — it all looks so different now.'

The woman nodded in silent agreement. 'Did you come through St. Clair?'

'Yes.'

'Gracious old town, isn't it? Settled by Loyalists in the late 1700's, you know. Now, of course, it's a popular tourist spot. Seems every year a new craft shop or art gallery opens up. Pretty in summer, with all the boats dotting the bay.'

'Yes,' Rachael said, not really up to discussion about the merits of tourism in St. Clair, or lack thereof.

'Plenty of budding photographers about. The older Gothic style homes with their widow's walks are a great subject of interest. Many a wife would stand on a widow's walk hoping to catch a glimpse of her husband's ship on the horizon. Of course you know all this if you visited here as a girl. Can I offer you a cold drink?' she asked, coming out from behind the counter, her skirt shifting about her ankles as she moved. 'You look a bit pale, my dear, if you don't mind my saying so. It is humid, to be sure.' Getting a lime-colored fruit drink from the cooler, she unscrewed the top, dropped in a straw, and handed it to Rachael. 'Have you been on the road long?'

'A while,' she replied noncommittally. 'How much do I owe . . . ?'

She raised her hand in protest. 'My treat.' The firmness in her warm, deep voice left no room for argument. 'Not much business now. It's nice to have someone drop in, even if it *is* just to ask directions.'

As Rachael gratefully sipped the cold, tangy drink, the woman turned her gaze to the storefront window. 'It has indeed changed,' she said wistfully. When she turned back to Rachael there was a knowing sympathetic smile on her lips. 'People and places do have a way of doing that, don't they?'

On the surface, an innocent enough remark, Rachael supposed, the sort of thing people said. But it unnerved her, just the same. As did those intense blue eyes that seemed to see into her very soul. *Something of the Gypsy about her. Something ageless.*

'But back to those directions. Bay Road is right where it always was. You passed it about a quarter of a mile back. The Reverend Willie Long's house used to be on that corner, but both he and it are long gone now. Replaced by a welding shop. I don't mean Willie was replaced by a welding shop,' she chuckled, 'only the house.'

Just then a Siamese cat slinked around a partly open door of a back room, blinked sleepily at Rachael out of eyes as blue as its mistress's. Then it sat on its haunches, looking remarkably like a sculpture of itself and studied her.

'What a beautiful cat,' Rachael said. She'd always had an affinity with animals, but made no move to pet this one, who was presently regarding her with haughty eyes.

'That's Cleopatra. Cleo for short. Doesn't keep her humble, though.' She smiled indulgently at Cleo then turned her attention on Rachael. 'You know,' she frowned, 'you remind me of someone. I can't think who. You did say you lived here as a girl?' As the last word trailed off, Rachael saw a shadow of fear cross the woman's features, her smile waver.

'Is something wrong?' Rachael asked.

'No. It's — nothing.'

She's lying. She looks as if she just saw a ghost. Except that it's me she's looking at. 'Only visited,' Rachael said in answer to her question, suddenly anxious to be on her way, beyond the scrutiny of those piercing blue eyes. But the woman had been kind; she owed her courtesy. 'I spent a few summers at Jenny's Cove with my grandmother,' she offered. 'It was a long time ago.' Another lifetime, she thought. 'Not so surprising that it would look different. I don't know what I expected.' Her laugh sounded hollow in her own ears.

Placing the empty bottle in the crate on the scrubbed-wood floor, Rachael started for the door.

In a move that seemed almost supernatural, the storekeeper was suddenly in front of her, holding the door for her. The scent of wild roses cut through the apple smell.

Rachael moved past the woman, down the steps. 'I do remember now seeing that welding shop on the corner,' she said over her shoulder. 'Thank you again.'

'I knew some of the people around here back then,' the woman said after her. Rachael had no choice but to turn around. The storekeeper looked as if she was trying to work out some complex problem in her mind, but the fear still lingered in her eyes. 'I'm Iris Brandt, by the way.'

Rachael knew she was expected to respond with her own name. When she didn't, the woman added in an ominous tone, 'Most of the summer people are gone now.'

3

Backtracking to the welding shop, a squat structure with dark green corrugated siding, Rachael turned onto Bay Road.

Just past the shop were a tarpaper shack, a couple of junk cars and a blue half-ton in the yard. The mailbox was nailed to a post at the end of the drive, the name N. *Prichard* printed on the side in red childlike letters.

The dusty, white Cavalier bumped along the narrow tree-lined road, groaning with the need of new shocks, forcing Rachael to slow down.

Fall was still more than a week away, but already the leaves were turning color. As a child, she used to imagine tiny elves skipping down this road with pots of paint, brushing the leaves with scarlets and golds. She'd even made up a poem about it. Not much she didn't pay poetic tribute to back then.

The road was narrower than she remembered, trees hemming her in, forming a lacy canopy overhead, moving her in and out of shadow. The salty mist of the ocean wafted through the open window.

Gradually, the trees on her right thinned,

revealing shimmering patches of blue, stirring old memories, buried emotions.

She passed a summerhouse, remembered the children — a boy and girl — who lived there one summer. Towheads both, they would wave to her as she flew past the house on her bicycle. Now the windows were boarded over, the porch leaning drunkenly, overgrown with weeds and shrubbery. She passed a few more cabins and cottages along the stretch of road, a couple recalled, most not.

At last the bay burst into full view. The rocky shore sprawled past, broken here and there by smooth sandy beaches. Overwhelmed with conflicting emotions, Rachael pulled to the side of the road, switched off the engine and got out.

She walked to the grassy bank and gazed out at mossy islands rising out of the bay like the backs of grey whales. On the farthest island, the pulsing light from the lighthouse guided the safe passage of sailors as it had done for more than a hundred years.

Enduring. Steadfast. Unlike her marriage. Her life. She fought back a fresh welling of tears, angry with herself. Surprised there were any tears left.

Once, she'd been downtown and looked up to see a man staring at her and realized the tears were streaming down her face. She couldn't seem to stop them. Another time, she actually started running as if she might outrun the pain. *Well, enough of that. Enough.*

She turned away and went back to the car.

She was about to open the door when suddenly the hairs on the back of her neck prickled. As if someone were watching her. She looked around.

But she saw no one.

4

The house appeared before her so suddenly that she gasped, the sight of it as startling as turning a corner and coming face to face with someone you'd believed long dead. As if on some level she had not expected it to be there at all — its existence only in her memory, and in some faded, yellowing snapshots.

But there it was — tall windows overlooking the bay, small open front porch where she had so often sat reading, or scribbling in her notebook.

As the road had seemed narrower, so the house appeared smaller, the way places often do when you revisit them years later. Once white shingles were weathered now, but nothing a coat of paint wouldn't fix. If it had been in A-1 shape, she wouldn't have gotten it at the price she had.

Rachael parked in the drive. As she made her way up the sloping path to the house, the salty breeze from the bay brushed her face like the hand of an old friend. Gazing wistfully up at the eaves of the house, she smiled to herself, wondering if that old gutter still held any of the rubber balls she'd lost to it over the years. But surely there'd been other children who'd played her solitary game since then. ' ... claimsies, clapsies, rollies, crossies ... ' she recited softly, almost hearing the phantom ball thump against the house.

A house she had bought sight unseen, deciding the instant she saw it up for sale in the paper. She knew a lot could happen to a house in over a quarter of a century, but she also knew that somehow it would be all right. The house had called out to her. Or perhaps she had called out to it.

She'd telephoned Greg at his office. Give me a quarter of what our place is worth, she'd said, and I'll sign it over to you. To his credit, he tried not to show his eagerness in complying, but Greg knew a deal when he heard one. He brought a certified check that same afternoon, and the appropriate papers to sign. She was surprised he'd been able to have them drawn up so quickly.

'You're in no mental state to make major decisions like this,' her friend, Betty, had said, when they had lunch at the mall a few days later. 'That's why insurance people like to negotiate right after a house fire. You can be sure if Allan threw me over for some tramp, I'd take the son-of-bitch for all he was worth.'

Of course, Allan would never betray Betty.

He adored her. Rachael had a bitter, jealous moment, followed by shame. Betty was her friend. She deserved her happiness.

Fitting one of the two keys the real estate woman had given her into the hole she turned the lock. The door creaked open, and Rachael stepped over the threshold into another lifetime.

The shadowy living room smelled dank and musty. Yellowing newspapers, held by bits of crumbling masking tape, hung over the two long windows facing the bay. The one nearest her was askew, letting in a shaft of sunlight to reveal dust motes in the air.

She stood very still, listening. *For what, Rachael? No one is here. No one is coming to greet you.*

Even the room's dim light couldn't disguise the battered furniture, the worn tweed carpeting, or the tired brown couch flush against one wall. Rachael flicked on the light-switch, bathing the room in light.

In the far corner, a fifty's floor lamp stood beside a sagging stuffed chair, its torn, fringed shade tilted at a jaunty angle, like a drunk's hat. Out of habit, she crossed the room and straightened it. She remembered a similar lamp from her childhood.

The brick fireplace took up most of one wall. Above it, on the mantle, a pickle bottle held a faded plastic rose. She ran her fingertips over the mantle's gritty surface. Once, it had been lined with photographs — Rachael in short hair with bangs, a tooth missing from her shy grin. Next to that, a black and white photo of her father in a baseball cap, hefting a bat too heavy for the thin boy he had been. She touched her fingertips to the spot where her parents' wedding picture had been.

Right here. Right in the middle. How young they were. Her mother's face soft and sweet, framed with dark hair, styled in a pageboy. Her father smiling, barely resembling the gray, somber man she remembered.

As Rachael climbed the stairs to the upstairs rooms, a strange sensation came over her — a sense that she was not real, not quite flesh and blood, but merely a ghost returned to haunt old stomping grounds. A haunted creature herself, belonging to neither past nor present.

The oak railing felt smooth and warm beneath her hand. She gripped it hard, until her hand tingled hotly, giving her evidence of her own substance, her own existence.

Her old room was situated across from her grandmother's. A small cozy room. An iron-framed bed much like the one in which she had slept, stood against the wall, beneath the sloped ceiling. Through the small window above the bed she could see the woods and a slice of bay.

She remembered lying in her bed, palms pressed flat against the ceiling, fancying she was holding it up, like Hercules holding up the Heavens. A wonder she hadn't felt claustrophobic with the ceiling crowding in on her like that, but she hadn't. Rather, she'd felt safe and snug under the patchwork quilt, like a small animal curled up in its den, the battery-operated radio playing beside her. How often she had fallen asleep listening to the old radio program, *Music in the Night*.

She still loved the songs from that time: Patti Page's *Old Cape Cod*, Tony Bennett's *Rags to Riches*, Ella Fitzgerald, Sinatra. Greg had no interest in things past, including music. Or a wife, she thought wryly.

Suddenly overcome by exhaustion, Rachael took off her shoes and lay down on the bare mattress. A nubby blue blanket lay folded at the foot of the bed; ignoring its musty smell, she drew it up over her, curled into a fetal position, and was soon asleep.

5

For the first time since the teenager was rushed into St. Clair Hospital, the victim of a brutal assault, her swollen eyelids twitched, as if she were trying to wake up. The nurse taking her pulse felt her own heartbeat quicken in response. She watched for other signs that her young patient just might make it through this horror. The wrist she held in her hand felt cool and fragile as a sparrow's wing.

'Miss Myers? Heather?'

The only answer was in the steady beeping of the monitor beside the bed.

'Heather? Can you hear my voice?'

The girl moaned faintly, her eyes fluttering open, at least as far as was possible, swollen near shut as they were. She peered up at her through mere slits in a face so horribly battered it made Nurse Janet Lewis wince inwardly just to look at her.

As the girl struggled to speak, blood beaded on her lower lip. The nurse gently blotted the wound with a cotton swab from the tray on the night table. *She's trying to tell me something.*

She tracked Heather Myer's gaze to the aqua plastic carafe beside the tray. 'Of course. You're thirsty.'

Pouring water into the glass, she then cupped the back of her patient's head, raised it just enough to allow her to take a few sips through the L-shaped straw.

When she had taken sufficient liquid, the nurse asked, 'Do you know where you are, Heather?'

The girl tried to answer, but nothing came out.

Seeing the panic in her eyes, the nurse said quickly, 'Don't worry. Your voice will return. I'm sure it's a temporary condition brought on by shock. You're going to be fine, Heather. It's just going to take a little time.'

Gently, she lowered the girl's head back on her pillow, smoothed the blanket around her then hurried for the doctor.

6

Iris fished a cigarette from the pack of Benson & Hedges she kept under the counter. Holding it unlit between her long fingers, she looked out the storefront window. In the elongated shadow cast by the Coca-Cola sign, a crow hopped and pecked at something on the ground. Probably a potato chip or a Taco dropped by some child.

As if sensing her watching it, the bird fixed its beady eye on her. A chill passed through Iris. *A crow at the window means death.* Not that she really believed any of those old superstitions.

Barely conscious of the jazzy tune bouncing from her radio, Iris' thoughts returned to yesterday's lone customer. *Unless you counted a three dollar purchase of gas from a teenage boy driving a wheezing Chevy.* She'd seen the woman somewhere before. But where? Though that wasn't the only reason she couldn't seem to get her out of her mind, or even the main reason. What had so unsettled Iris Brandt was the danger she'd sensed around the woman — a cold, malevolent energy. The energy wasn't coming *from* her, though — it accompanied her, like the demon dog from hell.

What was wrong with her today? Dogs . . . crows . . .

But it was not exactly an unfamiliar happening. Iris had gotten feelings about things and people since childhood. Not that she considered herself clairvoyant or psychic, or whatever was the in-term these days. The very notion of second sight, as her mother used to call it, was distasteful to her, right up there with snake charming. She was a simple woman, of German peasant stock, who ran a store during the tourist season, and dabbled in pottery-making whenever time allowed. A practical, no-nonsense person.

Still, she had learned to pay attention to the bad feelings, essentially because there was no way she could ignore them. Sometimes they were so intense they didn't let her sleep or eat. And when she did sleep, she would dream — terrible dreams that followed her into waking. And the feelings would stay with her, boring deeper and deeper inside her skull and her skin, until the awful thing happened.

Just like that time when — no, she wouldn't let herself dwell on that. Though she did often think of Ethel, wondered how she was getting on in Florida. Was George still alive? He'd seemed so feeble that last time

26

she saw him. Not so surprising considering what that boy did to him.

'We interrupt this program to bring you this news bulletin.'

Iris turned the volume up on the radio.

'We have just received a report that seventeen-year-old Heather Myers of St. Clair, was brutally assaulted in Steve's Convenience Store where she was employed part-time. Myers was discovered unconscious in the back room by owner and operator, Steve Poulis, who, following a frantic phone call from the girl's mother, drove back to the store to investigate. The condition of the teenager is listed as serious. Unable to speak, she is unable to describe her attacker. If anyone has any information, please — '

'My God,' Iris whispered, snapping off the radio. That poor, dear child. How terrible this must be for Helen and Bob.

'The devil walks among us,' Iris' grandmother used to say. If she were alive today that would probably be 'The devil runs amok,' or something similar.

Iris dropped the unsmoked cigarette into the deep pocket of her skirt. Retrieving the dust cloth from beneath the counter, she grimly attacked the already spotless display case as if through sheer physical effort she might banish the bad feelings inside her. She feared the savagery inflicted on Heather Myers was only the beginning.

Then it came to her. Now Iris knew who the woman was.

Or at least who she was kin to.

7

The instant Rachael opened her eyes she felt disoriented, confused at the unfamiliar, and at the same time familiar, surroundings. Shouldn't the window be facing her, the cedar chest in front of it? And the walls were too close. Then, like water gushing from a poisoned well, memory flooded her mind and heart.

She looked at her watch — 11:20. But it was daylight. At first she thought her watch must be wrong. But the slant of sunlight into her room told her otherwise.

Whatever, not nearly long enough, she thought, drawing the blanket back up over her head. A minute later, she listlessly threw it back. She had to use the bathroom. A dull pain prodded behind her eyelids. She allowed herself a few seconds longer, watched the sun's rays through the trees create a lacy, moving pattern over the blue blanket. Then, sighing, she slipped out of bed, used the washroom, then went downstairs.

She looked at the newspaper hanging crookedly over the window. She would hang curtains. A simple decision. Yes, she could manage that much.

⋆ ⋆ ⋆

In the kitchen, she rummaged through the crusted mess of cans and bottles under the sink, found a battered kettle, rinsed it under the hot water tap and put on water for tea. An electric range had sensibly replaced the old cast-iron stove.

The tile beneath her feet was bottle green, patterned with black streaks, like roads on a map. Roads to nowhere.

Knotty pine cupboards where no cupboards had been now flanked the small window over the sink. Through the glass she could see the old elm tree she used to climb and swing in as a child. It was taller now, its branches thick and gnarled as arthritic limbs.

How old was she when the man put up a swing for her in that tree? Seven. Yes, she remembered now; she'd been excited about turning eight in September. The seat was painted candy-apple red. She could still feel her small hands clutching those rough ropes, as higher and higher she would go, imagining that at any second she would fly right up into the clouds. When the fear grew too exquisite to bear, she would bring herself back down, heart thudding in her chest long after her sneakered feet had skidded to a stop in the grass.

A million years ago.

Leaving the kettle to boil, Rachael went outside to bring in the boxes from the trunk of her car, which held the few staples she'd brought with her, including teabags, necessary for the barest survival.

The bay stretched calm and blue before her. Birds chirped in the trees. No cars backing out of driveways, no kids calling to one another as they waited for the school bus. So quiet.

The air hung warm and still and heavy. Dark clouds were moving in from across the cove. Rachael unlocked the trunk and the lid groaned open, the sound amplified in the morning quiet. She lifted out one of the boxes.

Back inside, she ferreted the teabags from the box, dropped one into a chipped, blue mug she found in the cupboard. The few dishes she brought from home were in another box. She opened the door to the walk-in pantry and stale moldy air rushed out at her.

A three-legged chair lay on the floor on its side, near a torn window-screen propped against a wall. Half a dozen pickle bottles in varying sizes were lined up on the bottom shelf. No pretty cornflower edged paper here, just the blackened wood. She closed the door, opting to put the few groceries in the kitchen cupboard, although they too needed a good cleaning.

Well, that's your thing isn't it, Susie Homemaker?

A scream ripped the quiet, and she whirled. The damn kettle! The insanely shrieking kettle. She took it off the burner and with a shaky hand poured the bubbling water over her teabag.

Rachael wandered from room to room with her mug of tea, gazing out of windows, moving off again. She went outside, stood on the porch step and surveyed her surroundings.

A blue jay, perched on a nearby tree, scolded her. 'Hello to you too,' she said.

The jay let out a screech and flew off, leaves trembling in its wake.

'Don't take it personally, Rachael,' she said. The instant the words were out, she darted a look to her right, fully expecting to be embarrassed at having been caught talking to herself. But there was no one there. She was quite alone.

Late in the afternoon, she walked down the worn path to the beach, tall grasses whispering against her jean-clad legs as she went. There, she sat down on her favorite rock with its sheered off top, the site of many a well-enjoyed peanut butter and jelly sandwich, and sipped her tea.

The sun was setting, staining the water red and gold. Though she could appreciate the beauty of Jenny's Cove, she was unmoved by it. A part of her wanted to simply walk into the water, keep on walking. But she knew she didn't have the courage. She'd already proven that much to herself. She wanted to live. That's why she was here.

Had she been only fifteen the last summer she spent here? Her grandmother must have been ill even then for she died that following spring. Her father made her go to the funeral; she hadn't wanted to. She remembered barely glancing at the woman in the coffin with her hands still and folded in death. *I was so angry with her for leaving me.*

After high school she went to work at Halston's as a steno. It was where she'd met Greg. Handsome and charming, there wasn't a girl in the office who didn't flush and flutter whenever he stopped by her desk. Maybe it was because she didn't that he'd asked her out. Certainly there were prettier, more interesting girls at Halston's. When two months later he proposed, she accepted without hesitation. 'I want a real wife,

Rachael,' he'd told her. 'I want you there for me when I come home.'

She'd quit her job without complaint or regret. Jeff was born the first year, Susan the next. Life was complete. She wanted nothing more than to be a good wife and mother — the mother she herself had been denied — and was content to hold the ladder while Greg climbed it.

Betty kidded her about being reincarnated from a past era. Women weren't content to keep the home fires burning anymore, she said. They had their own dreams to follow.

But she'd never thought she was missing anything. Oh, there were a few times when Betty popped in, dressed like she'd just stepped out of *Career Woman*, while Rachael herself was up to her elbows in formula and dirty diapers, that resentment stung. But mostly she was grateful to be a stay-at-home mom, to watch her children grow under her guidance, not to have to hand them over to someone else.

At an excited chatter behind her, Rachael turned to see dark shiny eyes observing her from the trunk of a pine. Not waiting for her side of the conversation, the squirrel gave a flick of its red bushy tail, leapt to a higher branch, vanishing among the lush, green needles.

She set her cup beside her on the rock, impulsively took off her Nikes and socks. The feel of sun-warmed sand between her toes stirred something within her — a response from the child she had been.

After rolling up her pant legs, she walked down to the water's edge. As an icy wave broke over her feet Rachael jumped back. Beneath her bare feet, the sand shifted, made snicking sounds as it receded.

Once, she had raced down that hill, eager to challenge the numbing cold of the Atlantic, filled with a sense of her own power. Whatever happened to that girl?

She stayed on the beach until the sun was almost down, the water darkened and distant thunder rumbled in the sky. Then she emptied the cold dregs of her tea into the sand.

Even through the fleece-lined *Save the Whales* sweatshirt, that Susan left behind when she went off to college, Rachael had begun to feel chilly. As she bent to gather up her shoes and socks, a drop of rain slapped the back of her neck, ran under the sweatshirt on insect legs.

It was then that she noticed, about ten yards to her left, footsteps leading out of the water. *Strange, I didn't notice them before.* She followed them to where their edges blurred in the drier sand, disappearing in the tall grasses on the level above her.

Scanning the beach in either direction, she looked for a matching set of prints leading *into* the water, but there were only her own. Though she could hardly boast of tiny feet, the others were much larger, made by someone wearing shoes or boots. A man, she thought, noting that the prints nearest the water, where they were more deeply embedded in the sand, were distinctly patterned in circles and half-moons.

Fat raindrops pelted down, slowly at first, striking her face and arms. Lightning flashed over the water, backlighting swollen black clouds, chasing the mystery of the footprints from her mind, and Rachael raced up the hill. She'd no sooner closed the door behind her than the sky opened, unleashing a torrent of rain that fell in straight, violent sheets.

She'd almost forgotten the late summer storms that visited Jenny's Cove.

★ ★ ★

Like a bad dog with an unsuspecting deer in its sights, he watched her run up to the house. His narrowed eyes tracked her movements until she was inside. Then he lowered the binoculars and grinned.

Soon.

8

The bell above the door of Iris' store chimed. Iris looked up from her book, *Modern Techniques in Pottery Making*, and smiled experiencing the same warm pleasure she always did at the sight of her nephew.

'Peter, how wonderful. What can I get you? Coffee, a cold drink?'

His hair was wet from the rain and Iris noticed for the first time that it was beginning to recede. He'd had such beautiful thick hair as a boy, the color of corn silk. She remembered Heather Myers telling her that the girls at school thought he looked like Harrison Ford. Iris couldn't see it herself. She thought Peter was better looking. But perhaps she was biased. Thoughts of Heather lay heavy on her heart.

'Not a thing, thanks. Just dropped by to see if I couldn't interest my favorite aunt in joining me for dinner. I happen to know Hartley took Kathy in a nice catch of flounder today.'

Kathy was Kathy Burgess, who owned *Kathy's*, a café noted for its good home-cooked food and the fact that it stayed open year round. It was also licensed and Iris could have done with a good shot of whiskey just about then. Reluctantly, she declined the invitation. 'Best offer I've had all day, but I'm going to have to ask for a rain-check. There's something . . . I have to do tonight.'

'Sounds serious.'

'It . . . could be. Make it tomorrow and you've got yourself a date.'

'Well, can't promise the flounder will be as fresh,' he kidded, 'but you're on.' His lighthearted note did not hide his disappointment. She suspected this was one of those nights when going back to an empty apartment held little appeal. Ever since Mary Ellen's death, three years ago, Peter spent most of his time at the school where he taught English. His students had become his purpose in life. Hearing the awful news about Heather couldn't be helping his mood. She'd been one of his favorites. 'I — uh, heard about Heather. Do you know how . . . ?'

'She's in pretty bad shape, Aunt Iris,' he said, with a mix of sadness and anger. 'Only time will tell.' He hunkered down to pat Cleo, who was rubbing against his leg, demanding attention, purring like an old washing machine.

'I wrote a note to Helen,' Iris said. 'It's so hard to know what to say.'

'There are never adequate words for something like this. But I know Helen will appreciate it.'

After Peter left, Iris donned her coat and scarf, scooped Cleo up in her arms and left the store. While fumbling for her keys in her pocket and trying not to lose Cleo, Iris darted out into the rain.

Wet, but safely inside the car, she'd driven only a short distance when Nate Prichard's old pickup rumbled toward them, water splaying from the trucks big tires. Cleo sprang up on her hind legs, front paws propped against the windshield. As the truck roared past, she let out a low, anxious growl.

'I know, Cleo. He's not my favorite person, either.'

★ ★ ★

Across the cove, in the village of Harding, Peter parked his car in a small clearing and made his way to the log cabin. The sound of someone chopping wood traveled to him as he tromped through thick brush, navigating gnarled roots and brambles, fallen branches. The smell of sawdust, pine and rain hung in the air. The rain had let up, but by the look of those clouds, not for long.

Hartley was intently splitting his winter

wood. Not wanting to startle his old friend, Peter called out, 'Hey, Hartley, you're getting a pretty good pile stacked up there.'

Only when Luke let out a short excited bark and bounded over to Peter, did the old man look up. Luke's tail wagged happily and the black and white Collie mix gave him a big doggy grin. Peter scratched behind his ears. 'Hey, Luke, fella.' Luke was getting on in years, but clearly hadn't lost his puppy zest for living.

As Peter came into view, a wide grin broke on Hartley's face. 'Hey, Peter, good to see you, boy. How you gettin' on?'

'I've felt better,' Peter said, speaking louder than his normal volume, knowing Hartley's hearing wasn't what it used to be. Though Hartley'd be too proud to admit it and get himself a hearing aid. 'Glad to see you got your boat back.'

'Yeah, me too.' Hartley spat over his left shoulder into a pile of sawdust. 'It was drifting toward town, ya know, over t'other side.' He was near to shouting, the way folks tended to do when they began to lose their hearing. 'Elton got the call, and motored out after it.' White spokes of hair sprang loose as he pushed the Red Sox cap to the back of his head. 'Good man, Elton Sorrel. Bit of a hot dog, maybe.'

Peter agreed on both counts.

'Goddamn kids, more 'n likely,' Hartley said.

As much as he'd like to have argued the point, Peter wondered if Hartley might not be right. There'd been a rash of criminal activity lately. The week before school opened, vandals climbed in through a basement window, trashed computers, kicked in walls and upturned desks. Walking into the classroom that morning, he'd felt sick, almost as if he'd been personally attacked.

A couple of hard cases had come to mind, but he couldn't let himself believe that any student of his could be capable of such a willful destruction. Then, two Sundays ago someone tossed a firebomb through the post office window. And last night a house on the edge of town was burgled. Thankfully, the owners were away.

And now Heather.

'Heard about that poor Myers' girl,' Hartley said, picking up on his thoughts. 'What kind of sick bastards are running around loose out there anyway? If that poor kid does get her voice back and says who done it, the cops oughta fire a warning shot between his eyes, ask questions later.'

Fingers were already pointing to Tommy Prichard, also a past student of Peter's.

Suspicions not so surprising, perhaps, considering the violent nature of Tommy's old man. Tommy had been dating Heather. But Tommy was nothing like his father; Peter was absolutely sure of that.

'Think I'll pack 'er in for tonight,' Hartley said, giving the axe a final swing, chunking its steel blade into the chopping block. Grimacing, he massaged his left shoulder. Peter remembered Aunt Iris mentioning that Hartley's arthritis was giving him trouble. He was pretty sure Hartley wouldn't have willingly shared that information; sometimes his aunt just knew things.

'Will you come inside and sit a spell, Peter? I'll brew us some coffee. Or maybe you could do with something a mite stronger.' Fishing a red polka-dotted handkerchief from his back pocket, he wiped the sweat from his tanned, creased brow.

'Don't mind if I do, Hartley.'

A half-hour later, as they walked outside together, Hartley said, 'Hear tell some woman from Deering up and bought George and Ethel's old place.'

'That right?'

'Rumor has it.'

'Well, that's good then. The place needs work, but it's too fine a house to be left to the elements and the squirrels.'

The old man nodded as he lifted his gaze to the rolling dark clouds. 'Getting ready for another downpour.' He met Peter's eyes squarely. 'You ever figure Jimmy Ray'll come back here?'

'Dawson?' Peter said, surprised at the question. 'No, why would he? Ethel and George are long gone from here. Anyway, Jimmy's probably cooling his heels in a jail cell somewhere. What made you think of him?'

Hartley shrugged. 'Don't rightly know. Talking about the house, I suppose. Thinkin' of that lady over there alone. Maybe Jimmy Ray doesn't know they moved. It would be like the little slimeball, you know, to come back here. Expect a light in the window. Kick a dog and expect it to lick your fingers.' He patted Luke on the head, as if to reassure the dog that such a thing would never happen to him. Then he looked out at the bay.

A light wind had come up, turning the water choppy.

'Margaret used to like to sit on the porch and look out at the water,' Hartley said, his voice thoughtful with memory, speaking more to himself than to Peter. 'Used to say it was always different. Just like the sunsets — no two ever the same.'

Peter said nothing, sensing no reply was

required or expected. Feeling his presence an intrusion, he headed back to his car, leaving the old man looking out at the bay and thinking about his long departed wife.

He glanced over his shoulder once to see that Luke had settled devotedly at his master's feet, warm golden-brown eyes barely glancing at Peter's retreating form.

9

The house was damp and chill from the rain, so after washing and putting the dishes away, Rachael set about lighting a fire in the fireplace. She was about to put a match to the paper when someone knocked at the front door. *Who could that be? I know no one here.* The paper took and she tossed the match into the flame, went to answer.

She was startled to see the storekeeper standing in the doorway, grey hair blowing about the scarf she wore, and clutching two bags of groceries. Rachael could see the box of Oreos peaking from one of the bags.

'Mrs. Brandt?'

The woman gave a tentative smile. 'I'm flattered you remembered my name. I do hope I'm not intruding, though I'm sure I am. You probably have a million things to do, getting settled in and all. But I promise I won't hold you up. I just wanted to see if — well, I've brought a few things from the store. I thought you might not feel up to cooking right off. And please — call me Iris.'

Just what I needed, Rachael thought ungraciously. The welcome wagon. 'This is very generous of you, Mrs. — Iris. But I couldn't possibly . . . '

'I'll be closing up the store in a few days and some things just won't keep.' Her smile held a small plea. 'Really, you'd be doing me a favor.'

A gust of wind sent the skirt of her long, black coat flapping about her legs like giant bat wings. Behind her, lightning snaked across an angry sky.

'Please, come in,' Rachael said, forcing a smile. 'I was just about to have a bit of supper,' she lied. 'Nothing fancy — soup and a sandwich maybe.'

'I've got the fixings,' Iris said cheerfully, looking relieved. She stepped inside bringing with her the blended scents of damp wool and wild roses. 'I'm sorry, but — I'm afraid your name has slipped my mind.'

I never gave it to you, Rachael thought with a stab of resentment. *So how did you find me?* She took the bags from the woman's arms. 'Rachael. Rachael Timm — Warren.' *I don't even want his damn name.*

The keen blue eyes — eyes that missed little — took in their surroundings.

'The place is a mess,' Rachael said. 'I haven't had chance to . . . '

'Of course you haven't. Actually, it hasn't

changed all that much since your grandmother lived here. Or perhaps I'm just
recalling the way it was. Of course there have
been changes. The last owners, Ethel and
George Bates, were friends of mine. A tragic
story there,' she said sadly. 'At any rate, I'm
so glad someone will be living here again.
And I'm especially delighted it's you,
Rachael.'

'You knew my grandmother?'

'Oh, indeed. You favor her, you know.
Especially around the eyes. They're deep set
like hers were — intelligent. And you have
that same regal bearing. I knew when you
were in the store that you looked familiar. It
just took a little while to register why.'

She followed Rachael into the kitchen. 'I
didn't know her all that well, mind you. But
like everyone who lived around here then I
certainly knew who she was. And that she was
kind. Once, when I was canvassing for the
heart fund, she invited me in for a glass of
lemonade. But Emily Warren kept her own
counsel.'

'Please, sit down.' Rachael pulled out a
kitchen chair. 'Let me take your coat.'

'Oh, don't bother yourself. I'll just put it
here,' she said, draping it over the back of the
chair.

Rachael switched on the overhead light and

three tulip-shaped bulbs shed a weak amber glow over the rectangular wood table. 'I'll make us that tea.' She set the kettle on the burner. Then, opening the can of tuna Iris brought, she said, 'I can't believe you actually knew my grandmother. I would have thought all her contemporaries were . . . ' she caught herself. 'I'm sorry, I didn't mean . . . '

'I know what you mean,' Iris chuckled, thankfully taking no offense at the careless reference to her years. 'It might also surprise you to know that I have an Emily Warren seascape hanging above my fireplace at home.' This information was divulged with a hint of pride.

'Have you? Not that she was famous or anything. I'm afraid I have no milk.'

'No problem. I take my tea black. Maybe not famous, dear, but wonderful just the same. And not entirely unknown.'

Rachael busied herself setting out cups and saucers, bowls, triangular tuna sandwiches on a plate, the Oreo cookies, all the while listening to Iris' chatter about the way things used to be. She couldn't deny the pleasure it gave her to be talking to someone who had actually known her grandmother.

Ladling the steaming tomato soup into the bowls, she envisioned her grandmother at her easel — the intense concentration of her face, the way her hand would move absently to tuck back an errant strand of hair that had escaped the bun she always wore at the nape of her neck.

'I remember you, too,' Iris said, surprising Rachael yet again. 'I'd often see you down on the beach with her. Sometimes you would content yourself with just watching her paint, other times you'd be sitting on your rock, writing in your notebook. I used to wonder what you were writing about.'

'Nothing of great importance, I'm sure,' Rachael said, pouring the tea. Odd, it was the sounds she remembered most — the sighing of the bay, the birdsong, the whisper of brush on canvas, the contented beat of her heart. 'I'm sorry, but I'm afraid I don't remember you . . . '

Another soft chuckle. 'Oh, I think you were a child who tended to live in your own world. But you weren't always writing in your book. Sometimes I'd see you riding past our cottage on your bike, those long, sun-browned legs peddling for all they were worth, dark hair flying out behind you.' Rachael stifled an impulse to touch her hair — short now, streaked with grey, which she'd only noticed lately. 'Such a free spirit you were,' Iris said. 'Made a body feel good just to watch you.'

Uncomfortable with herself as the focus of

the conversation, she said off-handedly, 'Such a long time ago.'

'Seems only yesterday to me,' Iris said, and sipped her tea. She held the cup away from her lips, gesturing with it to Rachael. 'As it will to you too one day. Of course, you're much too young . . . '

'Not so young,' Rachael said quietly. Weariness had crept up on her again, and the headache she'd wakened with this morning was finding new legs. As much as she'd enjoyed Iris' company, which was a surprise in itself, she wanted — needed — to be alone now.

'Iris, I do wish you'd let me pay you for the groceries,' she blurted, a clumsy hint for her to go. The statement hung limp and awkward.

Iris smiled. 'Of course, Rachael, if you'd feel more comfortable.'

Taken aback at the quick acceptance, and further embarrassed that it probably showed, she reached for her purse on the refrigerator, accidentally knocking it to the floor. Coins clattered and bounced, and disappeared under things. A tube of lipstick rolled under the table.

Down on her hands and knees, she waved off Iris' attempts to help her, while trying not to burst into tears. Everything collected, she handed Iris a twenty. 'Will this cover it?'

Her headache was now a railing tyrant inside her skull. The tuna she'd eaten was swimming upstream in her stomach.

'That's fine,' Iris said easily, slipping the bill into her skirt pocket without looking at it. A hard gust of rain shook the window, and Iris turned slightly in her chair. 'These storms can get frightening at times.'

'I never used to mind them.'

She turned back to Rachael, gave her a mysterious smile. 'Yes, I can tell that about you. The wilder, the better. You love the feel of that power all around you, the energy.'

'And what else can you tell about me?' Rachael asked in a tight voice, beginning to feel like a bug under a microscope.

'I'm sorry,' Iris said, her smile vanishing. 'I've upset you. Please don't think I'm prying.'

'I don't know what to think. You keep implying you know things about me. At the store you — '

'Do I? I didn't realize . . . I am sorry. It's just that — well, you seemed to need a friend. One doesn't need special powers to see your pain, Rachael. It's in your eyes, in your every move.'

'My every clumsy move, you mean. Just because I dropped my purse . . . '

'Oh, no, of course not. I recognized myself

in you, Rachael. After my husband died, I was a lost soul, wandering in an alien world. There were no colors in that world, just varying shades of grey. It was all I could do to put one foot in front of the other. I felt as if I were standing on the edge of an abyss with a strong wind at my back.'

'I can assure you, my husband is very much alive.' Hot tears pressed behind her lids. *I don't need this, dammit!* The hammering in her head was working itself up to a crescendo, vying with the storm outside her window. Unexpectedly, Iris reached out and placed a hand over hers. Warmth and understanding flowed from her touch.

'There are many kinds of deaths, Rachael. A lot of little deaths in a lifetime.' Withdrawing her hand from Rachael's, she reached into her pocket and brought out a business card that she handed to her. 'Just in case — well, if you ever need anything. Perhaps just to talk.'

Rachael glanced at the words on the buff card with its raised chocolate lettering. 'You're a potter.'

'Yes. I became interested in the craft after John died. A long time ago, now. I found working with the clay helped to ease the grief. I suppose it also gave me a sense of having control in my life. If I didn't like the way a piece was shaping up, I could always change it. Work it differently. Take off a little here, add a little there. If you ever want a lesson — no charge of course — I'd be happy to . . .'

She's really a very nice woman, but I don't want these confidences. I have no energy to give to a new friendship. I just want to be left alone. Unconsciously, Rachael pressed her fingertips to her throbbing temples.

'Rachael,' Iris said, concerned. 'Are you feeling unwell? You've gone terribly pale.'

'Nothing serious. Just a headache.'

'Oh, I'm so sorry. I have some aspirin out in the car. I'll just get — '

'No, It's all right. Really. I'll take something later. I do think I *will* lie down for a while, though. I don't mean to rush you, Iris, but . . .'

Iris rose at once, put on her coat and buttoned it. 'Forgive me. I hadn't intended to take up so much of your time.'

'I'm glad you came,' Rachael said, and it was mostly true.

At the door, Iris hesitated. The fear was back in her eyes. The same fear Rachael saw in them when she was in the store.

'Rachael . . .'

'What is it? Is there something you want to tell me, Iris?' Her hand on the doorknob was damp, her legs felt shaky. She really did need to lie down.

Sighing, Iris said, 'Yes, I'm afraid there is. I'm not even sure how to say this. I don't want to frighten you needlessly. I may be wrong, but — '

'Please, Iris. Just say it.' Rachael could not imagine anything making her feel any worse than she already did.

'Yes, I suppose it is the only way.' She took a mental breath, then said, 'You are in danger here, Rachael. Terrible danger.'

'Danger. What are you talking about, Iris?'

'I know how insane it sounds. But I do sometimes get these — my mother called them forewarnings. I wish to God I didn't get them, believe me. But the feelings are so strong this time. I felt the danger all around you when you were in the store. I . . . still feel it.'

'Are you telling me I shouldn't live here?'

'I — I don't know. At least keep your door locked, Rachael. The world is a far different place from when your grandmother lived in this house.'

Rachael stood on the porch as the taillights of the station wagon swept the wind-bowed trees in a wide arc of drizzly light, then vanished into the night. Hugging herself against the cold rain that blew into the open porch, she hurried back inside and closed the door. With one thought foremost in her mind — the Tylenol with codeine, the only item in her purse that hadn't spilled onto the floor.

As she filled her glass with water from the kitchen tap, Iris' words replayed in her mind: 'Keep your doors locked, Rachael. The world is a far different place from when your grandmother lived in this house.'

Setting the glass of water on the counter, palming the pills, she went back into the living room and snapped the lock on the door. *No point in tempting the fates.* She was about to turn away when she heard something outside — a shuffling sound — like footsteps on the porch floor. An icy hand touched her heart. *Was someone out there?* Her eyes fixed on the door; she strained to hear. Even her pounding headache seemed to lower in volume to cooperate. But she heard nothing further, only the wailing of the wind in the trees, and the crashing of waves down on the shore.

She washed down the two Tylenol with water. She was spooking herself, letting Iris' warning get to her.

Back in the living room, she fed a new chunk of wood into the fire. As she sat on the floor hugging her knees, watching the flame curl hungrily about it, Iris Brandt's words echoed — *my mother called them forewarnings . . .*

Just so much superstitious nonsense, Rachael told herself. Iris had cited recent acts of vandalism and break-ins, but that had nothing to do with her. Crime happened back in Deering, too.

She would not let herself think about a girl in intensive care Iris told her about, the victim of a brutal attack that had left her unable to speak — *you could only process so much.*

The flames leapt higher, cracking and snapping, casting flickering shadows on the ceiling and walls. Yet, despite the heat from the fire, they failed to warm her.

But at least the Tylenol was kicking in.

10

It was after one in the morning when Bob Myers came downstairs to find his wife sitting in the living room in the dark. Lightning flashed in the picture window, silhouetting her small frame on the sofa. Bob turned on the tri-lamp, touched a hand to her shoulder. 'Helen, honey, are you okay?'

Her 'No' was barely audible as she lifted her gaze to him. She looked so pale and drawn in the lamplight, tormented he knew, by visions of that monster's savage attack on their only child. The good Lord knew he wasn't coping all that well himself. But at least Heather was alive; she was still with them. Not that it dulled his rage at the animal who did this to her. No. Not for a minute. And he knew who that animal was, too, even if he couldn't prove it. Not yet anyway. Heather couldn't help them. Doctor Halstead said that even when she did regain her speech, which he'd all but guaranteed would happen, she might have no memory at all of the attack.

'That bastard will pay, Helen. I promise you.'

Helen said nothing. He knew she didn't believe Tommy was Heather's attacker. Tommy was a good boy, she'd said, his only crime being born Nate Prichard's son. But then, Helen found good in everyone. It was one of the things he loved about her, while at the same time it made him crazy. Unfortunately, their daughter had inherited her mother's trusting heart. But as far as Bob was concerned, Tommy and his old man were cut from the same cloth. Not in any obvious way. The kid was smarter, smoother, that was all.

Without telling Helen, he'd made sure Tommy Prichard wouldn't be going anywhere near their daughter's hospital room. Not that she was in any state to have visitors anyway, other then her parents. A cop had been assigned to guard her door, just in case Prichard decided to sneak in to see her. Maybe silence her once and for all.

He knew he wasn't alone in his suspicions of Prichard, either.

'Come on up to bed, Helen. It's late.'

'No. But you go ahead. You have to get up for work in the morning. I just want to sit awhile.'

Sighing, he eased himself down beside her and put his arm around her. She was trembling. 'Bad dream?' he asked gently, smoothing her hair with his other hand. But

58

for the silver patch in front, it was exactly the same shade of chestnut brown as Heather's.

For a moment Helen was silent, then, not looking at him, she said, 'It — it was so awful.'

'I know, honey, but — '

'No. No. The dream, Bob. In the dream, I was looking down at my little girl — in her coffin.' As Helen spoke the words, a cold shiver, like a spasm, went through her into him. 'She was so still, her skin like wax. And her hair was neat — not crinkly and wild the way she wears it. I touched her hair . . . ' She reached out a hand and stroked the empty air in front of her, began to cry. 'I couldn't bear it if . . . ' The soft weeping quickly escalated in harsh, gut-wrenching sobs and Bob had to fight back his own tears.

'She's going to be fine, Helen,' he said hoarsely. 'Doctor Halstead practically promised she'd make a full recovery. You were there, sweetheart. You heard him.'

Soon, her sobs subsided, and she dabbed at her eyes with the cuff of her robe. 'I know you're right,' she sniffed. 'I'm sorry. I'm sorry I woke you.'

'Don't be silly,' he said, holding her tightly against him until he could feel her heart beating against his own. Helen would still be at the hospital if Dr. Halstead hadn't insisted they both go home and get some rest. He'd practically had to drag Helen away from Heather's bedside. 'Look, we'll get her some counseling. Hell, we'll all get counseling. We'll get through this, Helen. We will.'

The tick of the antique clock on the mantle seemed louder somehow. Beside it, Heather smiled out at him from an oval pewter frame. *I'm sorry, baby. So sorry Daddy couldn't protect you.*

Rain pattered softly against the window.

'I can still smell those flowers,' Helen whispered. And her words, breathed into the hollow of his neck, chilled him to the core.

★ ★ ★

The nurse had left the door propped partly open, letting in a narrow swath of light from the corridor. Heather managed to turn her head just enough to see a navy-blue broad shoulder, a pant-leg, and the splayed polished shoe of the policeman sitting outside her door.

Laughter drifted to her from the far end of the corridor, sounding echoey, as if she were in a church with a door opening and closing somewhere. Bits of conversation rising and falling, waves washing in and out, like when she and Tommy walked along the beach. No, don't think about Tommy. She listened to the voices.

' . . . but then she said he wouldn't let her sponge him . . . ' A woman's voice. She couldn't make out anymore words. A gale of laughter melted into a drone of fading voices. Heather imagined white-clad figures briskly turning a corner, now beyond her hearing.

Those nurses didn't know about her. Didn't know about her life. *Like when you see an airplane flying high up in the sky and you know the people on it don't know you exist.* Though she sometimes imagined the lives of the passengers, wondered at their destinations, their hopes and dreams. Mr. Gardner said that was because she had the soul of an artist.

'Doctor Whalen . . . Doctor Whalen . . . ,' came a nasal female voice over the intercom, piercing the quiet of her surroundings. 'Please report to . . . ' She heard the soft ping of an elevator stopping, the ring of a phone.

Physical pain drew her attention from the sounds, and life outside her door. She tried to find a more comfortable position when there wasn't any. There seemed no part of her body that didn't shriek at every movement, no matter how small, how careful.

Her head hurt, too, where he had wound his powerful fingers into her hair, forcing her onto her knees, whispering ugly things to her. Heather squeezed her eyes shut, tried not to think about him, about the awful things he had done to her. Made her do to him. She couldn't ever go back to school. How could she face anyone? Tears spilled from her closed eyes, stung her eyes, her cheeks. Everyone will know.

He'd seemed so nice at first — gentle, really soft-spoken. Not like the other one. 'Just give me what you have in the till. Don't be afraid. No one is going to hurt you.'

She'd believed him. Believed that if she did what he asked, he wouldn't hurt her. Mr. Poulis always said, 'Anyone comes in here demanding money, you just give it to them. Don't try to be a hero. We can always make us more money. Can't make us another Heather.'

Neither of them had really thought it would happen though. It was just talk, just in case. But it wasn't money he'd wanted.

The heady smell of flowers wafted through the hospital smells. Heather looked at the huge bouquet of pink roses on her night-stand. She seemed to remember someone saying they were from Mr. Poulis.

'Heather?' came a soft voice from her doorway. The nurse approached her bed, preceded by a thin beam of light. 'You're awake,' she said, switching off her flashlight and turning on Heather's overhead bed-lamp. Seeing her tears, she asked, 'Are you in discomfort, dear?' She checked her pulse.

Discomfort. Is that what they call what I'm feeling? She tried to answer, but again, nothing came out, no sound whatever. What time was it? How long had she been here? She had a vague recollection of her mother sitting by her bedside, her face pale and anxious. Her father crying, tears pouring down his face as he looked at his daughter lying in the bed. She had never seen her father cry before; it had frightened her. *I must look awful. When was that? Today? Yesterday?*

It was nighttime now. Yes, the middle of the night and everyone was asleep but her. That was why the nurse was speaking so softly, so as not to disturb the other patients.

'Do you know where you are, Heather?'

She's trying to get me to speak. Why can't I? What's wrong with me?

As the nurse fluffed her pillow, Heather read the name Janet Lewis, R.N. on the gold bar pinned to the pocket of her white nylon uniform. Her eyes were a soft brown, kind. Heather wanted to cooperate, wanted the comfort of her own voice more than anyone, but it was like the words were trapped inside her head. Like she'd forgotten how to speak.

Forcing back a wave of panic, she focused on that simple sentence, 'I'm in a hospital.' Concentrating all her will and effort into forming the words, getting them past her tongue, she struggled to speak. But it was no use. Tears of frustration seeped from her eyes.

'Don't try to force it,' the nurse said gently. 'Your mind and body have undergone terrible trauma. The important thing now is to rest. Everything will be all right. Give yourself a chance to heal.'

Yes. She needed to heal. Her throat was raw and sore when she tried to swallow or speak. She could still feel the pressure of his hands around her throat. When she tried to pry them away, he beat her with his fists. Memory ended there. Why? Why did he want to hurt her? What had she done wrong?

The nurse had said everything would be all right. But how could it be? Even if her speech did return, how could anything ever be all right again?

Through the slightly open drapes, a black starless sky was visible. Raindrops wriggled down the glass.

She thought of Tommy out there some-where. Was he awake too? Did he know? Shame burned inside her. What would he think? What would Tommy think of his sweet Heather now?

Pushing thoughts of Tommy from her mind, she tried to concentrate on Nurse Lewis' brisk, efficient movements as she went about the room silent as a ghost, straightening this, smoothing that. Heather followed her with her eyes as she took a banana-colored blanket from the white metal cabinet next to the washroom and laid it gently across the foot of Heather's bed. Heather could feel its light pressure on her feet.

Her thoughts went back to Tommy. Mom liked him, she could tell. Daddy was another story. He didn't come right out and say he disapproved of Tommy, but she knew he didn't think Tommy was good enough for her, that he thought he was some kind of loser. It didn't help that Tommy had dropped out of school and gone to work in the scrapyard. But that wasn't his fault, either. Just like it wasn't his fault he had a rotten father. She'd never met Mr. Prichard, but she'd heard plenty of awful stuff about him, and most of it not from Tommy.

So Tommy worked in the scrapyard. Big deal. At least he worked. Anyway, it wasn't like he was planning on staying there his whole life.

Daddy didn't really know Tommy. If he

did, he'd know that he was a really good person. He wasn't like a lot of the guys at school, out for one thing. He never once tried anything with her. 'I want us to wait until we're married,' he always told her when things kind of got out of control. She was the one who didn't want to stop. He'd gently push her away, though, even while she could feel him trembling with wanting her. So how could she face him now? She felt so dirty. So small inside herself. I'm sorry, Tommy. I'm so sorry.

She tried not to start crying again because the tears smarted too much, but they came anyway.

The nurse was at her bedside. 'Doctor Halstead left orders for pain medication, Heather,' she said, misinterpreting the reason for Heather's tears. 'There's no need for you to suffer needlessly.'

She plucked tissues from the box on the night table, gently wiped away her tears. 'I'll be right back.'

Listening to her soft footsteps fading down the corridor, Heather closed her eyes.

★ ★ ★

Tommy slipped through the double-doors of the emergency room of St. Clair General

Hospital, glanced up at the hexagon-shaped clock on the wall. The big second hand clicked to 2:07 a.m. The molded, blue plastic chairs were bolted to the floor in a semi-circle, in front of the large windows. Maybe a dozen people waited to see the doctor on duty. Tommy made his way to the chair closest to the stairs. You had to pass them on your way to the elevators.

At the far end of the row a woman sat rocking a little boy who sounded like he might cough up his lungs at any second. The poor kid's face was beet-red and he was crying. He'd get a little break, and then the coughing fit would be on him again.

In the chair next to the empty one beside him, an old man in a tweed cap pulled low over his brow, was nodding off. How he could sleep with the kid howling and hacking in his ear like that was a mystery to Tommy. Maybe he was dead.

Turning a careful eye to the receptionist behind her kiosk, he waited his chance to bolt for the stairs. Mrs. Myers told him Heather was on the third floor, room 314. He'd telephoned as soon as he heard what happened, grateful it wasn't Mr. Myers who answered the phone. He was watching TV when he heard it on the news. They didn't release Heather's name, but there was only one store in Harding that was open all night.

Why? Why did this happen to her? She'd been working so hard, saving every penny she could earn to go to one of those famous acting schools, maybe even Julliard.

Would she blame him? Hate him for not being there for her? God knew he hated himself. Why hadn't he sensed that she was in trouble, that she needed him?

The receptionist was on the phone, but she was keeping a steely eye on her flock, forcing him to wait her out. A big woman, she looked like she could pick him up by the ear if she took a mind to, and toss him out of here.

A young guy was limping in his direction, grimacing with pain. He eased himself down into the empty chair between Tommy and the old man. He was a muscular type about his own age, hair tied back in a skimpy ponytail. Tommy glanced down at the dirty wad of blood-soaked cloth he was pressing against his outer thigh. He acknowledged Tommy with a slight nod, his heel tapping a nervous staccato on the floor. A wave of sourness rose off him, a brew of sweat and pain.

We're like people trapped in a broken down bus in the middle of nowhere, Tommy thought, waiting for someone to come and get it going again.

The receptionist paged a Doctor Whalen

on the intercom. Her voice was bored and whiny, not at all how he'd expected it to sound. The kid had started coughing again, wide blue eyes panicky. The old man woke with a jerk and looked around, as if surprised at finding himself in this place, with these strangers. The guy beside him let out a grunt of pain.

★ ★ ★

Up on the third floor, the elevator stopped and a man stepped off. He wore a doctor's white coat, wire-rimmed glasses, and carried a patient's chart in his hand. From his confident stride and easy manner, no one would have guessed he did not belong here, or that he was not a doctor.

Except for the girl in room 314.

★ ★ ★

The dragon-lady finally broke down and brought the kid a glass of water. She'd barely turned her back and Tommy was on his feet heading for the stairs. He forced himself to walk casually, bracing himself for that nasal voice behind him, commanding him to 'Stop — stop now!' It took all he had not to break into a run.

But there was no command for him to stop, no sound of urgent feet tromping behind him. Home free. He was on the other side of the door now, and it was swinging closed behind him. He took the metal stairs two at a time, landing on each step as softly as possible. In just a few minutes he would be with Heather. He would help her through this. He loved her.

Oh, God, Heather, I'm so sorry.

★   ★   ★

Approaching the nurses' station, the bespectacled man in the white coat spoke pleasantly to the nurse on duty. It mildly amused him when she snapped shut the book she was reading, to see her country-girl cheeks turn nearly as red as the lettering on the book's dust-jacket that spelled out *Summer's Passion*.

She glanced at the chart in his hand. 'Good morning, Doctor,' she said, her greeting coming out high and timid.

'Morning, nurse. Quiet night?'

'Yes, doctor. Pretty quiet.'

He spoke softly, earnestly — a man who inspired confidence, and obedience. 'Have they transferred the Myers girl to Psych yet?'

It was not a large hospital, only three

floors, not counting the basement where the morgue was located. Not much ground to cover.

'No, I — she's still in intensive care.'

Having already noted the numbers on the door, he took a stab. 'Still in 302, then.'

'314,' she corrected him.

He looked down at his chart. 'Right. 314. Good book?' He winked conspiratorially, moved on down the corridor, checking the numbers on the doors as he went. His step faltered when he saw the cop sitting outside her door. Adrenaline coursing through his veins, he assessed his situation. A rookie, maybe in his twenties. With an animal's keen sense of danger, he patted the knife in his belt, under the coat. Just in case. A last resort.

Drawing nearer, he saw the cop's mouth agape, heard his snores, and almost laughed out loud. Not that he'd been too worried. He was quite prepared to handle whatever stood in his way, one way or the other.

'Evening, Officer. Long night?'

Mel Willis jerked awake, straightened in his chair. He adjusted his hat. 'Wasn't sleep,' he said, relieved it wasn't Sorrel; he'd be walking a beat tomorrow if the old man had caught him. Might anyway, if this doctor ratted on him. 'Just closing my eyes for a minute or two,' he said.

71

'Well, it's that kind of night.'

'Yeah, I guess.'

'I'm going to be in there for a few minutes,' the doctor said, patting Mel's shoulder in empathy. 'Why don't you go down and grab yourself a coffee, pal. You look like you could use one. I know the feeling. I'll hold the fort till you get back.'

'Oh, I don't know if . . . ' Hot coffee sounded awfully tempting.

'Give yourself a break while you've got the chance,' the doc said. He gave Mel a knowing grin. 'I'm guessing you've still got a few more hours of duty before you're out of here, right?'

Seconds later, the nurse glanced up from her book as Officer Willis passed by her station, but it never occurred to her to question his leaving his post.

11

A shadow fell across her bed and Heather opened her eyes expecting to see the nurse standing there with her medication. But it was not Nurse Lewis, nor Doctor Halstead, either. Doctor Halstead was older than this doctor, and had white hair and chubby cheeks. He'd always reminded her of the doctor in Norman Rockwell's illustration hanging in her father's muffler shop. She took in the graying hair, the glasses and mustache. Something familiar about him. Also familiar was one of the voices she'd heard outside her door only moments ago. Or was that a dream?

As his eyes held hers, the pattern of her heartbeat peaked on the monitor beside her. Why doesn't he say something? Then he smiled, a slow smile devoid of humor, and a paralyzing terror filled her, flooding her mouth and throat with the taste of old pennies long buried in the earth.

'Ah, yes. I see you do remember me.' Thin lips stretched further over predatory teeth as he smiled his death grin. Behind the glasses, his eyes were cold and merciless. 'I thought you were dead when I left you,' he said matter-of-factly. 'You looked dead enough. Well, we'll just have to remedy that.'

He slid the pillow from under her head.

Oh, no. Please, please dear God, somebody help me. She fought to escape the confines of her bed, but three broken ribs refused to allow it. In her struggle, she did manage to tip over the I.V. bottle on its stand, was rewarded with a flicker of panic on his face. But before it could crash to the floor and summon help, he caught and righted it. Heather opened her mouth to scream, could feel it stretched in its silent cry, but again, no sound came.

He cocked a mocking brow at her. 'What's the matter?' he whispered. 'Cat got your tongue?'

'Excuse me, Doctor,' came a voice from the doorway. 'May I ask what you're doing? This is Doctor Halstead's patient.'

Relief surged through Heather, tears of gratitude rolled down her cheeks as the nurse, frowning, came further into the room, carrying a miniature cup containing a small white pill. 'She's also supposed to be under police guard,' she said. Her voice was firm, but Heather heard the vague uncertainty underneath. 'Why is Officer Willis no longer outside her door?'

'So many questions. Well, for your information, I sent the poor man for a coffee. He was asleep on the job.' He spoke easily, with just the right note of annoyance. 'And I'm well aware of whose patient she is. Doctor Halstead asked me to look in on Miss Myers. Since I'm going to be out of town for a few days, and since I was in the building — I'm Doctor Whittaker, by the way, Nurse . . . ' His eyes flicked over her name bar, ' . . . Lewis.'

★ ★ ★

His broad back was to Heather, white in its doctor's coat. Her panicked gaze moved upward to the queer indentation where his hair ended, and she realized he was wearing a wig.

He sounded so convincing. Just the way he did in the store. 'Just give me what you have in the till, and you won't get hurt.' *Oh, please don't believe him, Nurse Lewis.* Past his shoulder, Heather tried desperately to catch the nurse's eye. *Look at me. Please look at me.*

But Janet Lewis was intent on what the doctor was saying. He spoke respectfully to her, but with a certain professional reserve that said he was a man quite willing to go out of his way to oblige a colleague, but he was also a busy man.

'I'll be out of your way in just a minute, Doctor,' she said, pouring water into the glass. 'She's been experiencing some discomfort tonight.' Her attention focused on her task, she did not see the horrified disbelief in her patient's eyes, or the desperate plea within their depths. Although when she turned to give Heather her pill she did notice with some dismay that the I.V. needle had slipped out of the back of her hand.

She replaced the needle. 'Don't know how that happened,' she muttered. After practically force-feeding her patient the pill, she quickly exited the room, closing the door after her.

No! The voice inside Heather's head screamed. *Come back. Don't leave me!*

He waited a few seconds to be sure the nurse had really gone. Then slowly, he turned to Heather, picked up the pillow once again. Smiling down into the wide, terror-filled blue eyes, he said with deadly softness, 'Almost got away. And I was kind of rooting for you too. Really.'

Heather mouthed the words, *Please no*, as the pillow slowly came down onto her face, blocking out all light, all hope.

* ★ ★ ★

At exactly 2:26 a.m., Iris Brandt bolted upright in her bed, clutching her chest and gasping for air, with the horrible sensation of being suffocated.

★ ★ ★

Hearing footsteps on the landing below, Tommy froze where he was. When he was satisfied that the clanging feet were racing to the lower level, he let himself breathe again.

Then he was facing a grey metal door with the number three painted above a narrow rectangular pane of fireproof glass. At the sound of an approaching gurney, he shrank back against the wall. A white-haired black man pushing an empty gurney rattled past the door and on down the corridor.

Tommy wiped sweaty palms on his jeans, and slumped down on the top step. Had to get himself together. His nerves were jumpy as hell.

The last thing Heather needed was for him to go in there and lose it. She needed to concentrate on getting better, so he had to be strong for her. He would help her make it through this. He didn't know how, exactly, but he would.

Right now he just wanted to see her, to hold her and let her know how much he loved her and that he was there for her. He would also vow that the creep who did this to her would be punished. But the first thing he had to do, he thought, getting to his feet, was to make it to her room without being seen. There might be a little problem with that especially considering that her mom had told him a policeman was guarding her door. He would beg if he had to. Throw himself on the guy's mercy. 'Just for a minute,' he'd say. 'You can come in with me.'

One step at a time, Tommy Prichard. You got this far.

Inching the door open a crack, he peered cautiously around it. Seeing a doctor headed in his direction, going flat out, Tommy eased the door closed, stood well back until he passed. Then he opened it again and, heart pounding like a trip-hammer, stepped into the highly polished corridor.

Complete quiet surrounded him — an eerie hush. While beneath it he could hear the faintest murmur of machines — that great technology that kept hearts pumping, lungs breathing. Or maybe the sounds were just inside his head.

The air was heavy and too warm, filled

78

with unspoken dangers. Tommy hated hospitals at the best of times. He hated the smells, the sounds. He knew it was because of that time when he was five and an ambulance had rushed him in here in the middle of the night with an attack of appendicitis. He'd never forget his terror at waking up in the shadowy quiet of his room, peering through the bars of his bed, like a trapped rabbit. He'd been crying for his mother, when suddenly a monster in white loomed over him, clamped a big hand over his mouth, cutting off his cries, terrifying him. 'Quiet,' she'd commanded before thrusting a big needle into his arm.

When he woke the next morning, his mother was at his bedside, smiling tenderly down at him, stroking his damp hair, telling him he'd just had a bad dream that was all. There were no monsters — especially monsters in white.

Her smile floated from his mind as Tommy looked up at the red numbers on the wall. Red arrows pointed left and right, guiding him in the direction he needed to go.

Creeping ghost-like down the corridor, Tommy's sneakers were soundless on the floor. He checked the numbers on the doors; even numbers were on his right.

300 . . . 302 . . . 304 . . .

Her room had to be just around the next

turn past the nurse's station. Luck was with him. The nurse had her back to him, flipping through a box of files. He slipped quickly past her, worried that she might sense him there, but she didn't. So far, so good. 306 . . . 308 . . . 310 . . . 312 . . .

314 . . .

He stopped, his heart seeming to stop with him. So where was the cop who was supposed to be guarding her door? While he was relieved that no one would be keeping him from Heather, he was also angry that no one was looking out for her. What if the guy decided to come back? Didn't anyone give a damn?

What would he say to her? For the millionth time, he blamed himself for not being there when she needed him. Why didn't I know? He wiped impatiently at a tear. Knock it off. She damn well doesn't need you blubbering all over her like a baby, Prichard. What was he waiting for? Someone to see him standing here? Tommy pushed the door open. The room was dark. 'Heather?' he said softly.

As he took a tentative step forward, steel glinted in the sparse light coming from the window, outlining her bed. Taking another step into the room, the scent of flowers wafted to him. Nearly tripping over the blanket puddled on the floor, his heart gave a small skip. He picked it up.

Something's wrong.

Approaching her bedside, his bewildered eyes took in the hair spilling from beneath the pillow that lay over her face — her smooth pale arm hanging limply by the side of the bed . . .

Though Tommy's brain snapped frantic photos of the scene, it had not yet had time to process them. The unthinkable did not yet register. That would take a few more seconds.

'Heather?'

★   ★   ★

Officer Mel Willis was just returning with his second cup of coffee, which tasted only a tad better than he imagined the cleaning agent in Sam's scrub bucket would. But at least it woke him up. And it was hot. He'd passed a minute or two, fifteen in real time, chatting with the old man on whether or not Tyson still had the fire in him. Sam was a die-hard fan of the bad-boy boxer.

Mel's steps halted at the sight of the young man stumbling wild-eyed out of Heather Myer's room. Dread and horror slammed through him, turning the coffee in his gut into acid. He'd heard it said that before you die, your life flashes in front of you. It was

81

exactly like that for Mel, except that it was his career that flashed before his eyes.

The boy turned to look at him. As their eyes locked, Willis' training went into gear. The coffee in his cup splattering its dark liquid against the wall, Mel went for his gun, simultaneously assuming the crouch position.

12

At 2:51 a.m. Rachael woke to the wailing of sirens. She'd fallen asleep on the sofa listening to the storm rage outside her window. The wind howled beneath the eaves, moaned down the chimney, and Rachael was strangely lulled by its mad symphony.

The room was still warm but the fire had waned. She rose and placed another piece of wood on the burning embers. She watched until it caught, then went out to the kitchen.

More sirens. They seemed close. She looked out the small window over the sink, wondering what had happened, but could see only her own pale reflection in the rain-battered glass.

Lightning flashed silent and eerie in the window, casting the old elm tree in unearthly light. So stark were its tortured branches, it no longer resembled the tree she had climbed and swung in as a child, but some evil apparition. Like a tree in one of those old Bela Lugosi flicks that had held her spellbound.

You saw too many of them. Feeling the headache returning, she washed down a couple more Tylenol to hopefully ward it off. She'd been living on the damn things lately.

The sirens had stopped. Silence now.

She went back to thinking about those old movies, about how the scary stuff always seemed to happen in the midst of a thunderstorm. As she stood there, a blinding flash of lightning turned night into day. Rachael's heart lurched at the sight of someone standing out by the old elm tree, staring straight in at her.

Darkness fell again and the watcher was gone. A fleeting silhouette caught in the blue-white glow, like a negative of a photograph, instantly swallowed up by the night. She could see nothing now, only the blackness, the rain streaming down the glass, and her own reflection. But she sensed him out there. Her pulses were racing, her mouth dry. The fine hairs on her arms tingled as if brushed with electricity. *I saw someone. I know I did.*

Moving closer to the window, Rachael waited for the next flash of lightning to confirm what her eyes had clearly seen. Iris Brandt's words echoed in her mind: 'You're in danger here, Rachael. Terrible danger.' She shivered involuntarily.

The next flash came but revealed only the tree in its contorted shape. No one standing beside it. Her imagination? A trick of the lightning, maybe.

You're losing it, Rachael.

Thunder cracked, reverberating through her body, giving her a sense of being caught in the eye of the storm. She moved away.

A torrent of rain rattled the windows in their casings. Lightning stabbed the objects in the room in otherworldly light, making them appear to jerk about in a mad, convulsive dance, as if alive. Drained and exhausted, as if the storm, rather than infusing her with its energy, was stealing what little she had left. *I need to go back and lie down. I don't feel well.*

As she was about to go into the living room, the bulbs in their three tulip-shaped shades flickered threateningly. She stood perfectly still. 'No, please,' she whispered.

She fixed the lights with her gaze, as if she might impose her will on them to remain bright and steady, but they flickered a second time — and again — dimming lower and lower, finally abandoning her to the darkness.

Damn! What next?

She felt her way long the edge of the counter, closed a hand around the last drawer handle. Pulling it open, she rummaged inside for the broken candles and the card of matches she'd seen there earlier.

Her fingers fumbled over curtain hooks, a corkscrew, an iron caster from a long discarded item of furniture, its owner apparently figuring it would come in handy at some point. At last her hand closed around a short, chunky candle. The smooth, waxy feel of it lent comfort. She came up with four candles of varying lengths. She found the matches, lit one of the candles and set it on the kitchen table, dispelling a layer of the thick, inky darkness.

She placed two more candles at either end of the counter, bringing welcome light into room. The flames made wavering circles on the ceiling. The last candle, she took into the living room, letting the small flame guide her step. She was about to set it on the mantle, when someone knocked on the front door. She spun around, the movement creating a draft that blew out the flame. Now only the glow from the fireplace kept her from being in total darkness.

The silhouetted figure by the elm tree leapt to the forefront of her mind.

★ ★ ★

Iris sat on the ash rose sofa, a double-shot of whiskey in hand, still shaken from her awful nightmare. Sensing her mistress' distress,

Cleo crept next to her and licked her hand. Iris stroked the warm, silky body, more out of her own need for contact, but eliciting a grateful purr from Cleo just the same.

Iris had quit smoking three weeks before. Now she slipped her hand into the pocket of her robe, found the lone cigarette she kept there, and in other pockets, in case of emergency. This damn well qualifies, she thought.

Rain pattered insistently against the window, sounding like the tapping of fingers of someone wanting to be let inside. In the far corner of the room, the grandfather clock ticked away, as it had through three generations. Tick tock . . . tick tock . . . like a time bomb. *Time running out.* Crazy. Why was she thinking like this? The nightmare, that was why.

But it wasn't the only reason. Her gaze wandered to the Emily Warren landscape hanging above the fireplace. Looking upon it usually had a calming effect on Iris, but not tonight.

It was not an ordinary landscape, but one that took you in after you'd kept company with it awhile, let you feel the salt-sea air on your skin, know the heave and sway of the ship beneath your feet, hear the wind filling the massive sails. She wasn't the only person to experience its effect.

Looking at it now though, she heard the faintest whisper of accusation. *You have to help her.*

Is it my fault your granddaughter won't listen? That she thinks I'm just a dotty old woman. I tried to warn her.

Iris took a swig of the whiskey, choked and sputtered on its fire. Great! Obviously, she was getting too old to take her booze straight up. She took the silver lighter from the end table and lit her cigarette. For a few seconds, she stared at its glowing tip with distaste, as much for her own weakness as for the cigarette. Then she proceeded to smoke it down to its filter, as if the tobacco might contain the precious oxygen her lungs couldn't seem to get enough of since she woke from her nightmare, gasping for air. Never mind that the thing tasted like scorched socks, and made her feel light-headed.

Iris' hand jerked as the cat let out an ungodly howl. Sparks flew from her cigarette, one landed on the back of her hand; it burned like the devil. Uttering a mild curse, Iris leapt to her feet, frantically brushing at it. Mashing the cigarette out in the ashtray, Iris said, 'Cleo? What the — ?'

In answer, Cleo sprang up behind her to

the back of the sofa, hackles raised, teeth bared in a deep, steady growl as she stared at a spot above the fireplace. Goosebumps raised on Iris' arms as her own gaze followed her companion's.

Another nightmare, she told herself, as in disbelief she watched the clouds in the painting. They were moving. *It can't be.* Black clouds, sun-yellowed at their edges, boiling into one another. Iris blinked, shook her head to dispel what had to be an hallucination. She had to be losing her mind, didn't she? Because this could not be happening.

But it was. As the clouds raced across the painting, entering into some mysterious dimension beyond the frame, new angrier clouds took their place. And beneath them, the ship rode the giant swells, sails billowing in the wind.

'Impossible,' Iris whispered, unable to look away. At last she squeezed her eyes shut. Maybe it's the whiskey, she thought, grasping for some reasonable, sane explanation. After a moment, she took a deep breath, forced her eyes upon the painting once more. A shudder of breath escaped her lips as relief replaced her dread. The clouds were still now, mere images painted on a flat, canvas surface.

Some sort of hallucination, she thought

again. That was all. But Cleo had seen it too. She reached for her glass. As she tipped it to her lips, some of the liquid trickled from the corner of her mouth. She wiped it away with a tissue, was visited with a vision of herself sitting with a covey of other old women, staring with glazed eyes at a flickering television screen in some nursing home, while an impatient hand wiped spittle from her palsied chin.

The phone rang and for the second time in a few minutes, Iris nearly jumped out of her skin, almost knocking over her drink. Cleo bounded from the sofa in fright, tried to scramble from the room but her feet were traveling so fast she was running in place, nails clicking madly on the hardwood floor. She looked so hilarious, so like a cat in a cartoon, that Iris laughed with weak release.

She picked up the receiver. Who could be calling at such an hour?

'Aunt Iris,' her distraught nephew said. 'Something horrible has happened. I'm sorry if I woke you. I just didn't want you to hear it on the news . . . '

13

The knocking grew more insistent. Whoever was out there wasn't planning on going away.

I have no phone. I can't even call for help.

Thunder rumbled and cracked around her. She thought about the sirens, now silent. Perhaps someone other than herself was in need of help. The storm was a bad one; maybe there'd been an accident. She took a single, tentative step forward. 'Who's there?' she called, keeping her voice calm, even.

'Rach, it's me. For God's sake, let me in before I drown out here.'

With a mixture of relief and astonishment, Rachael quickly opened the door to her soggy, yet still glamorous friend standing in her doorway, the hood of her raincoat drawn up over her head.

The lights came back on as Betty apologized for showing up in the middle of the night, explaining that she'd gotten lost trying to find her way here. 'I drove miles out of my way,' she said.

'I got lost myself,' Rachael said. 'Easy to do. It's great to see you, Betty. Please stop apologizing and come in.'

Ten minutes later they were sitting in Rachael's kitchen over coffee and Betty was relating the events of her summer sale. 'They ripped every last scrap of clothing from the hangers,' she said in mock complaint. 'How women do love a sale.'

Rachael laughed dutifully, knowing that Betty was doing her best to cheer her up. No surprise to her that the lights had come on the second Rachael opened the door to her. How attractive she looked in her bronze silk shirt, the brown suede skirt ending at mid-calf. Her lips and nails were painted in the same shade of bronze, her short red hair worn sleek and saucy, freckles expertly hidden beneath makeup. Her spicy perfume scented the air. Betty was the epitome of the successful career woman.

When they were kids, Betty once said that Rachael was like black and white TV while she was like color TV. Not a bad analogy, now that she thought of it. Betty had exhibited more than the usual teenage interest in makeup and fashion. And she was smart. Not so surprising that she would end up owning her own dress boutique. They were an unlikely pair.

'This road must be the darkest, scariest one I've ever driven on,' Betty said, changing the subject. 'I kept expecting some hideous thing to come shambling out of the bay, dripping in seaweed.'

'You have an overactive imagination,' Rachel said.

'Yeah, maybe. But it didn't help hearing about that poor girl being murdered in her hospital bed.'

'What girl?'

'They didn't give the name. But apparently she was a victim of assault, which was why she was in there in the first place. Guess the guy came back tonight to finish the job. Didn't you hear the police sirens.'

'Yes. I did.' A memory nudged Rachael. She pushed it back. 'How horrible. Can I get you something to eat — a sandwich?'

'No, thanks. I had a greasy cheeseburger at a truck stop earlier. It's still with me, probably will be till Christmas. Come, sit down, Rachael. Stop fussing. And more to the point, when was the last time you ate? You look like hell, if you don't mind my saying so. You've lost more weight.' She looked searchingly at her. 'I've been worried about you, Rach.'

'I'm okay. I just need some time.' One more word or gesture of sympathy and she would come apart. 'Are you cold, Betty? You just have that thin blouse on. I'll put more wood on the fire. We can set in there, if you like.'

'I'm fine, honey. But whatever you want.'

Rachael's next words tumbled out in a rush. 'He tried to lie his way out of it at first, you know. But I knew he was relieved to have it out in the open.' Pain rose like a fist in her chest. 'He told me Lisa saw me that day I drove to the office. She recognized me from the photo on Greg's desk.' Kept there, she suspected, because Halston was big on family. 'He said Lisa felt bad. Why did he need to tell me that, Betty?'

'Because he's a jerk. What can I say? I always thought you were too damn good for him.' She paused. 'I tried to call you. I dialed information for the number.'

'I don't have a phone.'

Betty raised a finely arched brow. 'Gee. No kidding.'

'I'm sorry. On both counts. I didn't mean to dump on you like that. At least you know why I didn't get a phone installed. Your shoulder is damp enough. I'll have to get a phone though. I need to call Jeff and Susan. This will be hard for them. I'm just — not ready.'

'I know. Remember, Rachael — this isn't your fault.' She looked around. 'Funny, after you told me about this place, I remembered you used to summer with your grandmother 'at the shore', you said. I never knew what shore. I used to wish you would ask me to go with you.'

Rachael said nothing. She had no explanation. She'd told no one about Jenny's Cove, other than her children, and her grandmother was long dead when they were born. And even in the telling, it had seemed a fairytale place, even to her. Like the magical places in the books she had read them.

I wanted to keep it for myself, she realized. *My secret place.*

Betty darted a look toward the window, gasped.

'What? What's wrong?' Rachael peered through the dark glass. 'Did you see something?'

She was silent a moment, then she laughed and shook her head. 'Yeah, my own reflection. Rach, if you're determined to live here, you should at least get some curtains on those windows.'

'I plan to,' she said, feeling a twinge of defensiveness. 'I'm really sorry you felt a need to drive all the way down here and check on me, Betty.' Seeing the hurt on her friend's face, she immediately regretted her words. 'I'm sorry. I don't know why I said that.'

'Apology accepted. But sometimes I don't understand you, girl. We've been there for each other since we were kids. When I got hit with the news that I would never have kids, no matter how badly I wanted that, you were there for me. I don't know what I would have done without you, Rach.' Tears glimmered in her green eyes. 'If not for you . . . '

'You give me too much credit. I — '

'No, it's true. And I want to be there for you now. Please, don't shut me out. I had this awful feeling that when you left Greg, you left me, too. I know it sounds crazy, but — '

'It is crazy. I just needed to be by myself for a while, that's all.'

'You should be back in your own home,' Betty bristled. 'It was Greg's place to leave, not yours. You're not the one who's screwing around.'

A familiar refrain. As much as she appreciated Betty being in her corner, she really didn't want to hear this now. 'I don't give a damn about the house,' she said. 'It, and everything in it, was always more Greg's than mine. This place is more my style.'

Betty shrugged. 'Okay kid, if that's how you feel I'll shut up about it.'

'Thanks. Would you like to see the rest of the house?'

'Sure.' She stood and draped an arm around Rachael's shoulder. 'Need to stretch the old gams, anyway. You know,' she said, looking around her, 'this place is kind of cozy at that. Rustic. Kind of grows on you.'

'I know it needs work, but it's basically sound. I'll make up a bed for you, Betty.'

'Oh, no, I'm not staying. I just wanted to be sure you were okay.'

'Don't talk nonsense. Of course you're staying. It's the middle of the night for heaven's sake.'

'Well, if you're sure.'

'I'm sure.'

'Well, okay, then, if you really want me to. It'll be like old times.' She grinned. 'Like a slumber party.'

Rachael could only shake her head and smile. 'C'mon, you can help me make up the bed.'

''Member when we used to sit up all night talking. Let's pretend we're kids again. Unless you're tired. I'm keeping you up, aren't I? Just call me Miss Sensitivity.'

'Don't be silly. So, should we take a drive so you can phone Allan and let him know? There's a phone booth at the end of the road.'

'You forget, I have a car phone. Anyway, I already left Allan a note.'

'Oh.' Rachael suppressed a smile.

'So then,' Betty said, 'since we're going to pull an allnighter, how about we celebrate — albeit a tad belatedly — your birthday. Or at least give it the good old college try. We'll save the tour for later.' With that, she reached into her leather bag on the floor, and produced a small wrapped box, topped with a silver bow.

'Happy birthday, Rachael,' she said, handing it to her. 'But we need to make a toast before you open it.' Not waiting for a response, Betty headed for the front door. 'I've got something a little extra special out in the car. Be right back.'

Rachael envisioned the girl Betty had been — red curly mop, though not as vivid a red as now, the quick grin. Always in a hurry like she was afraid she might miss that new adventure right around the next corner. Never afraid to go after what she wanted. Never imagining that she might not always get it. Which had to make finding out she would never bear children all the more devastating.

As Rachael waited for Betty on the porch, something just beyond the car caught her eye — a mound of deeper darkness near the edge of the road.

Something crouched there? Every nerve in her body tensed as Rachael strained to make it out. A few seconds later, she shook her head at her foolishness. A tree, she realized. Only a tree felled by the storm.

It seemed both their imaginations were working overtime tonight.

★   ★   ★

Minutes after Rachael and Betty went back inside, Tommy Prichard came staggering up from the beach, clutching a pint of Johnnie Walker's by the neck. He'd swiped it from his old man's stash.

The storm had moved out to sea, the rain dwindling to a fine bone-chilling drizzle. Though Tommy was soaked to the skin, the booze he'd consumed had chased most of the cold out of him.

It had all happened so fast. One minute he was looking at his beautiful Heather lying dead in her hospital bed, the next he was pounding back down the metal stairs, his footfalls echoing all around him, and the cop on his heels, bellowing, 'Halt or I'll shoot.' Tommy didn't stop running until he was deep in the woods. The woods — where he'd always felt safe and hidden.

Planting his feet apart for balance, Tommy uncapped the bottle and took a long swallow of the scalding liquid. Its warmth spread to his belly and limbs. But it couldn't touch his pain at losing Heather. Brought no relief from the knowledge that she was gone from him forever. Gone from the world. There was this huge, cavernous hole in his heart, so big it seemed impossible that his heart could go on beating.

He heard the murmuring of the bay behind him, the wind sighing in the trees like they understood and shared his pain. Rocking on his heels, Tommy made a couple of fumbled attempts to screw the cap back on the bottle. Finally succeeding, he slipped it into the inside pocket of his jean jacket, and with a mad lurch, reeled toward the house like a shipwrecked sailor, drawn by the lights — beacons that guided him to safe harbor.

Once there, he crouched at a window and peered through the narrow slit where the newspaper did not quite reach the sill. A sofa came into view and across from it a fireplace with a low burning fire. He shivered, jealous of its warmth as the cold began to cut through the boozy haze. He could see the pickle bottle on the mantle. The bottle had a rose in it. Instantly, the bottle split into two bottles, the rose into two roses, four, then a whole damn bouquet. He rubbed his eyes, tried to refocus them.

He could hear voices drifting from another part of the house. Mrs. Bates? No. George and Ethel Bates moved away last year. No one lived here now — did they?

In a sober corner of his brain, a voice was screaming at him to 'Get the hell out of here.

Get away now!' If the cops found him here, he'd be behind bars before he could turn around. His fate would be sealed.

Earlier, the woods had been swarming with cops, but he'd easily managed to evade them.

Not that it mattered. He'd heard the whispers in town. How could Heather's father think he would hurt Heather? How could he think I'm the kind of sick creep who would beat and rape a girl? And now he'll think I killed her to keep her from telling.

Staying low, Tommy crept past the porch to the other window, toward the voices. No newspaper covered this window, nothing to obscure his view.

Two women were sitting at the kitchen table, drinking wine, talking. He wondered if they were talking about him. Trying to position himself for better advantage, he abruptly lost his balance and sat down hard, with a *splat*, in the muddy trough beneath the window. The cold muck seeped through his already wet jeans. Hearing a car coming up the road, Tommy scrambled to his hands and knees. Clutching the house for support, he struggled to his feet at the same moment as the car came into view, cutting a swath of misty yellow light through the darkness. In his panic, he went down again, this time sprawling headlong in the mud.

Regaining his footing, he pitched forward, smacking his head on the sill. The crack resounded inside his skull, churned the whiskey in his gut to bile. Bright lights dancing before his eyes, Tommy took off, running in a wild zigzag pattern into the woods behind the house.

★ ★ ★

At a sharp thump against the house, Betty was on her feet. 'What the hell was that?'

'I don't know,' Rachael said, rising too. 'Betty, I'll just turn this light out, see if I can see anything. I think I saw someone out there earlier tonight.'

Betty looked at her. 'You're kidding, right.'

'No.' After a few seconds, she turned the light back on. 'But I probably imagined it. Anyway, there's no one out there now. Probably just a branch blown against the house. The storm seems to have passed over.'

'Well, that's something anyway,' Betty said uneasily, turning her attention from the window to refill their glasses.

★ ★ ★

The ground spun upward at Tommy as he grabbed for the nearest tree, sinking to his knees. The sour taste of whiskey rose in his mouth and throat, and he thought for a moment he was going to barf. But he didn't. Gradually, his racing heart slowed to normal.

The bark was wet and rough against his palms, but warm and welcoming, too. Tommy liked the company of trees. It was nice in the woods, kind of like being in a church. Ever since he was a little kid, he would hide out in the woods, sometimes to escape the old man's fists, but often just to be alone, to think. He would tell the trees his secrets, his innermost thoughts. And the trees would listen; they were his friends.

'Hi, good ol' friend,' he greeted the one he was presently clinging to, thinking that if it were up to Heather's father, he'd be hanging by his neck from it right about now. Resting his cheek against the trunk, he closed his eyes.

She can't be dead. She can't be. It was just a dream. But he knew it wasn't.

The blood from where his head had struck the windowsill trickled down his face, mingling with his tears and the fine, cold rain.

Tommy sat on the ground, his back resting against the trunk of the tree. Now and then he dozed only to be jolted awake from the bad dream, the awful vision of Heather lying dead in her hospital bed, lingering behind his lids. He feverishly patted his pocket for his pint, but it wasn't there. *Must have dropped out when I fell. Damn!*

Seconds later, he emerged from the woods, crab-walked round to the front of the house, to the window, where he groped about in the mud for his bottle. When his hand finally closed around it, he grinned to himself, a foolish, drunken grin.

Drawn once more by the voices inside, he looked through the window.

Not dressed up like her friend, the dark-haired woman wore jeans and a baggy sweatshirt. She was unwrapping a present, smiling like she thought her friend was a little ditzy, but pleased all the same. Must be her birthday, Tommy thought. She had a gentle smile that made him think of his mother, the way she used to smile sometimes when she looked at him. There was sadness in the smile.

Their voices comforted him. He wondered what they'd do if he went right up to the front door and knocked. Maybe they'd invite him inside. His mind conjured up their welcoming smiles at the sight of him standing in the doorway. 'Hey, look, it's Tommy.'

He would sit with them at the kitchen table

and tell them about his life. About Heather. How he promised her he would go back to school and get his diploma. He'd even planned on talking to Mr. Gardner and seeing if it would be okay if he started back next term. He would work part-time and pay his own way. He'd been doing that all along anyway.

Heather was smart; she wasn't about to spend her life with a loser who worked in a scrapyard. She said she didn't care, but he knew she did. The funny thing was, he probably wouldn't even have *that* job now. Mr. Gabriel wouldn't want someone working for him who everyone thought was a murderer.

So who cared? *He* had. Once.

A wave of dizziness sent Tommy weaving for the back porch, where he sagged down on the bottom step. Trapping the pint between his knees, he gazed mournfully at it. Around him, wet leaves rattled in the biting wind. The booze having lost its ability to warm him, Tommy shivered in his cold, wet clothes. When the shivering stopped enough to allow him to uncap the bottle, he finished it off in a couple of swallows and tossed the empty into the darkness.

Coughing against the harsh taste, he wiped his mouth with the back of his hand, looked longingly at the closed door behind him. 'Oh, look how wet you are, poor boy. Come inside this minute and let me get you a towel.'

The voice became his mother's voice, and the words played in his mind like a sweet, painful lullaby. Tommy hugged himself in his sodden clothes and began to rock to and fro, like a child, trying to comfort itself. Slowly, slowly, his eyes closed, his head dropping down and down to his chest. His last thoughts before sinking down into the dark womb of sleep were of his mother, as she'd been the last time he saw her, when he was seven years old. So pretty with her shiny brown hair, wearing the powder blue coat with the double row of pearl buttons. She had smelled so good, like the violets that grew in the woods.

Her suitcase had been open on the bed and she was throwing things into it, stuffing them down, crying. When he saw her take his picture down from the wall, gaze on it, then quickly slip it between her dresses in the suitcase, terror and panic had filled him, and he begged her to take him with her. As she turned to put her arms around him, he saw that the old man had given her another shiner. Her eye was puffy, all dark and purple and ugly.

She stroked his hair, saying, 'You under-stand, don't you, sweetie. Momma's got to go. I'll send for you as soon as I get us a nice little place. I promise, baby. You be good now. Don't make your papa mad. Do what he says, and stay out of his way when he's drunk. I'll write, I promise. And I'll put money and a bus ticket in the letter, and you can come to me.'

Everyday, for weeks and then months, he'd run home after school and look eagerly in the mailbox. But no letter ever came. After a while he stopped looking.

He wondered where she was living now.

Soon, memory faded and he was snoring softly, unmindful of another watcher — a deadly watcher — moving through the night toward him.

14

'Like 'em?' Betty grinned, pleased with herself. 'They're 18-karat.'

'What's not to like?' Rachael said, admiring the hammered-gold hoop earrings nestled on royal blue velvet. 'They're beautiful. They must have cost a fortune.'

'Just a small one. But you're worth it. You would have gotten them sooner, but — anyway, many happy — happier returns, my friend.'

Dear Betty, always so generous. And they really were lovely. She tried to sound enthusiastic. 'I love them. Really. Thank you so much, Betty.'

'You're welcome. So, why didn't you call me before you took off?'

Rachael sipped the champagne. It was dry, very good, and knowing Betty, outrageously expensive. She ran a thumb over the velvety surface of the box then snapped it closed. 'I almost did. But I knew I had to start relying on my own inner resources. Find out if I have any,' she laughed wryly. The words sounded good, almost as if she had a plan.

'C'mon, Rach, you're the strongest person I — '

'No, that's not really been tested. For a good part of my life I've found my identity in being a wife and mother. I'm not sure I have any beyond that. Susan and Jeff are grown, and Greg has, forgive the bad poetry, *flown*. At this moment, I feel as if vital organs have been removed from my body without the benefit of an anesthetic.'

To Rachael's dismay, Betty immediately got out of her chair and put an arm around her shoulder. 'You are strong. Stronger than you think. If you want my opinion, you wouldn't have looked at Greg Timmins twice if your mother hadn't died when you were four days old, and if your father had been available to you emotionally. If he had — '

'Betty, please don't psychoanalyze me,' she said, standing so that Betty's arm dropped away. She wiped the counter for want of something to do with her hands. For some reason, the scent of Betty's perfume was suddenly cloying. *Any second now and I will shatter into a million pieces, like old china.* 'Anyway, you're wrong. I love — loved — Greg. I was happy in my marriage.'

'At the risk of evoking your wrath, dear friend, I think you were as happy as you thought you deserved to be. I — '

An explosion of glass cut off her words, the missile smashing through the window barely missing Betty's head. Cold, wet air blasted into the room. Both women leapt to their feet as glass tinkled to the floor, and the rock thumped to rest beside the refrigerator.

Before either of them could speak, a second explosion sounded from the living room, propelling Rachael to action. She dashed from the room, Betty behind her.

This rock, a boulder really, had landed in the fireplace, sending up a shower of sparks and ash. Bits of burnt wood were strewn across the carpet, giving off an acrid stench of old rags burning.

As Betty stomped about the floor in her good leather boots, trying to trample out the live sparks, resembling a frenzied, primitive dancer, Rachael looked dazedly up at the wet newspaper flapping in the smashed window.

Shock giving way to a rage she didn't know she possessed, she flung open the front door and cried into the night, 'You bastard! This is my home. How dare you? How dare you?'

'Take it easy, Rach,' Betty said, maneuvering past her and down the porch steps. 'I'll call the police.'

Out on the road, Rachael could make out someone moving on fast but unsteady feet. He soon disappeared from her sight.

Betty, having made the call to police, had just set foot on the porch step when a car pulled into the drive. 'That's gotta be a record,' she said, as they both stood watching the car come to a stop, and a man get out. He was tall and walked with an easy gait.

'Good evening, ladies. I hope I'm not intruding. I'm Peter Gardner.' He explained that he'd been taking a drive, and thought he saw someone crouching outside the kitchen window. His glance took in the broken window that was letting in a cold rain, the large rock on the floor.

'Are you all right?' he asked, looking from one to the other of them, genuine concern on his face. 'Was either of you hurt?'

They assured him they were fine.

'It didn't register at first,' he said, directing his conversation mainly to Rachael. 'A branch broken in the storm, I figured. But something wasn't setting right with me. Actually, I was quite a ways past the house, when I decided to turn back and check it out. And then I heard the call on the police band. I volunteer with the department. Or at least I used to. Did you get a look at the man?'

'No, not really,' Rachael replied. 'I did see someone staggering down the road, but I couldn't even swear for a fact that it *was* a man.'

The three stood in awkward silence as Rachael looked about her, again at the newspaper in the window hanging by its one piece of tape. It seemed a perfect metaphor for her life. The room smell vaguely of a house fire. A shiver slipped through her, and she hugged herself against the cold chill of the house.

'If you'll allow me, I'd like to make arrangements to put you ladies up at the motel in town. We'll get these windows replaced first thing in the morning.'

'That's very kind of you, Mr. Gardner,' Rachael said, surprised at his offer. 'I'm sure it's not part of your service with the police department, but I'd be most grateful.'

As she spoke, the whirling dome lights of a police car pulsed through the window into the room. Rachael opened the door to two burly policemen. The older one, hard-eyed and with an air of arrogance, gave a brief nod of greeting to Peter Gardner. After taking their statements, they left. As the two policemen headed back to the cruiser, Rachael heard the younger one say, 'Prichard, do you think?'

'Put your money on it,' the older man replied, sliding into the driver's seat.

'Prichard?' Betty repeated in a hushed, frightened voice when they had driven away. 'Isn't that the guy the cops are looking for? The one who murdered — ?'

'He's not been convicted yet. But yes, one and the same. Tommy Prichard. He was a student of mine. He's basically a good kid. I don't believe he killed anyone.' He turned back to Rachael. 'Ms. Warren, you have a small cut under your eye. Maybe you should let me drive you to the hospital and have it looked at.'

Rachael's hand went instinctively to her cheek, felt a sharp sting at her touch. 'Probably just a splinter of glass. Nothing serious.'

'Are you sure, Rachael?' Betty said.

'I'm sure.' Betty's own face was so pale her freckles seemed to jump out from beneath her makeup. She'd come very close to being seriously injured by that rock, Rachael thought. Anger returned, and bewilderment. *Who would throw rocks through my windows? Why?*

'Well, at least let me see what I can do about that splinter,' Peter Gardner said, already heading for the door before she could make any protest. 'I have a first-aid kit out in the car. Comes in handy in the classroom. Don't worry,' he grinned, 'I'm an old hand at this.'

'He's cute,' Betty said the instant he was out of earshot. 'A teacher. He reminds of that actor — what's his name? And those blue eyes . . .'

113

Rachael was relieved to see Betty back to her old self. Even her color was returning. 'He seems very nice. Quite a night, huh? Bet you're glad you came to visit.'

'Hey, I can use a little excitement in my life. You're the one I'm worried about. I get to go back home. You — oh, damn, someone should sew my mouth shut. Rach, I'm s — '

'It's okay. I know how you meant it. Really, Betty. You don't have to walk on eggs with me.'

Peter Gardner returned just then, kit in hand. Placing a firm, yet gentle hand under Rachael's chin, he tilted her head to gain better advantage with the tweezers. Looking into those intense, deep blue eyes, Rachael felt herself relaxing. He seemed to know what he was doing. Something familiar about those eyes. After a moment, she asked, 'Are you, by any chance, related to a woman named Iris Brandt?'

'That I am. Are you acquainted with my aunt?'

'We've met. An interesting woman.'

He grinned at her choice of adjective. 'That sounded ominous. But indeed she *is* interesting,' he said fondly. 'There.' Sliding the barely visible sliver of glass onto a tissue, he then dabbed the tender spot on her cheek with a cotton swab. The odor of antiseptic drifted

114

about Rachael's face as the swab joined the sliver of glass on the tissue.

He stepped back to appraise his work. 'Good as new,' he said. 'Won't even leave a scar.' He included them both in his smile. Well, shall we head out?'

Rachael and Betty followed him into town in their separate cars.

★   ★   ★

He sat behind the wheel of his car, parked beneath a streetlight, directly across from the motel. He'd followed them, staying well behind the Marquis, circling a couple of times until it was gone from the parking lot then pulled in here.

A light showed behind the drapes in their room, and now and again he would catch a fleeting shadowy movement in the window. Visions of her taking off her clothes brought memories of another time, another place and a slow heat began to build in him.

The best part had been her not knowing he was there. Being secret from her, invisible. But one night she caught him, and beat him with her small fists, furious, indignant, tearful. At first, he was afraid, not sure what would happen next. But nothing did because she never told. And then he was glad she knew, because now he didn't have to pretend anymore. He grew bolder, entering her room whenever the urge came over him.

After they locked him up he dreamed of her every night. And when he got out he looked for her everywhere — on the streets, in the stores . . . a few times he thought he'd found her. He'd been wrong. *He was not wrong now.*

Closing his eyes, he could almost hear her soft breathing in the darkness. Sense her sudden waking. Feel her body beneath his, warm and soft. So much better when she stopped fighting him.

The fire was raging through him now, centering in his loins, pulsing there, evoking a muttering from his lips, drawing his hands between his legs. With a sense of urgency, he unzipped his pants and began to stroke himself, his breathing raspy in the small confines of the front seat.

At a sudden high-pitched giggle, his eyes snapped open and a far less pleasant heat traveled upward to his neck and face. Glancing in his rearview mirror, he saw a couple headed toward him, and quickly righted himself.

The woman hung on her friend's arm, looking more than a little soused. Through his open window, he heard the sound of her unsteady step on the wet pavement coming closer. Then they were moving beneath the streetlight, passing him by without a backward glance, laughing together.

Had they seen him? Was it him they were laughing at?

Flushing hard, he snatched his cigarettes off the dash, lit one from the car lighter. He caught sight of himself in the rearview mirror, and was momentarily startled. The bright glow from the lighter cast his face in hellish light, reflecting for an instant, the demon that inhabited his soul.

He dragged hard on the cigarette, let the nicotine calm him. He sank back against the headrest, blew smoke rings at the grey plush ceiling. When next he looked across to the motel, her room was in darkness. At once, the old feeling of being 'shut out' swept through him, a chorus of ancient taunts summoning the rage that was his constant companion.

The broken windows are only the beginning. Soon you will understand how much you need me. How much you need me to take care of you. You won't leave me again. I won't let you.

'Marie is dead,' the voice said. 'You already killed her.'

He denied the voice, banished it.

'Hey fella, you look a little lonely,' said a sultry voice at his open window. He looked up to see a bleached blonde in clinging black leather grinning in at him, her neckline so low he could almost see her nipples. Her teeth gleamed obscenely between plump, wet lips. 'Want some company, Honey?'

'Take off, whore,' he said softly, almost pleasantly.

★ ★ ★

She had a sailor's vocabulary herself, and was about to give him a free sample, but then she saw something in his eyes that made her think better of it. The hooker who, in another lifetime, was a pretty cheerleader and wannabe model hurried down the deserted sidewalk, the lonely sound of her high heels clacking on the pavement loud in her ears, icy breath at her back. Once, she darted a look behind her, nearly tripping in her panic, but there was no one following her.

She was gasping for breath and sweating hard in her black leather outfit when she finally stopped and looked back at the car still parked beneath the streetlight two blocks away.

★ ★ ★

It was nearly dawn when Peter let himself into his apartment. He shrugged out of his jacket and hung it in the closet. Then he looked around the room as if seeing it for the first time — the tweed sofa, his recliner chair from the house, the tables, the lamps, a couple of generic pictures on the walls. The brass clock Aunt Iris gave them as a wedding present sat on the mantle, ticking faithfully. He hadn't put much thought into decorating when he moved here, but at least everything didn't remind him of Mary Ellen.

For a while he had wanted that, had drawn comfort from being surrounded by those things that reflected their life together. But later he sold the house, and, but for a few things, gave most of what there was to his son and daughter-in-law out in California.

His briefcase lay on the coffee table, thirty-two papers inside waiting to be marked. Ignoring them, he went out to the closet-sized kitchen, got a beer from the fridge, and took it into the living room. Slumping into the La-Z-Boy, he clicked on the remote. No point in going to bed now; it would soon be time to get up.

The picture came up slowly, like some exotic fish surfacing in murky water. The TV was an old Philco, on its last legs.

Jay Leno was bantering and giggling with a stunning black woman in a gold lamé dress. Though he referred to her as the newest singing sensation, Peter had never heard of her. A sure sign he was getting old. He used to know them all — Lena Horne, Tony Bennett, Johnny Mathis, Ella — and, of course, Old Blue Eyes. On their second anniversary, he took Mary Ellen to Las Vegas to see Sinatra perform live at MGM. Who cared if he messed up a couple of lines; he was still 'The Boss.'

As he sipped his beer, he thought of Tommy. He was worried about him. Tommy had been one of his best students. After he suddenly dropped out of school Peter went out to the house, determined to talk him into coming back. He might as well have been talking to a stone wall for all the good it did. Peter knew it was because of Tommy's father, who let Peter know in no uncertain terms that he didn't appreciate the interference.

'I was out working when I was fourteen,' Nate Prichard had ranted. 'If it was good enough for me, it's damn well good enough for my kid.'

Did Tommy break those windows tonight? Why that particular house to vent his rage on? Because Peter was pretty sure that *rage* had to be what Tommy was feeling right now. God knew the kid had every reason to be angry. His own mother had abandoned him. And Peter had seen the evidence of Nate

Prichard's brutality on more than one occasion. Tommy always blamed his bruises on a door, or some other inanimate object, but Peter knew better, even if he couldn't prove it. Calling in the authorities would have been futile. He'd been teaching long enough to know that kids protected lousy parents all the time.

Peter had actually entertained the thought of going out to the house and taking his chances with Nate. He'd been a pretty fair boxer in college. But even if he did manage to get in a lucky punch or two, it would only make things worse for Tommy. Besides, there was a law against teachers knocking parents about, no matter what kind of jerks they might be.

And then there were the good parents, like Helen and Bob Myers, who cared about their kids, and in the end, it didn't seem to make a damn bit of difference. Their babies got murdered and were buried in dark, cold graves, along with their hopes and dreams.

Tommy had to be grieving right along with Helen and Bob. Unless . . . Peter massaged the bridge of his nose. He was tired. It had been a long day.

He closed his eyes, and was soon asleep in the chair, the television show playing to other audiences.

15

It was nearly dawn when Tommy jerked awake at the sound of his father's truck rumbling into the yard. The motor cut to silence, and Tommy tensed as the door opened. Cold night air poured into the room where he lay on his cot in the kitchen, unmoving, feigning sleep. He was still in his clothes; the mud had dried on them, leaving grit on his skin.

The door closed behind Nate, and in the lengthening silence Tommy could sense his father standing at the foot of his bed, could feel those small, mean eyes boring into him. The sour smell of sweat and booze wafted to him. Hearing the old man's breathing, he concentrated hard on not letting himself blink. *Leave me alone. Please just go to bed and sleep it off.*

Without warning, Tommy was yanked off the bed, sent careening across the room where he crashed into the wall. A picture fell, shattering glass.

Tommy was down on his hands and knees, crawling close to the baseboard, more shocked by the suddenness of the attack, than physically hurt. As his eyes met his father's, he knew that wouldn't be the case for long. The old man was in a crouch position, looking like some mad sumo wrestler going in for the kill. Tommy looked frantically around the room for something to defend himself with, but saw nothing. Nor was there any avenue of escape. His father was a wall between him and the door.

'You stole liquor off me, didn't you, boy?' he said, his voice dangerously soft. Before Tommy could answer, Nate's hand shot out, backhanding him, snapping Tommy's head to one side. Fire bloomed in his cheek; tears stung his eyes.

'I'll teach you to steal from me, you little punk. You're no damn good, just like your whore of a mother.'

Something inside Tommy broke then and he leapt to his feet, fired a straight right to Nate's nose. Connected. Nate looked as surprised as Tommy felt. More so as he wiped a hand under his nose and it came away smeared with his blood. For a moment, he simply stared at it in bewilderment and disbelief. Then, Tommy's own blood ran cold as those cruel eyes lifted to meet his. Only fury there now.

Before Tommy could even think about blocking the punch, or maybe he'd just been too scared to move, Nate hit him a hammer blow to the side of the head that made his ears ring, and sent the room spinning like a nightmare carnival ride.

Just as suddenly, the room began to fade from Tommy's vision, growing smaller and smaller, like a pinpoint of light on the television screen just after you flick the off button on the remote.

I can't pass out. He'll kill me. I'll die here in his godforsaken dump.

And then it came over him that he didn't really care. *Do it, you bastard!* he thought, the side of his head throbbing with pain, warm blood trickling down his face. *Just get it over with.*

He lay there pretending to be unconscious, which was only half-truth, listening to Nate moving about the room, opening and closing dresser drawers, raising and slamming the lid on the washing machine, mumbling to himself the whole time. Tommy knew he was looking for other booze he might have hidden on himself. Through his mumblings, Tommy caught the familiar words, 'whore' and 'faggot.'

At last the door closed again and the truck tore out of the drive. Slowly, painfully, Tommy drew himself to his feet, his mouth and throat tasting of stale whiskey, bile and blood. He forced himself to take several deep breaths through his nose, determined not to puke his guts up right here on the floor. He'd cleaned up after his father too many times to let that happen.

Putting his stomach on uneasy hold, Tommy made it the bathroom, and dropped to his knees before the toilet bowl just in time.

When there was nothing left to bring up, he gripped the edge of the sink, and in a cold sweat and shaking, spasms of pain shooting through his ribs, he struggled to his feet. He turned the tap on full and splashed his face with handfuls of the icy water, until his head cleared enough to let him think.

Tommy caught his reflection in the small cracked mirror above the sink. The skin in front of his ear was split and bleeding, the flesh surrounding it already rising even as he looked at it, turning red.

Tearing a strip of tissue from the roll on the rusting toilet tank, he wadded it and held it gingerly to the cut, wincing with the pain. The ringing in his ears had settled to a low whine. The imprint of his father's huge hand blazed on his otherwise ashen face.

It was a face inherited from his mother — a male version of hers — light brown eyes, full mouth, straight nose, not pugged like Nate's.

He even had that same weak nerve that, when he smiled, tugged the right corner of his mouth down ever-so-slightly. He'd always been self-conscious about it, until Heather told him she thought it was sexy.

An image of Heather lying dead filled the screen of his mind. He blocked it out, thought instead, of his mother. Funny, he'd been thinking about her a lot lately.

You knew what he was like better than anyone, Mom. How could you leave me with him? Why, Mom?

He'd been called 'nothing' and 'fag' so often, that in some deep part of himself, he almost believed it was true. He'd begun to feel differently with Heather. But Heather was gone now.

Tommy went into his father's bedroom. He lifted the .32 special rifle down from the crudely made gun rack above the bed, gasping from the knife-sharp pain that stabbed his right side, forcing him to remain very still until it eased. It was agony just to breathe, and he wondered if the old man had managed to crack a rib or two.

A memory of Nate holding the gun to his mother's head came unbidden. She was crying, her hands covering her head, 'Oh, no, Nate, please, don't. Please. Don't shoot me.' Nate laughing his ugly, mocking laugh at her terror, her helplessness.

Strange how he'd forgotten about that, tucked it into some small compartment of his brain and closed the door. The door was open now, revealing its ugly contents. Now he saw the small boy he had been, screaming in the background, 'Don't kill Mommy. Don't kill Mommy, Daddy.' He'd buried that memory, buried it deep. But the terror of it had echoed inside him all these years.

No more, damn you! No more.

Easing himself back down on the cot, breathing his shallow, cutting breaths, Tommy positioned himself with his back against the wall, the rifle raised. He took careful aim at the door with its peeling shit-brindle paint.

And waited for it to open again.

★ ★ ★

The ringing phone jarred Peter out of fitful sleep. He picked up the receiver. It was Aunt Iris.

'I'm sorry to call you so early, Peter, but I couldn't sleep. It's been on the news — '

'I know. I couldn't sleep either. I went for a drive.' Hardly the time to tell her about someone smashing out Rachael Warren's windows. She'd find out soon enough. After talking to her for a while, securing her promise that she would try to get some sleep, he hung up and went into his own bedroom for his robe. Might as well shower. Maybe he'd even get some of those papers marked.

Mary Ellen's likeness smiled softly up at him from her picture on the nightstand. Peter studied her lovely face for a time, feeling a need to reinforce his memory of her, angry with himself that this could be so. Yet when he took his eyes from the photo, it was Rachael Warren's face he saw.

And it made him feel like the worse kind of Judas.

★ ★ ★

Tommy had not long to wait for his father's return. About an hour later, he heard the truck drive into the yard. Heard the truck door slam shut. Tommy drew himself up in the bed. Ribs shrieking, he cocked the gun. It made a small click. Resting the rifle butt against his shoulder, he set his sights where his father's heart would be.

The door opened and Nate stood reeling in the doorway, clutching a brown paper bag in his hand. By its familiar shape, Tommy knew it was a forty-ouncer. He's not taking any chances of running out, he thought contemptuously. By the look of him, he'd swilled back a good share of the whiskey on the way home.

His faded plaid shirt hung partway out of his pants, the open vee revealing a mat of course black hair. *What are you waiting for? Do it!*

Nate gave a sudden lurch forward and Tommy braced himself for the full impact of his father's weight on top of him, knowing it would kill him for sure. But after a couple of involuntary steps, Nate managed to steady himself.

Nate's unfocussed eyes were on the gun-barrel, which was aligned with the third rust-colored button on his shirt. But Tommy knew he was too drunk for it to register.

He doesn't really see the gun. He won't even feel the bullet's impact when it slams into his body, tearing through flesh and bone. He'll just be dead.

The stench of booze and sweat coming off his father was stronger now, filling Tommy with hatred and disgust. Do it! A voice commanded him. *What are you waiting for?*

But the moment when he might have pulled the trigger came and went, as his father went reeling into his bedroom. The bedsprings groaned in complaint as Nate sprawled heavily on the bed. He was out for the night. So what else was new?

Tommy relaxed his fingers on the trigger,

lowered the gun. And wept.

As on so many nights in his seventeen years, he lay listening to his father's drunken snores through the thin wall. Gradually, those snores and grumblings faded into the background as Tommy's thoughts took a different turn.

Gazing down at the rifle lying across his lap, he thought, *Why not? It would be so easy.* He would be with Heather then.

But who would find her killer? If I kill myself, everyone will think I did it out of guilt and the real murderer will go free. Eventually, Tommy fell into a restless sleep and dreamed of barking dogs chasing him through grasses so tall they blocked out the sky.

Sometime in the night he woke to see his father standing in the doorway between their rooms. Backlit by scant light coming through the window, he seemed at first not a man at all, but a monster — an evil, grinning apparition. He wondered if he was still dreaming.

'No guts,' his old man sneered. 'Didn't have the guts to pull the trigger, did ya, boy?'

And then he heard pounding on the door, followed by the bellow of, 'Police. Open up.'

And he knew he was quite awake. The old man had turned him in to the cops.

16

Showered and dressed, in search of breakfast, Rachael and Betty entered the motel lobby. The desk clerk, a pretty blonde with a frosted pink mouth, chatted animatedly on the phone.

'Yeah, ain't it awful? My brother worked with him, ya know, over at Benny's scrapyard. He says Tommy Prichard kept to himself, didn't joke around with the other fellas, or nothin'. Just does his work. Well, he's locked up now, thank the good Lord for that. Ralphie says it's the quiet types you gotta watch out for.' She flicked a glance at the two women waiting at the counter. 'Gotta go. Talk to you later.' She hung up. 'Mornin', ladies, what can I do for you?'

'Know of a good place where we can grab a late breakfast?' Betty asked. The girl smiled and proceeded to give them directions to a place called *Kathy's*.

They stepped out into a clear, crisp day — streets and buildings polished from the rain, the sky an almost surreal blue. Leaving Betty's car in the parking lot, they drove to the restaurant in the Cavalier. 'Peter Gardner doesn't think the boy is guilty,' Rachael said as they turned onto Water Street.

'From what that desk clerk was saying, he might be alone in his convictions. Maybe he's in denial. He did say Prichard was an ex-student of his. Hope they got good food at that restaurant. I'm starved.'

Driving along the quiet tree-lined street they passed brightly fronted craft shops, some closed for the season. A small art gallery displayed a sculpture, in the window, that looked to Rachael incredibly like a bouquet of elbows, each at an opposing angle. Further on, a woman in a lilac pantsuit was unlocking the door to a beauty shop.

'Reminds me,' Betty said, checking her reflection in the rearview mirror, 'I'm due for a cut.'

'You look great,' Rachael said absently, watching for the restaurant the girl had recommended. A minute later, she drew the car to a stop in front of a café with the name *Kathy's*, written in gothic scroll on a blue and white striped awning.

Getting out of the car, Rachael glanced across the street where a slightly overweight boy in an orange-glo cap industriously raked leaves off the church lawn, stuffing them into the green plastic garbage bag he dragged behind him. The sight of him brought thoughts of her son, Jeff, and of how enterprising he had been at that age. And reminded her that she needed to phone her kids.

They entered the café to an excited buzz of conversation and good smells. It was small and cozy with blue and white décor, a slender vase holding a blue flower adorning every table. Betty made a beeline for a table by the door. They'd barely sat down when the waitress approached, smiling, eyes huge behind granny glasses. 'I'll just be a moment,' she said, handing them their menus.

'Smells fabulous in here,' Betty said, scanning the menu.

In the conversation that hummed around them, Rachael heard Tommy Prichard's name mentioned. Something country played on the jukebox.

Betty moved the vase aside to better see Rachael. 'So, how are you?'

'Fine. You?' Averting her gaze, and more questions, Rachael studied the paintings hanging on the walls. Seascapes, mainly. Better than amateur. Probably done by locals. A woman at the next table was filling in a crossword puzzle, the other hand groping blindly around it for her coffee.

Betty'd been about to say something else when the waitress returned. 'Lovely morning, isn't it? Nip of fall in the air. Nice change after all the rain. Have you ladies decided what you'd like? The sausages are excellent.'

Rachael grimaced at the thought, opted for orange juice, a bran muffin and coffee.

'Can't build muscle on that,' Betty grinned, and ordered the special, which included juice, pancakes and sausages, toast and coffee. 'Trauma always makes me ravenous.'

She said little else until she'd mopped up the last of the maple syrup on her plate with a scrap of toast, after which she daintily blotted her coral mouth with her napkin. 'Don't do this all the time, you know. I'd weigh a ton. Excellent food.' She placed the unfolded napkin on her plate. 'Okay, Rach. Talk to me.'

'I thought we were talking.'

'You know what I mean.'

'I don't — '

A commotion in the doorway drew their attention. The waitress hurried to let in a customer who seemed to be having trouble negotiating his way through the door. Looking embarrassed, the man gestured to his cane. 'Thanks. Haven't quite gotten the hang of this thing yet.'

Betty turned back to Rachael. 'So? How do you propose to live while you're waiting for the courts to decide what a dumped wife is worth? And please don't tell me you're going to cut down trees for firewood, and hope the fishing is good.'

Rachael laughed in spite of herself. Subtlety was not Betty's strong point. 'Actually, it doesn't sound all that bad. Seriously, Betty, I'll be okay. I bought the house for a good price, so I've got enough left to last me the winter. Come spring, I'll get some kind of job. I want nothing from Greg.'

'Are you nuts? You're entitled to half of everything, legally. You contributed as an equal partner in the marriage, more than equal. You better make damn sure you've got a good lawy — '

Rachael was grateful when the waitress interrupted with fresh coffee. Bless Betty, she meant well, but Rachael was wearying of the subject. You'd have thought it was Betty who'd been dumped, as she'd so delicately put it. When the waitress turned away, Rachael said, 'Let's talk about something else, okay?'

Betty shrugged and sipped her coffee.

Rachael wondered if the broken windows had been replaced yet. Right now, all she wanted to do was go home and crawl into bed. But Betty was intent on doing a little shopping while she was here, so she would bear up. It was the least she could do. The last thing she wanted was to become one of those

135

bitter, joyless women who dragged everyone else down with them. Better to avoid people for a while, she thought.

The breakfast crowd was thinning. Rachael looked about her. Her eyes met those of the man who'd needed assistance getting through the door. She looked away, not wanting him to think she was staring. She drank her coffee; it was hot and strong. Maybe the caffeine would pump a little energy into her.

'Maybe I'll open a craft shop,' she said, setting the cup in its saucer, relenting in the face of Betty's hurt silence.

Betty took the offered thread warily. 'Not a bad idea,' she said, with something less than conviction. 'You'd have to cater to people who live here year round though to eke out a living. Even a meager one. Supply and demand, you know.'

'I could carry artists' supplies,' she said, and heard a note of defensiveness in her voice. 'There are a lot of artists living in St. Clair.'

'Sure. You could always take a business course.'

The comment was intended to remind her that she knew nothing about business. And she was right. Greg had always taken care of their business affairs. *I've been so stupid.*

'Mornin' ladies,' an elderly man hefting a

wooden crate on his shoulder, and smelling of fish grinned down at them. The grin revealed tobacco-stained teeth. 'Saw you and your friend comin' out of the motel earlier, Ms. Warren. Danged if Iris wasn't right — you do take after your grandma, God rest her soul. Name's Hartley McLeod, not that you'd know it. Don't s'pose you'd remember that time your grandma got me to hang you a swing in the old elm tree. You was just a little tyke. And 'course I wasn't such an old geezer myself back then,' he chuckled.

Rachael assured him that she did indeed remember that swing. Seeing him cock his head to better hear her, she raised her voice a notch, as she said, 'The seat was painted red.'

It touched her to see how pleased he was that she remembered the swing. 'Sorry 'bout your windows getting busted out like that, before you barely got moved in. Doesn't give a body a real good impression of the place, does it? But they're back in now, good as new. Mayhaps better,' he added with a craftsman's pride. 'Finished up about an hour ago. Some of these kids can get up to no good and that's a fact. But the Prichard boy's not a bad boy at heart. Mighta broke a few windows in his time, but I don't think he did what they're saying he did.'

As they were leaving the restaurant, they

heard yelling across the street. Amidst a chorus of catcalls and jeerings, three older boys were harassing the boy who'd been raking leaves when they drove up. One of them was scooping up armfuls of leaves from the plastic bag and tossing them into the air, while the other two played catch with his orange-glo cap, whipping it back and forth between them, its owner leaping and leaping again, trying to snatch it out of the air.

'C'mon, guys, knock it off. C'mon, okay . . . ?' Although he was doing his darndest not to cry, Rachael could hear the tears in his pleas.

Betty raised an eyebrow at her. 'You be Cagney. I'll be Lacey. Okay?'

They crossed the street.

Keeping her tone pleasant, Rachael said, 'Why don't you boys let him be? Three on one is hardly fair, do you think?'

Two of the boys eyed her nervously, one small and pale, the other with greasy hair and raging acne. The latter shifted his gaze to the third boy for direction, or perhaps moral support. Despite the chill morning, this one, clearly the ring-leader, wore a sleeveless black tee shirt, intended to show off his physique. 'Muscle-shirt' she'd heard Susan call them, Charlie Manson's likeness imprinted on the front.

Apparently having received his unspoken instructions, the younger one leveled his eyes at her. 'Why don't you just butt out, lady.'

'Yeah,' his cohort chimed in, the air of bravado hollow, unconvincing.

'You got business here?' their leader drawled softly. His insolent gaze swept over Rachael, the orange-glo cap dangling from one finger. He let it sway back and forth there, as if to say, 'You want it, come and get it.'

His mocking young eyes made her feel uncomfortable, but she forced herself to hold his gaze, refusing to allow herself to be intimidated by a mere boy. Nonetheless, she wasn't sorry to hear the sudden wail of a police siren, and saw her own relief reflected on Betty's face. Three pair of eyes darted in the direction of the siren, fear and uncertainty replacing the earlier insolence. Their leader suddenly looked like the kid he was, maybe not so tough after all.

'C'mon, Derek,' the thin boy whined. 'Let's split.'

'Smart idea,' Betty said.

'Yeah, man, I'm out of here,' the other squeaked, almost dancing in his panic, but making no move to leave without permission from Derek, who was trying to maintain his image as fearless and blasé before his underlings. As the siren's wail grew louder, he tossed the cap back to the younger boy. 'Here ya go, wienie.' He gave Rachael a long, hard look. 'Catch you later, lady.'

They watched after the trio now running hell-bent up the street, finally piling into a black sports car parked at the corner, then speeding off in a cloud of oily smoke, tires squealing.

'Not exactly the Mayberry it appears to be, is it?' said a faintly familiar voice. They both turned to see the man with the cane limping heavily toward them. With each step, the camera slung about his neck bounced lightly on his chest. The man had longish dark hair, a pleasant face.

'Sorry I was so slow in getting here, but you seemed to have handled the situation just fine without my help.'

'It was the sirens that did it,' Rachael said, looking toward the boy now adjusting his cap on his head, eyes downcast. 'I just hope we didn't make matters worse,' she said quietly.

The young man mumbled a dutiful thanks, clearly not too thrilled at having been rescued by a couple of women. But it might have escalated into something more serious if they hadn't intervened, Rachael thought.

'If you see those fellows coming back,' he said to the boy, 'You just hightail it out of here, okay? You and I both know you could have taken them one at a time, but three is asking for trouble. Remember the old saying, 'He who runs away, lives to fight another day?' Okay, partner?' He gave a conspiratorially wink, bringing a slow grin to the gentle, pudgy face.

'Okay,' the boy said shyly.

'That was sensitive of you,' Betty said.

He smiled vaguely at her. *He has that distracted look of someone who has a rich inner life,* Rachael thought, her eye reflecting on the camera. An artist, of course. As he left them, she noted the ungainly gait favored his right leg. A recent injury, she thought idly, recalling him telling the waitress he wasn't used to the cane yet.

Their shopping finished, they were on the way back to the motel when they saw the man again. He was taking pictures in the park.

Rachael helped Betty stow her treasures in the Honda, among them a tweed vest for Alan, a red plaid coat for Baby, their poodle. She thanked Betty for coming, and for the beautiful earrings.

'You're a wonderful friend. I'll call, I promise. You drive carefully now.'

'Sure. But you're the one who needs to be

careful, Rach. I didn't much like that little hoodlum saying he'd 'Catch you later.''

As they were talking, a man rushed through the doors of the motel, briefcase in hand, coat flapping open. He had that jowly, flushed look of someone on the verge of a stroke. Rachael wondered if he knew that about himself. So much of life came as a surprise. Or maybe we just don't pay enough attention to the signs. She knew she was thinking more about herself than the man, who had already gotten into a waiting cab and driven off.

Rachael followed Betty to the junction of the highway, waved goodbye. Then she sat for several minutes in the car, feeling both relief to be alone, and an acute sense of emptiness.

She glanced at the bags on the back seat. Mostly items for the house, cleaning supplies. It was a small step, but a step just the same. Something.

She was still sitting in the car when a police siren went off behind her, startling her. She pulled off to the side of the road to let it pass.

She was nearing Bay Road when up ahead the cruiser pulled into the small parking lot of Iris' store, where a small crowd had gathered. Alarmed, Rachael stepped on the gas, bypassing her turn-off.

Amidst the throng of onlookers, Iris was

easily recognizable in her long black coat, the silvery, blunt-cut hair. Hands buried in her pockets, she was deep in conversation with a tall, fair-haired man in stone-washed jeans and a leather jacket. On closer inspection, she saw it was Peter Gardner, Iris' nephew. Unconsciously, Rachael's hand moved to her cheek, touched the spot from where he had removed the sliver of glass.

'Rachael,' Iris said, her smile warm if weary. 'It seems we're having something of an epidemic around here. I hope the siren didn't scare you. Elton doesn't get to use it much since leaving the big city.' The lightness draining from her voice, she added, 'Though I suppose that's not exactly true of late.'

Iris' store had been broken into. 'They didn't get much of value,' she told Rachael. 'But they took my radio, damn them. Peter gave it to me when he was still in school. Best little radio I ever owned.'

'Cost me all of ten bucks,' her nephew said. 'I'll get you another one.'

'Can't. They don't make them like that anymore.'

'The main thing is that you're okay,' Rachael said. Iris' gaze shifted past her shoulder, and Rachael turned to see a big man in an overcoat making his way toward

143

them. Iris introduced him as Sergeant Sorrel.

'Prichard must have hit here after, or maybe before, he wreaked havoc on your windows, ma'am,' he said to Rachael. 'But not to worry; he's behind bars where he belongs.'

As he spoke, his shrewd eyes studied her. His big shoulders were hunched inside the overcoat like a man who could never quite get warm.

'Whoever burglarized my store, Elton,' Iris spoke up, 'it wasn't Tommy Prichard. There might not have been a lot of stock left, but certainly whoever took it would have needed a car to haul it away in.'

Rachael immediately envisioned three boys piling into a black sports car.

'Or a truck, Iris,' the policeman said pointedly.

'You're out in left field on that one,' Peter Gardner said. 'Nate would have had Tommy's hide if he touched that bucket of bolts of his.'

'You didn't see him this morning, Peter. I'd say the old man did a pretty good job on him.'

Rachael saw Peter's mouth tighten, his blue eyes go hard as flint.

'Would you like to come back to the house, Iris?' Rachael asked impulsively, a hand on her shoulder. 'I'll make us some tea.'

'Good idea,' Peter said before his aunt could reply. 'A cup of hot tea will do you good. Settle your nerves, Aunt Iris. There's nothing more you can do here.'

Iris' chin lifted perceptibly. 'You're wrong about that, Peter,' she said a tad stiffly. 'Rachael, thank you for the offer, but I want to take a more careful inventory of what's been taken for my insurance adjuster. May I take a rain check?'

'Yes, of course.'

Rachael didn't miss the grin that touched the corners of Iris' nephew's mouth, or the raised eyebrow at the mild, but definite, rebuke. His expression said he should have known better. He seemed to enjoy his aunt's spunkiness, her independent nature.

Rachael didn't like to think about what trouble that spunkiness might have gotten her into if she'd happened to catch the culprits in the act. Iris was definitely not the type to cower in the face of danger. No doubt the same thought had already occurred to Peter Gardner.

Should she mention the incident with those boys this morning? Yet, she had witnessed only a classic case of bullying. And bullying wasn't against the law. Bullies had reined terror against those smaller and weaker when she went to school, and no doubt would continue long after she was gone. She suspected most bullies grew up to be model citizens, with little, if any, recollection of their victims. While the kids they tormented bore the scars to their graves. Well, not much she could do about it. And the 'Catch you later' comment was no doubt just some empty grandstanding in front of his friends.

Still, they did have a car. And they were definitely fitting candidates to any variety of offenses.

At a sudden rumbling and banging, she turned to see a truck pulling into the parking lot and a man in greasy overalls and a faded plaid shirt shamble out. He bulled his way through the crowd, parting it like the Red Sea. Glowering up at the door, at the circular hole someone had punched out with a rock, just big enough to allow a hand to pass through and turn the lock, he raved, 'Damn little jerk gives me nothing but trouble, just like his old lady. She took off and left me with the kid. Probably not even mine.'

'That's Nate Prichard,' Iris said quietly beside her. 'Meanest son-of-a-bitch you'll ever meet.'

'Show's over, folks,' Sorrel said, as he worked his way through the murmuring crowd which, sensing a juicy scene about to erupt, was miffed at being deprived of it. 'Go on back to your homes, now.'

Approaching Nate Prichard, who was still ranting to whomever would listen, Sorrel clapped a friendly hand on his shoulder. 'Okay, let's move it along, Nate. Your boy ain't been charged with nothing yet. We're just holding him for questioning. And I don't want to charge you with anything either. But I will if you give me any grief. Assault and battery, for starters.'

'I never touched that kid. He's lyin'. Hey, remember I called you guys. He did that Myers girl and — '

'Go home, Nate,' Sorrel spat, looking as if he had just bit down on something bad. 'Just get the hell out of here.'

Iris walked Rachael to her car. 'I really do appreciate your stopping by, Rachael. *And* for the offer of tea. It was kind of you. And I would like to talk to you soon. Actually, I was going to call you. I wonder if I might come by . . . perhaps one day next week.'

'Sure. That would be fine. For a — visit, you mean?' she added foolishly. Rachael wondered what she was letting herself in for.

Her eye followed Iris' to Nate Prichard, who was now getting back in his truck, his meaty face sullen and hostile. Sergeant Sorrel stood close by, keeping an eye on him. Rachael had the idle thought that Nate

Prichard would have liked nothing better than to stomp the gas pedal to the floor, but couldn't quite gather up the nerve.

When the truck was no longer in view, Iris turned to Rachael. 'Yes, Rachael,' she said pleasantly, 'for a visit.'

17

After spending the morning in a cell, Tommy now sat on a hard-backed chair in a windowless room watching Captain Sorrel circle him like a hawk, talons poised for the big kill. Tommy's eyes flickered over the other two cops in the room. The one with the cold eyes — Detective Mason — leaned against the wall by the door, beefy arms crossed over his chest. The bald one had narrow shoulders, and a gut hanging over his belt. He looked a little less redneck.

Thumb-tacked on the greasy green wall above the bald cop's head, a yellowing wanted poster showed a picture of a guy not much older than Tommy, but with an old-fashioned mustache that drooped down on either side of his mouth. The caption said he shot four people in a bank holdup.

The room reeked of stale cigarette smoke mixed with sweat and fear and desperation. Or maybe the desperation was coming from him. Meeting Sorrel's eyes, Tommy had to breathe shallow quick breaths to bear the pain in his ribs. He tried to block it out, but that was impossible.

Behind the opaque, glass door, he could make out silhouettes moving about on the other side. He could hear the muffled ringing of telephones.

'I know how you feel, Tommy,' the sergeant said in a tone intended to be fatherly. 'But like I told you, you gotta tell the truth. It'll make a difference in what happens here.'

'I told you the truth,' Tommy said.

Sorrel's hound-dog eyes hunted Tommy's. Just as if he hadn't spoken, Sorrel said, 'So, now, why not come clean and make it easy on yourself? She didn't want to go all the way? You find out she was seeing someone else? Was she trying to break it off with you? You know, Tom, a classy girl like Heather Myers couldn't have been too thrilled at having a boyfriend who worked in a scrapyard.'

Tommy felt numb from sitting, his mind equally numb from answering the same questions over and over, each time with a slightly different spin. Questions meant to trick him into confessing to something he didn't do. Aside from his shrieking ribs, his eyes felt as though someone had rubbed sandpaper over them, and the place beside his ear, where his father's fist had landed, throbbed like a toothache.

'Listen,' the police captain said, laying a hand on Tommy's shoulder, 'It's not that hard to understand, you know? Women can do it to you. Make you nuts. Ain't that right, Mason?' The detective gave a nod of agreement, a smirk touching his mouth.

Tommy shrugged the captain's hand off his shoulder, which brought a swift anger to Sorrel's eyes that Tommy ignored.

'Why don't you believe me?' he said. 'I want Heather's killer found as much as anyone. Maybe more. It's just a job to you guys.' Every word he spoke was an excruciating effort, draining him a little more. 'If you got anything on me, then arrest me. Otherwise, I'm walking out of here.' If I can, he thought miserably. 'Look, I need to see a doctor. I think — I've got a couple of busted ribs.'

The stalking ceased, a bushy eyebrow lifted. 'No kidding. And how did that happen? Did she manage to get in a good kick when you were holding that pillow over her face, smothering the life out of her?'

'Yeah, right.' Tears sprung to his eyes at the horror of the image. 'And then she beat the hell out of me.' He could say no more. Beads of cold sweat broke out on his forehead. The killer's face on the wanted poster wavered in front of his eyes like he was seeing it through water. He was going to pass out.

'You *are* looking a little green around the

151

gills, lad,' Sorrel said, sounding like he almost gave a damn. 'You just take it easy. We'll have a doctor look at you. In fact, I'm going to personally see to it that you have plenty of time to heal, with no one to disturb you. Not for a long, long time.'

18

Rachael's phone was installed on Wednesday morning. No sooner did the blue van from the phone company drive out of the yard than the instrument rang. A soft trill, but it startled her just the same. She picked up the receiver.

'Hello?'

'Mom?'

'Susan, darling — '

'Are you okay, Mom?' Her voice sounded small over the line, a child's voice, uncertain. 'I got the number from information. You're using your maiden name.'

Rachael only replied that she was fine. A small lie, necessary. Susan was in her second year of college, studying marketing and communication, at the top of her class. Though she'd inherited Rachael's grey eyes, and high cheekbones, she had Greg's gregarious nature, his gift of persuasion. She would do well in her chosen field. *She doesn't need to be worrying about me.*

'Dad loves you, Mom,' she was saying. 'He's just going through some kind of mid-life crisis. Maybe if you got your hair done differently. Bought some sharp new clothes . . . '

She's telling me this is somehow my fault. It hurt, but came as no surprise. *She loves me, but she's first and foremost, her daddy's girl. And why not?* Greg was handsome and fun to be around. Rachael had always encouraged their special relationship, had nurtured it.

Listening to Susan's so-simple solutions, from the corner of her eye Rachael caught a movement down on the beach. Inching aside the new lace curtain, she recognized the man from the restaurant. He was leaning on his cane, snapping pictures of a piece of driftwood. His longish hair blowing in the breeze, he turned, aimed his camera at a lone seagull standing skittishly on Rachael's flat-topped rock. She watched a moment then let the curtain drop from her fingers.

Allowing herself a moment to regroup after hanging up the phone, she dialed Jeff's number. Getting the machine, she left a message, relieved at the reprieve. When she looked out the window again, the man was gone. The beach was deserted. She was about to turn away when she saw Iris Brandt's car pull into the yard.

She instinctively looked around her. The carpet didn't look half-bad after a good shampooing. The musty house-fire smell was gone, replaced by a clean piney fragrance. She'd replaced the torn lampshade with a new one, hung a couple of inexpensive Victorian prints.

After she got home from the scene of Iris' break-in, Rachael had launched into a marathon of housecleaning that lasted until twenty minutes ago. She'd heard somewhere that the best weapon against feeling powerless was action. And it worked — at least temporarily.

'I'm beginning to feel like the proverbial bad penny,' Iris said, when they were sitting in the living room sipping wine from long-stemmed glasses. Rachael had angled the chairs toward one another, facing the windows, and the bay. Iris' eye strayed there now. 'But I thought I should tell you a little about the last family who lived here.'

'George and Ethel Bates?' Rachael had never met the previous owners, only read their names on the transfer of deed. As far as she knew they were an older couple who decided to move to Florida for the climate. Iris had alluded to some kind of family tragedy.

'Yes. Oh, I know all the focus right now is on Tommy Prichard, but I've never known Tommy to be violent, and in fact I don't recall he's ever been in any kind of trouble. I can't say the same for the Bates' nephew.'

'Nephew?' Rachael repeated, having no idea who Iris was talking about.

'Yes. His name is Jimmy Ray Dawson, a no-account boy, unfortunately, and also unfortunately, Ethel's blood nephew. Jimmy Ray got it in his head that his Uncle George had money stashed somewhere in the house, and was determined to find out where. I doubt George had any money, though that is hardly the point. Anyway, Ethel told him if he ever darkened her doorway again, she'd have him thrown in jail.'

Rachael nodded for Iris to go on, curious as to what all this had to do with her.

'Ethel loved that boy with all her heart, but she'd reached her limit when he hurt George.'

The Chantilly lace curtains fluttered gently in the screened-in windows, letting in the scent of the sea, and a momentary chill. Rachael closed the window, let her eye linger a moment on the calm blue bay.

She sat down again, picked up her wineglass. 'He assaulted his uncle?'

Iris' blue eyes were at once sad and angry. 'By the time I got here, it was all over,' she said. 'Ethel was cleaning the blood from her husband's face. She'd been crying. George was moaning, half-conscious.'

'My God.'

'My reaction exactly. She begged me to keep her secret. It was only because she was a registered nurse herself that I agreed, although against my better judgment. She was ashamed, took it as her own personal failure. A black mark on the family name.'

'But it wasn't her fault.'

'No. It wasn't. They were good people. Jimmy Ray was just twelve when they took him in. They treated him like the son they never had, doted on him. Especially Ethel. Maybe that had something to do with it. Maybe not. Anyway, he repaid them with not a moment's peace. Ethel always blamed it on the fact that he came from a broken home.'

'Iris, I think I'm getting a sense of where you're going with this. But this place was vacant for a year before I bought it. Surely, he knows — '

'That's just it, Rachael. I'm not sure he does know they sold the house and moved away. Peter thinks he's probably spent time in jail without Ethel's help. The good Lord knows he was headed in that direction.'

'And you think he'll be furious when he finds out they took off without leaving a forwarding address. Sounds like an old joke.'

'But not very funny, I'm afraid. Like most

cowards, he's a bully. It wouldn't be beneath him to take out his anger on whoever opens that door to him. Especially someone vulnerable like a woman alone.'

Fear touched Rachael's heart. 'You really think he'll turn up here.'

'I don't know. It's possible. It's also possible I'm making far too much of the whole matter. But I did think you should be aware. It seemed more important than keeping Ethel's secret. This is excellent sherry, by the way.'

'I'm glad you like it.' Her mind envisioned the silhouette out by the elm tree she'd seen on the night of the storm. *Could it have been the Bates' nephew?*

Shaking her head as if to erase the incident from her mind, Iris looked around the room approvingly. 'You're spinning a cozy cocoon for yourself, Rachael. A safe haven, I'm sure,' she added, too heartily. 'Truly, it is not my intention to frighten you. Only to alert you to possible danger.'

The words had a familiar ring. 'I know that, Iris. Thank you for telling me.' Like Iris, she too, wanted to dismiss the subject of the Bates from further thought or conversation.

Her gaze wandered to the mantle and the matching off-white candleholders Iris had brought her as a *proper* housewarming gift.

Rachael had arranged them at either end of the mantle, flanking the vase of silk daisies — a fitting replacement for the pickle bottle with its plastic rose. Beautifully crafted, the exact thread of moss green ran through the candleholders as was in her new chintz chair covers.

Maybe Iris really is psychic. Rachel smiled to herself.

After Iris left, Rachael looked up Hartley McLeod's number, dialed it. The phone rang a few times before he answered. She could hear a dog barking in the background. She should get a dog. It would be good company, and could also let her know if anyone was lurking around outside. When the kids were little, they'd wanted a pet, but Greg was allergic.

'This is Rachael Warren, Mr. McLeod,' she said. 'I wanted to thank you so much for replacing the windows. If you'll just let me know how much . . . '

'Glad to be of service,' he interrupted. 'Couldn't very well live in a house without windows, now, could you?' He gave his raspy chuckle. 'But don't you worry none about money, you hear, we got a victim's fund set up for just that sort of thing. Thought we should what with all the vandalism.'

'I see. Well, I'm deeply grateful. Mr.

McLeod, I — uh, wondered if you wouldn't mind bringing my spare key by when you're — well, in the neighborhood.'

'Key?' he said, sounding surprised. 'I put that key on the ledge above the door, same as always, ma'am.'

'Same as always?'

He paused. 'I used to do a little work for George after he couldn't do it for himself no more.'

Had she hurt his feelings? She hadn't meant to. 'I'll have another look,' she said, and thanked him again for his good work. 'I must have just missed seeing it.'

But the key was not where he said. Nor was it under the mat, or anywhere else she could think of as a possible hiding place. Had someone been watching him when he put the key on the ledge, waited until he left, and took it?

But the Bates' nephew wouldn't need to do that, would he? He would already know where the key was kept.

And why didn't that make her feel any better?

Why was all this happening? She came here to heal, to try to find her way back to herself, and somehow she'd been drawn in to murder and mayhem, even becoming a victim of vandalism herself.

Not much she could do about it. Keeping busy was the only answer that came to her. Although the house looked considerably better than it had, it still needed papering and painting throughout. Not easy to summon the motivation or energy when all you really wanted to do was go to bed and pull a cover over your head, but she would put herself to the task. *Yes, a project is just what I need.*

When she was working, she didn't let herself feel or think. She operated on automatic. She functioned better in pleasant, orderly surroundings. She always had. Tomorrow she'd go into town and check out prices on paint and paper at the hardware store.

Right now though what was in order was a long, hot shower.

Upstairs, she slipped out of her jeans, shirt, bra and panties, letting them drop into a heap on the bathroom floor. Turning the taps on full, she adjusted the showerhead and stepped into the old-fashioned claw foot tub. Standing beneath the hot needle-fine spray, she closed her eyes, surrendering to the cascade of water. Gradually, the hot shower began to wash the tiredness from her body.

'*Maybe if you got your hair done differently, Mom . . . bought some sharp new clothes . . .* '

Susan wasn't the first one to have had that

thought. For a moment, Rachael had managed to convince *herself* that it would work. A few nights after Greg admitted to his affair with Lisa, she'd showered and slipped into the new negligee she had purchased that very afternoon. A lovely thing it was, of ivory satin, the bodice edged in fine lace, cut to flatter her small breasts, camouflage her less than washboard stomach. She'd applied make-up, layers of erase to hide the puffiness from so much crying, brushed her dark hair until it gleamed. Greg used to say she had nice hair.

Dimming the lights, she waited for his footsteps on the stairs. When she heard them, she panicked, tried to bolster her courage with thoughts of the two wonderful children they'd brought into the world. With the sheer force of her own love, she would bring him back to her. Make him understand that they belonged together. Lisa was a mistake; he would see that.

But it was she who had made the mistake. One that it was too late to correct. Despite the nightgown, she had never felt quite so naked as she did in that moment, with Greg standing in the doorway, looking at her. She saw embarrassment in his eyes, guilt, and most unforgivable of all — pity. She tried to look away, but some perversity within her made her unable to, as if at some level she needed to extract the full measure of this humiliation. Not spare herself one shred of it. When he was gone, she filled the tub with water and held a razor blade between thumb and forefinger for a good half hour, but could not summon the courage to slide it across her wrists. It was her lowest point. She'd heard it said you had to go there before you could start climbing back up.

She would not have wanted anyone to know about that night. Not even Betty. Maybe *especially* not Betty.

Rachael stepped out of the tub onto the cool tile floor. As she towel-dried her hair, she caught a glimpse of her blurred reflection in the steamy mirror and it struck her as somehow symbolic.

She was reaching for her robe on the door hook when a shadow fell across the threshold, blocking the light that came through the crack under the closed door. Her heart contracted in fright, sending a shot of adrenaline surging through her body. She tried to swallow, but her mouth was dry.

Was someone standing on the other side of the door? Someone who crept up the stairs while she was in the shower? Rachael tried to remember if she'd locked the back door after Iris left. Yes, she could visualize herself locking it. Heard in her head the lock click into place. She remembered again the missing spare key.

She imagined she could hear *him* breathing. Soft, measured breaths, mouth close to the door. Waiting for her to open it.

Behind her, water dripped . . . dripped . . . into the tub. She continued to listen for the breathing, and soon realized it was herself she was hearing. Her own breathing. As suddenly as the shadow had fallen beneath the door, it lifted, once again allowing light in from the window at the end of the hallway.

Rachael resumed drying her hair, slipped into her robe and, with only the slightest trepidation, opened the door. Stepped into the hallway

No one there. No sinister being lying in wait for her. Iris' talk of the Bates' nephew had gotten to her. She let out a long shuddering breath she hadn't known she was holding and went to the window. The sun was still shining, laying a path of light along the polished, brown linoleum runner

A cloud must have passed over.

19

Tommy sat listlessly on his cell cot, staring at the cement floor. He heard the footsteps approaching, but paid them little attention until they stopped at his cell door. He looked up, fully expecting to see one of the guards, was surprised when it wasn't.

'Hey, Tom. How's it going?'

'Mr. Gardner. What are you doing here?'

'I wondered if maybe you and I couldn't have a little talk. Are you up for that?'

'Sorrel thinks because you used to be my teacher you'll have better luck in getting a confession out of me?'

Peter remained silent as the guard unlocked the cell door. Close by, another cell door clanged shut. 'I got a right to make a phone call,' someone yelled in a slurred voice. 'Where the hell is the stinking justice in this place anyway?' This followed by a string of colorful expletives.

Stepping into the cell, Peter felt the walls closing in on him. 'Do you have anything to confess, Tom?'

'Shit. You mean the cops don't already have all the answers?' The hard-edged words were no sooner out of his mouth than the tears came. Grinding his fists into his eyes, he choked out, 'The old man's right. I am gutless. A goddamn baby.'

Peter fished a handkerchief from his back pocket, shook out the folds and handed it to him. 'It's no sign of weakness to cry,' he said. 'Your father might be a better man if he knew how.' He eyed the raised bruise on the side of Tommy's face. He also knew that beneath the shirt, his ribs were strapped up. Luckily, none broken, though badly bruised.

Paul Goldman, the lawyer Peter hired for Tommy, told him that when he first saw the boy, he'd been ready to sue for police brutality. Tommy had no choice but to tell him what really happened.

Peter sat on the cot beside him, tapped his breast pocket. 'Cigarette?'

Tommy accepted, trying not to look surprised at the offer. Peter lit two, averting his eyes from the brown-stained toilet bowl in the corner. 'At least you won't have to hide in the john to smoke this one,' he said. 'Considering you're already in one.'

'Funny,' Tommy said, unable to suppress a small grin.

'Just for my own curiosity, Tommy. Why did you bust out Rachael Warren's windows?'

'I didn't. I mean, I don't think so. Oh,

what's the use talking about it?' He stared at the lighted tip of his cigarette as if the answer might be inscribed there.

'Indulge me, okay.'

Tommy shrugged. 'I've been trying to get it clear in my own head. Not much else to do in here,' he said bitterly. When he spoke again, his voice had grown soft. He did not look at Peter, but at the floor. 'I know I was really out of it. I, uh, swiped a pint of the old man's whiskey. I wanted to get drunk, block out everything. I wanted to . . . '

'Run away?'

'Yeah. I guess.'

'I can relate to that. Do you drink often?'

'No,' he said adamantly, his head snapping up. 'I don't smoke anymore, either, if you want to know.'

'Good. Neither do I.' He took Tommy's cigarette from his hand, and dropped it with his own into the toilet bowl, where they sizzled, adding to the stench of the small space. He turned to Tommy, hands in his pockets. 'You ready to ditch this place?'

Twenty minutes later, they were setting in a booth in Burger King.

'How did you manage it, Mr. Gardner?' Tommy asked, spearing a French fry from his plate and swirling it around in the ketchup.

'I didn't. Your lawyer did. The evidence was circumstantial. Nothing a good defense lawyer couldn't poke holes through. Heather's father had you banned from visiting her so you snuck in during the middle of the night. Besides, Paul thinks you're innocent. For the record, so do I.'

'How come? Everyone else thinks I'm guilty.'

'Not everyone.'

Watching Tommy salting his fries so liberally, Peter winced inwardly. He was grateful when he finally put the shaker down. 'I wanted to see her,' Tommy said. 'I needed her to know I was there for her.'

Sensing Tommy's need to talk about it, to get it all out, Peter said nothing.

'I couldn't even go to her funeral.'

'I know. I'm sorry.'

'We were going to get married someday.'

Peter nodded.

'Funny thing is, we didn't get together until I quit school and went to work at the scrapyard. I just never figured someone as pretty and smart as Heather could ever be interested in me. She said she sent me lots of signals, but I guess I was just too dumb to pick up on them. Anyway, she was always nice to everyone. I thought that's all it was.'

'You sell yourself short, Tom. So,' he prompted gently, 'when did you finally get the message?'

Tommy smiled, and Peter noticed that the right side of his mouth tugged down slightly. A weak muscle. Odd, he'd never noticed that before. Then again, he'd rarely seen Tommy smile.

'She drove out to the scrapyard one day at lunchtime, said she was looking for a good used muffler for a friend. I was so thick I reminded her that her dad owned a brake and muffler shop. She smiled and said, 'Yeah, I know.' Then she handed me one of the Cokes she was holding. I thought I must be dreaming.'

'Not exactly subtle,' Peter smiled.

'Guess she figured I needed a sledgehammer. I'll never find anyone like her, Mr. Gardner.' He swallowed hard. 'Heather was special.'

'Yes, she was. And no one will ever take her place. But you're a young man. You will find someone else one day. Someone special in her own way.'

Tommy looked squarely at him. 'You didn't.'

The statement came out of left field, catching him off-guard. 'I'm an old man compared to you,' he said, brushing the comment off. He had no desire to get into his private life, or lack thereof, with anyone, much less an ex-student.

Tommy sipped his coke, speared another fry.

'Something's been bothering me, Tom. Mind if I ask you a personal question?'

'No.'

He paused. Then, 'Why do you continue to live with your father? You don't have to, you know. Until things are settled, you're welcome to bunk at my place. It's not fancy, but there's a pullout.'

'Thanks.' Tommy looked thoughtfully at the ketchup-smeared fry on his fork. 'But she wouldn't know where I was.'

'Who?' Was he talking about Heather? Did he think she was coming back? Maybe he was in serious need of grief counseling. Peter leaned forward, asked quietly, 'Who wouldn't know where you are, Tom?'

Tommy's reply was barely audible, almost a whisper. 'My mother.'

As Peter was trying to make sense of the words, the door opened. Sensing a new tension in the atmosphere, Peter turned to see Bob Myers standing in the doorway, crazed eyes scanning the restaurant. Peter's stomach clenched, knowing who he was

170

looking for. He looked even worse than he had at Heather's funeral. Bob's eyes found them, flared with rage. He made for their table. Peter sprung to his feet. 'Afternoon, Bob,' he said, putting out a hand, which Myers ignored.

'Saw your car outside, Peter. Thought I'd drop in and say thank you for taking such good care of my little girl's killer.'

News travels fast, Peter thought, and hoped this wasn't going to turn into an ugly situation, knowing with a sinking sensation that it already had. 'Bob, wait, you're jumping to conclus — '

'The hell I am. He's got you conned just like he conned Helen and me. Heather had a good heart. She was always picking up strays and bringing them home. Like this animal here.'

Tommy's color had gone from pale to a sickly grey. Suddenly the manager was there, threatening to call the police. Peter had to talk him out of it. They both did their best to calm Myers down, but there was no reasoning with him. Other than Bob Myers' hate-filled voice, the restaurant had fallen silent.

'You're a worse creep than your sleazy old man ever was,' he told Tommy. 'Smoother is all, smarter. But you don't fool me. It's not over yet. The cops know you did it.' His voice lowered dangerously. 'You put my baby girl in the ground, you bastard, and one way or the other, I'm going to see that you pay for it. You just keep looking over your shoulder, boy,' he said, punctuating every word with a hard finger-jab to Tommy's shoulder, 'because one of those times I'll be there.'

Peter stepped between them. 'Okay, Bob, you had your say. Go on home now.'

'Sure, I'll go. But not because you say so. I'm not one of your worshipful students, Peter.'

Torn between concern for Tommy, and compassion for Bob Myers, he caught up with him in the doorway. 'Bob, can we talk about this? I won't pretend to know what you're feeling, but — '

Myers wheeled. 'Good. Because you don't know. If you had even the remotest idea, you wouldn't have gotten that murdering creep out of jail, and you wouldn't be mollycoddling him now. I got nothing more to say to you, Gardner.'

His cold fury shifted back to Tommy, who'd sat through the torrent of abuse like he was made of stone. 'I mean what I say, Prichard. You mark my words.'

There was a deafening silence at Peter's

back as he and Tommy exited. The instant they were out of here, he knew the place would erupt into a cacophony of gossip and speculation.

He was glad he didn't have to hear it.

20

Despite the sunshine, temperatures had dropped to below zero, and by the time Rachael reached Iris' house, she was shivering in her thin all-weather coat.

Iris lived just three blocks from where Rachel had abandoned her car. Or, to be more precise, where the car had abandoned her.

It was a pretty house, white colonial with hunter-green shutters, set well back from the road, fronted by a cedar hedge. Pocketing the business card Iris had given her three weeks before, Rachael started up the stone walk. But before she reached the door, it opened and Iris stood in the doorway smiling at her.

'I'm so glad you came, Rachael.' Just as if she'd been expecting her.

Maybe she put a hex on the car, she thought, knowing how ridiculous that was. Almost as ridiculous as sitting in her dead car feeling like a lost child because it wouldn't start. When the engine refused to turn over, she'd seen it as an act of betrayal, somehow deliberate. And how crazy was that?

'Thanks,' Rachael said, grateful to let Iris

lead her into the warm foyer.

Before closing the door, Iris looked past her, toward the street. 'Where's your car?'

What? You didn't know? 'Quit on me. About three blocks from here.'

'Oh, I see.' Mild amusement crept into her smile. 'The proverbial last straw, huh.'

'Something like that. But I've been planning on calling you anyway. I was wondering if you might consider telling me a little more about that illusory control in one's life you talked about.'

'Pottery making, you mean? Sculpting?'

'If you really think I could . . . '

Iris was fairly glowing as she took Rachael's coat. 'It's a wonderful idea, Rachael. And I'd be delighted to teach you what I know. And I'll drive you home after your lesson.'

'Thank you, but it's not necessary.'

'I insist,' she said, picking up the receiver. 'I'll get my mechanic to tow your car to the garage. And deliver it to you when it's ready. He's a good man,' she smiled.

For the next hour they sat in Iris' kitchen talking and sipping tea from china cups adorned with tea roses.

Cleo was curled up asleep on the braided mat at Iris' feet. Every now and then, as if one of them had said something that sparked her interest, she would open one blue eye.

Then she would yawn with boredom, stretch and settle back to sleep.

'When I was a girl,' Iris was saying, speaking about the changes in the area over the years, 'the streets in St. Clair weren't even paved. Most folks got about in horse and wagon. If you don't mind my saying so, you're looking much better today. Not so peaked. How are you feeling?'

'Actually not too bad. I've been running in the mornings. It helps.' It was true. She liked the rhythmic sound of her feet running on the sand, the wind in her hair. Running was a great stress-releaser, she found. Although that first couple of times she had to force herself out of the house then had run only a short distance before doubling over, the blood pounding in her ears like Niagara Falls. She hadn't realized she was in such lousy physical shape. But she was improving. This morning she'd jogged a good two miles before working up a sweat. Along her run, she ran into the photographer taking his pictures. They waved to one another, an oddly comforting exchange. Neighbors greeting one another.

She had her black moments. They came at her like tidal waves, unexpected, savage, dragging her into their undertow, leaving her weepy and fragile, as if she'd contacted some exotic illness.

A little death, Iris had termed it. But it would have been easier if Greg had died. She could have worn black, attended his funeral. There would have been dignity in that. My God, how could she even think such a horrible thing? *What kind of person am I?*

Iris was asking about her mother and father, if they were still alive. Rachael confided that her mother had died of a massive hemorrhage just days after giving birth to Rachael.

'How sad for you never to have known her. Surely your father . . . ?'

'My father never spoke of her. My questions were met with silences, or curt answers. I soon learned not to ask them.'

Maybe it was the car breaking down that shed her defenses. Or maybe it was just easier to confide in a virtual stranger. Whatever it was, Rachael found herself opening up to this woman who conveyed a quiet wisdom through her eyes, even by her very presence.

When they finished their tea, Rachael followed Iris through the long narrow hallway to the studio at the back of the house. Cleo padded behind them, nails soundless on the dark blue carpeting, alternately clicking on the hardwood stretches between.

As Iris opened the maroon painted door, Rachael bent down and patted Cleo, was rewarded with a deep, affectionate purr.

'She likes you,' Iris said. 'Cleo doesn't take to many people. She's a good judge of character.'

The compliment warmed her, probably more than it should have. When had she become so needy?

The studio was a rectangular room, dominated by a long wooden table strewn with various wooden-handled tools, brushes, drawings, and other items alien to her eye.

On the clay-spattered floor, an organized clutter of boxes, bags, clay pots, jars and other paraphernalia stood against the walls.

The room smelled pleasantly of something vinegary, and of paint and clay, and dry heat from the fired-up kiln across the room.

Portraits and drawings hung on three walls, while at the far end of the room, a large, curtainless window overlooked a brief stretch of field, coming up against the backs of houses. Sheets flapped on a line spanning two of the houses.

Flanking the window, an assortment of vessels and plates were displayed on floor to ceiling shelves. One plate in particular grabbed her attention. Painted a deep scarlet, it was edged in gold, centered with an Indian chief's profile in full headdress.

'Gorgeous,' Rachael breathed.

On the next lower shelf a small bowl decorated with bluebirds in flight, rimmed with intertwining silver leaves, drew her admiration. Some of the other pieces were bare of adornment, but striking in their own primitive rendering.

'I'm no expert, Iris, but even I can see you are a gifted artist. These are wonderful. By the way,' she smiled. 'I bought a set of your blue mugs the other day. Hand-painted with yellow flowers. I saw them in a little craft shop on Water Street.'

She had just left the lawyer's office after filing for divorce, and the sight of the mugs in the window had lifted her spirits.

'The mugs with the butter-and-eggs flowers from my childhood,' Iris said, clearly pleased that Rachael had fancied them. 'Toadflax, actually. Weeds, you know. But I've always rather liked them. What a lovely compliment that you bought them, Rachael.'

Iris turned her attention to the contraption on the table, referring to it as a *hand-wheel*. Propped on this hand-wheel, wrapped mummy-like in a white cloth, was what appeared to Rachael to be a work-in-progress.

Beginning to remove the wrapping, Iris said, 'I'd like your opinion on something I've been working on, Rachael. It still needs work, I know. I don't have the face quite right.'

Setting the cloth aside, she stepped back so that Rachael could view the piece in its entirety.

As she looked at it, a cold chill slid over Rachael. For the moment, she was at a loss for words.

'You don't like it.'

'No, no it's not that. It's just so . . . powerful,' she faltered.

'You don't have to patronize me, Rachael.' Iris sounded disappointed but not terribly surprised. 'I know the face is too broad,' she said, misunderstanding the reason behind Rachael's hesitation. 'Cleo has much finer bones . . . '

'Iris, I do like it. Really,' Rachael cut in, though not quite sure *like* was the right word to describe her reaction. 'It's just that Cleo always seems such a sweet, serene animal. What possess — moved you to sculpt her in this particular . . . '

'Pose?' Iris finished, contemplating the sculpture. 'Something frightened her one night — frightened both of us, actually.' She spoke quietly. 'I felt compelled — or maybe possessed *is* a better word — to recapture her in that moment. Maybe to remind myself I wasn't alone in my . . . ' She let the sentence drift off, shook her head, picked up a nozzled spray bottle from the floor.

Rachael continued to stare at the sculpture. *Yes, it is terror that I see in her eyes. Far more so than any threat against whatever it was.* In this rendering, Cleo's back was arched, her small teeth bared in a silent, eternal growl. A shiver passed over Rachael.

'What was it that . . . ?'

'Overactive imagination, I'm sure,' Iris laughed, a laugh that held a false and unconvincing note. 'On both our parts. What I'm doing now, Rachael,' she said, switching subjects, 'is spraying the piece with water so that the clay doesn't become too dry to work with. You want it to remain malleable,' she smiled, now fully the instructor imparting a lesson to her student.

The sculpture sprayed to her satisfaction, Iris rewrapped it in its cloth and set it on the shelf behind her. Reaching into a pail on the floor, she tore off a chunk of clay about the size of a bowling ball, and positioned it on the hand-wheel. Giving a theatrical sweep of her hand, she said, 'There you go, Rachael. See what you can make of it.'

'Oh, Iris, I don't know . . . '

'What's to know? You select your clay, which I've already done for you. You shape it, let it dry, then glaze it or not, as inspiration moves you. After that, you bake it in the kiln.'

She gave a delighted laugh at what must

181

have been a rather dazed expression on Rachael's face. 'Well, maybe there's a little more to it than that. But essentially, that's the process. And we all have to start somewhere.'

'I'm not sure I'm ready. Why don't I just watch you today, Iris? Maybe next time . . . '

'Nonsense, we learn by doing. You mentioned that you used to like to write poetry. Well, now, instead of words, you will express your inner vision, your emotions, through the medium of clay. The main thing is,' she said, taking a leather apron from a hook on the door and tying it around Rachael, 'is to relax. Let yourself get a feel for the clay.' She stood back and smiled. 'Perfect. You look like a natural to me.'

After a brief hesitation, Rachael stepped up to the lump of whitish-grey clay awaiting her at eye-level. Soon, a tingling started in her fingers, bringing with it a sense of anticipation, of possibility. At the same time, she feared looking foolish in front of Iris.

'Try to work it as a whole,' Iris said, moving to the far end of the table. There, she donned a paint-spattered, blue smock.

'Remember to turn the wheel every so often,' she said, as she took up her pen and turned to a new page in her sketchpad. 'That way, you'll be able to view all sides of the piece and it won't end up being one-dimensional.'

'I feel like a kid with play dough,' Rachael said, as she tentatively placed her hands upon the clay. The touch of it conjured memories of rainy days spent inside with Jeff and Susan. She recalled flowers and elephants and impossibly shaped dogs formed by small, industrious fingers.

'Good,' Iris smiled. 'That's exactly how you're supposed to feel. It's the state of mind we artists strive for, and so seldom achieve.'

As she worked, gradually everything else faded to some far place in her mind. Only the image she hoped to create and the clay beneath her fingers held any reality for her. So completely focused on the task at hand, Rachael jumped when Iris spoke to her.

'Sorry, but you've been at it for . . . ' Iris looked at her watch ' . . . over an hour now. Impressive for your first time. How about we stop for a little bodily sustenance. How did you get on?'

'I've been trying to do a bust of my grandmother,' Rachael said, kneading the knot of tension from her left shoulder. 'But I'm afraid it looks more like Richard Nixon.'

Iris laughed. 'Oh, I'm sure you exaggerate,' she said, coming round to look. She cocked an eye at it, and absolutely deadpan, said,

'You know, it does look like him at that.'

They both laughed.

The doorbell rang into the studio. There was urgency in the sound.

Rachael was getting into her coat as Iris opened the door to a frail looking woman with an anxious face and haunted eyes, an air of desperation about her.

'I need to talk to you, Iris,' she said, running a hand through hair carelessly swept back from her face. In her other hand she clutched a large canvas bag with a fierceness that suggested the bag held all she possessed in the world.

'Of course, Helen,' Iris said gently, drawing the woman inside. 'I'd like you to meet a friend of mine — Rachael Warren. Rachael this is Helen Myers — you remember . . . '

'Yes,' she said, extending her hand, knowing intuitively who the woman was even before Iris introduced them. 'I'm so sorry . . . ' Such empty, useless words. She wished she could think of something profound to say, something that would ease the pain so evident in this woman's face, but she knew no such words existed.

'I'm sorry to intrude,' she said to Rachael, 'but I must talk privately to Iris . . . '

'Please don't apologize. I was just leaving. It was nice to meet you. Iris, if you wouldn't

184

mind calling me a cab . . . '

'Rachael, I'm . . . ' Her eyes were full of apology.

'No problem. I'll call you.'

Bad enough to lose a child, Rachael thought, as Iris went to call her a cab. But to have one murdered . . . incredible what the human heart can endure and still go on beating.

★　★　★

Forty miles away, in Silverglade Nursing Home, an elderly woman in a navy print dress and pink fuzzy mules sat rocking in her rocking chair, and watching an old rerun of *Bewitched*. She'd been upset when they took it off the air, but it was back on now, these many years later, along with some others she'd enjoyed. *Programs you could watch without all the swearing and nastiness.*

James had left a fair bit of insurance, enough to allow her to have her own private room in this place, with her very own TV set. He'd been an accountant and had a good head for the markets, did James. A quiet man, he never once crossed her in all the days of their marriage. A saint. Though she had never quite forgiven him for leaving that boy so amply provided for. It was his own forgiving nature, she supposed, grudgingly, that misled him.

Most of the residents at Silverglade shared a room, and watched television in the common room down the hall. Occasionally, Ruth joined them just to be sociable, but mostly she preferred being on her own. That way she could watch what she wanted to with no one grumbling at her or changing channels. Besides, with her heart problems, she couldn't go too far anymore. Just walking down the hall could set her heart to scrabbling in her chest like some terrified little animal trying to escape.

During a commercial, Ruth's faded old eyes strayed to the night table, the windowsill, then to the dresser, surfaces on which were displayed evidence that she'd once had a real life. Personal belongings she'd been permitted to take with her when ill health forced her to sell the house and move in here.

The little ballerina regarded her from the windowsill. In her pink tutu, hands positioned over her head, she was frozen in time. Once, she had pirouetted to the tinkling of something by Mozart, but the innards had long since seized up.

The porcelain Japanese doll in her red silk kimono that James brought back from the war stood elegantly on the dresser beside the ebony jewelry box. Inside the box were the two medals he'd received for bravery, along with a few pieces of jewelry he had given her over the years. Sometimes people came to the home to entertain the residents, playing their accordions and such. Ruth would wear one of her nicer pieces on these occasions.

Eight framed photographs were also arranged on three surfaces, six black and whites she'd taken herself with her little Brownie, of her daughter at various stages in her short life. This one taken the day Marie was leaving for summer camp, a blue plaid canvas book-bag slung over her shoulder. Squinting into the camera, her sweet smile revealed a space where her two front teeth had been.

Ruth remembered the day like it was yesterday — the way the warm afternoon air had smelled, softly scented with lilacs. She'd been beside herself at the thought of her little princess going off on her own for a whole week.

The most recent photograph was an eight by ten, color. Ruth had snapped it just before Marie left for the prom that night with that nice Johnson boy, whose father was a dentist. It was the last time she saw her daughter alive.

There'd been mud on her white prom

dress. *Stop! Don't think about it.* The flowers in the corsage on her small wrist were crushed. *Don't! You know how your heart gets when you start thinking about it.*

I should have seen it coming. The way he was always looking at her, thinking I didn't know. I did hear something that night. *Why didn't I go downstairs?* A question that would haunt her right into the grave.

Tears spilled down her parched cheeks. Feeling her heart beginning to fret, she deliberately turned her gaze to the photograph on her bedside table — her wedding picture. Her trembling finger traced her husband's young, serious face. So handsome he was back then. Their child's murder did to him what the war could not. It killed him.

Unconsciously, she began turning her wedding ring round and round on her finger as the old hatred welled within her breast.

No pictures of *him*. She'd torn them all up. The boy was dead to her.

Fumbling for the wad of tissue in her dress pocket, Ruth dabbed at her eyes, sniffed, refocused her attention on the television screen.

Samantha was twitching her nose at Darren, and the old woman cackled as a horrified Darren shrunk to frog-size. Samantha, towering above him, gave one of her sheepish 'oops.' Ruth's chair creaked rhythmically on its rockers.

He was such a fool, that man. She loved Samantha. So pretty. Didn't care too much for the cousin, though — Sabrina. No, not that one. Didn't care for her at all. Always up to no good.

'Afternoon, sweetie,' said an irritating voice from her doorway. 'Guess what? You have a visitor.'

Ruth ceased her rocking, sure she heard wrong. Who would be coming to visit her?

'A man,' the attendant sang, her gleeful mocking tone an insult. 'Says he's an old friend from out of town. Not keeping something from us, are you, dear?'

Mamie Greerson weight well over 200 pounds, had a hairy mole above her upper lip and always smelled of garlic and the bags of peppermints she chewed, trying to cover it.

Ruth thought she was a disgusting thing, but she smiled her *sweet little old woman smile* anyway. You were at their mercy in here. Wouldn't do to let them know how you really felt.

Nonetheless, her curiosity was aroused. Who could it be? The few friends who came to mind had long since gone to their own reward. Still, she couldn't deny a stirring of excitement at the thought of a visitor. She could think of a few around her whose noses would be out of joint at her popularity.

Minutes after the attendant left, she heard footsteps in the corridor. As they approached her room, faces of old schoolmates passed through her mind like photos in a rogue's gallery. One, more vivid than the rest, belonged to a young man she'd been smitten with long before she met James — a school crush. But oh, wasn't he just the cat's meow. Aaron Walsh, his name was. He had curly dark hair and a grin that made her heart beat faster. Rumor had it he left school to marry a young woman he'd gotten in the family way. Perhaps Aaron's wife, like James, had gone on to meet her maker and . . .

Nonsense. She was behaving like the old fool Mamie Greerson took her to be. Still . . .

But it was a man of the cloth that stood in her doorway, a collared gentleman. Wasn't it just like that silly creature to leave out that little detail? Come to save my soul, she thought, a shaky, coquettish hand fluttering to her sparse, white hair. She was suddenly glad of the cross she'd brought from home and had the attendant hang above her bed.

The man entered her room and closed the door behind him.

Why doesn't he say something? She

wondered, with just the smallest stirrings of unease. Then he smiled at her and her heart skittered wildly in her chest. She couldn't breathe.

'Hello, mother,' he said.

21

The phone was ringing when Rachael got home. She picked up the receiver, sensing it was Jeff. She wasn't wrong. As she knew he would, he immediately took her side and, perhaps to her shame, she garnered some comfort in that. He was angry with his father, but she managed to talk him out of driving to Deering and confronting him.

'He's your father, Jeff,' she said. As it was, the relationship was strained. Father and son were very different.

'I hate him, Mom, for what he did to you.'

'Don't. Please, don't. It was no one's fault, Jeff. Whatever happened is between us. People grow apart. Your father loves you.'

'Mom, why are you always defending him? Do you think she's the first bimbo he's cheated on you with?'

She didn't let herself feel the blow fully. Yet neither was she entirely surprised. She didn't ask how he knew. Kids always know far more than we give them credit for. Sometimes wives do, too. The signs had been there. She just hadn't wanted to see them. If you knew, you had to do something about it. She hated her cowardice.

'Mom, are you still there? I'm sorry. I didn't mean — '

'I know. It's okay. But I want to talk about your life. How is Nancy?'

Nancy was pregnant. Rachael could sense Jeff's reluctance to show his joy when his mother was not exactly at a high point in her own life. She made it okay. How would Greg take the news that he was about to become a grandfather? She took pleasure in thinking about it.

She'd no more than hung up when the phone rang again. *Must have forgotten something he wanted to tell me.*

'Hello.'

No one answered. But someone was on the line; she could hear breathing. Probably kids messing with the phone, she told herself, hanging up.

She started from the room, stopped, noticing that the candleholders were on the coffee table instead of on the mantle where she'd put them. Had she set them there to dust the mantle and forgot to put them back? She must have. What other explanation could there be? She could think of one. The Bates' nephew.

She returned the candleholders to the mantle.

Then she called the locksmith to have the locks changed.

★ ★ ★

Iris led the pale, drawn woman into the living room. 'Can I get you something Helen? Perhaps a nice cup of chamomile tea? Chamomile is very calming.'

'No, nothing, thank you, Iris. I'm sorry about showing up like this, not calling or anything. I chased your friend away. I didn't mean to be rude. She seemed very nice.'

'She is very nice. And you weren't rude. Anyway, Rachael's a very understanding person, so you mustn't concern yourself.' Motioning Helen to the stuffed chair, Rachael sat across from her on the sofa, her eye moving involuntarily to the Emily Warren seascape.

Cloud and sea still today.

The calm before the storm?

Helen's hands were tightly clasped together in her lap, as if it might be the only thing keeping her from coming apart.

'Bob's out of town picking up some parts,' she said. 'I don't expect him home until late tonight.' Her voice was as frail as her appearance. Iris nodded, waited.

'I know you have a gift, Iris.'

194

'A gift,' Iris repeated, getting a hint of where this was leading, wanting to stop it in mid-stride. 'Helen, you — '

'No, please, hear me out.'

Iris sighed resignedly. 'All right.' She supposed it couldn't hurt to listen. She didn't have to act on anything, and she wouldn't. 'Please, go on.'

After a pause, Helen said, 'I want you to contact Heather.'

Well, there it was. Looking into those haunted eyes, Iris saw something savage, primal in their depths. This wasn't going to be easy. 'Helen, I can't — '

'I believe you can. I wouldn't be here if I didn't. I need to talk to my child, Iris. I know you can make that possible. I need her to tell me who murdered her.'

Iris cast about in her mind for the right words to diffuse this obsession of Helen's. Words that could convince her that what she asked was impossible, even dangerous.

'Helen, my dear, I can't even begin to imagine how devastating this has been for you and Bob. If there was anything I could do to ease — '

'But there is. I just told you. You have only to agree to do it.'

'Helen, you're wrong about me. I have no special powers. Please, believe me.'

'Everyone knows you're psychic, Iris,' she cut in. 'Even if you don't like to admit it. Remember that time you directed the searchers right to the exact spot near Brown's Creek where little Billy Trenton was found after being missing for two days? He would have died but for you. He very nearly did. You saved his life, Iris. And Ethel told me how you showed up on her doorstep just minutes after Jimmy Ray beat poor old George senseless. Just as if she'd called you on the phone, she said. It was like you knew she was in trouble.'

Iris was surprised to learn that Ethel had confided the incident to Helen, considering that she herself had been sworn to secrecy. You just never know about people. Iris left her own chair to sit down beside Helen, took both hands in her own. Helen's were like ice. 'That was mere coincidence,' Iris said quietly. 'That's all, Helen. Coincidence.'

'Why do you keep denying your powers? It's not all that strange, you know. Some people are born knowing how to play Mozart, or do long division in their heads, or paint like the masters.' She hesitated then said, 'Like Heather was a talented actress. I knew from the time she was a little girl she was going to be famous. Remember how wonderful she was in the role of Annie in the musical last year, Iris?'

Iris smiled sadly. 'She brought the house down. A standing ovation every night.'

Tears shimmered in Helen's eyes. 'She could have made it, Iris. I need to know who killed my baby. I want him punished.'

'Then you don't believe that Tommy — '

'I don't know what to believe. Though Bob is convinced. If he's right, then it's my fault our child is dead, because I'm the one who gave him her room number. If it's Bob who's wrong, then Tommy . . . '

She fondled the small gold locket nestled in the vee of her blouse, the same locket Iris had seen Heather wearing the few times she'd been in the store.

'Bob doesn't know I gave him her room number, Iris,' she said, tears spilling down her gaunt cheeks.

Iris could only wonder at all the tears she must have shed in the past few weeks, and felt her resolve begin to weaken.

'I don't know what he'd do if he found out. So you see, one way or the other, I have to know. Will you help me? I'm just asking you to try, that's all. As my friend.'

Peter had told Iris about the confrontation in *Burger King*, so she knew that Iris wasn't exaggerating Bob's hatred of Tommy.

Taking Iris' silence for consent, Helen slid the Ouija board from the canvas bag at her

197

feet, held it out to Iris with almost an air of reverence. 'I brought candles too,' she said, those hollowed eyes now emitting a feverish glitter as her words began to tumble over themselves. 'You have to have candles — white ones to keep away the dark entities. I bought them yesterday in that little candle shop on Bay Avenue. They have every sort of candle in there, you know.'

Leaving Iris holding the Ouija board, Helen rushed about the room arranging white tapered candles — eight in all — strategically about them. She set Heather's portrait in its pewter frame on the mantle, flanked by two of the candles. Backtracking, she lit them one by one.

Iris watched each pale yellow flame flare up, signifying the ancient, religious ritual they'd already begun, and wondered what in hell she was doing.

Now the two women sat facing one another, the Ouija board balanced between them, on their laps. The scene was set. Candlelight flickered over the black letters, highlighting numbers and symbols painted on the light, varnished wood.

The tension in the air was almost real enough to touch. Iris supposed much of it was coming from herself, stemming from her unease at this dark activity in which they were about to engage. She also felt more than a little ridiculous at having allowed herself to be cast in the role of medium. I'm about to conduct a séance, for Heaven's sake. Or perhaps *Heaven* was not the best choice of words here. She had never approved of this sort of dabbling into the unknown. Never. And now, against her better judgment, against all that was holy, she was flying in the face of her own beliefs.

She was about to call up the dead.

★ ★ ★

The press conference was held on the steps of the courthouse, a two-story red brick building. Peter stood at the edge of the crowd watching Captain Elton Sorrel field questions from clamoring reporters. Heather's murder had gained national attention mainly because of where it occurred. Pressure from high places was apparently being brought to bear.

'What about this phantom doctor?' a reporter from the local TV station yelled out. 'Anyone track him down yet?'

The nurse on duty at the time of Heather's murder had told police a Doctor Whittaker had visited the girl that night, *before* Tommy Prichard showed up. A check revealed that no Doctor Whittaker worked at the hospital, nor in fact was even listed in the yellow pages.

'Probably some intern wanting to get a look at her,' Sorrel said. 'Celebrities are always of interest. These days victims of violence rank right up there.'

When the conference ended, Peter followed Captain Sorrel inside the building, catching up with him in the corridor. 'But you don't *know* that's what happened, do you, Captain? That it was an intern who visited her room?'

Sorrel's hawk-eyes bored into his. 'Where you been living, Gardner? In a cave?' Peter had to walk fast to keep up with him. 'Take a look around you. Look at the Menendez brothers — blew their parents away without so much as a by-the-by, then lied through their teeth in court. And think about those two kids who tortured a two-year-old, then laid his broken body on some railroads tracks. Or the jerk that takes a gun to school and starts popping his classmates into oblivion. Kids ain't what they used to be, for Chrissake. They're a new breed.'

Peter followed him into his office. 'I know you see a good deal of the underbelly of humanity in your job, Captain. But there really are good kids out there. Why don't you come out to the school sometimes? Maybe give a talk on law enforcement as a career. Meet some of those good kids. You might be pleasantly surprised.'

Sorrel growled around the Tums he'd just popped into his mouth. 'Is that really why you're here, Gardner? To ask me to give a talk at your school?' He smiled an alligator smile. 'No, I didn't think so. I heard about the little fiasco in the restaurant. I don't blame Bob Myers one damn bit for having it in for your friend Prichard. It's a natural thing for a man to want to avenge the murder of his little girl. Let it be on your own shoulders, Peter, if anything happens to the kid.'

'There's a killer out there somewhere, Captain, but it's not Tommy Prichard. He's entitled to protection under the law the same as anyone else. Unless I'm mistaken, a person is still presumed innocent in this country until proven guilty.'

'You sound like Goldman, your lawyer friend.' He sat down behind his cluttered desk. 'They tell me you used to be a pretty damn good amateur cop, Gardner. So how do you explain Officer Willis seeing Prichard coming out of her room that night? Prichard fled the scene. He hid out. Now, I know you're the teacher, but when I went to school, two and two made four.'

'Circumstantial. Willis was threatening to shoot at him, for God's sake.'

A light knock at the door, and Detective

Chuck Mason, a stocky, broad-featured man with pale eyes that gave away little, swaggered into the office. Giving Peter a nod of recognition, he then dropped a report on the captain's desk.

Sorrel picked it up, scanned it.

'Domestic,' Mason said, snapping his gum, sending a whiff of spearmint in Peter's direction. 'She's in the hospital. Broken jaw, internal bleeding from her old man's boots. She just keeps coming back for more. One of these days they'll pick her up in a body bag.'

Sorrel tapped the paper with his forefinger. 'See, Gardner. Anytime you got a woman dead of other than natural causes, ninety-nine times out of a hundred it's the boyfriend or hubby who did it.'

Peter didn't bother to ask about the other one percent. Cutting his visit with Sorrel short by mutual unspoken consent, he drove around aimlessly for a while, ended up in the parking lot of St. Clair Hospital. It was quarter to six. Already the sky had turned a dusky purple, a smattering of stars visible. He needed to talk to the nurse who was on duty that night.

He was in luck. Nurse Janet Lewis was just about to start her shift. He knew he had no official right to be here, to be asking questions of anyone, but dammit, someone had to.

'I've already told the police everything I know,' she said, a trace of defensiveness, even weariness, in her voice. 'I didn't get your name, Officer . . . '

'I'm not a policeman, Miss Lewis. My name is Peter Gardner. I'm a teacher. Heather was my student.'

'Oh. I'm so sorry.' Her brown eyes were sympathetic. He also thought he saw guilt there.

'Yes, so am I. But it's not your fault.'

'I'm not sure that's true, but thank you for saying it. I feel so awful about what happened to her.'

'Miss Lewis. Janet. I wondered if, in the wake of all of this aftermath, there might have been something you missed. Or that the police missed. If you don't mind.'

The TV room was empty, so they went in there. She sat on the edge of the sofa, while he took the yellow, cracked leather chair facing her. He waited.

'As soon as I went into her room that night and saw him standing over her,' she said tonelessly, 'I felt something wasn't right. Something about the way he stood, the edge in his voice when he spoke. I ignored my own gut reaction to him. Oh, I asked him what he was doing there, and his answer seemed plausible enough. Sometimes Doctor Halstead *will* ask another doctor to check on a patient. It wasn't that unusual. Except that he didn't. Not this time. I didn't know that then, of course.'

'No,' he said quietly. 'You couldn't.'

'It was late and he was in a hurry. He was a doctor, or so I believed. I'm just a nurse.'

He couldn't help thinking that if she'd been able to summon more courage that night, Heather might still be alive. But he also felt sorry for Janet Lewis, who was obviously a caring, decent person. This must be very hard for her, thinking she might have left her patient in the hands of a murderer.

'I have to go now,' she said, checking her watch. At the door, she turned. 'There was one thing . . . ' A frown etched in her smooth forehead. 'Something I noticed. It's probably not important . . . '

'Please, Janet. What did you notice?'

'I think he might have worn a wig. I remember thinking it odd that someone would buy a grey wig. I could be wrong of course, but . . . '

'But you don't think so. Then you're not convinced Tommy Prichard killed her.'

'I don't know. I have to hope it was him. Otherwise . . . '

★　★　★

That night his sleep was haunted by a shadowy man in a grey wig stalking a hospital corridor. At some point, Mary Ellen entered the dream. She was sitting before the vanity mirror in their bedroom, trying on one of the wigs she was forced to wear in those last months of her life, smiling at him in the mirror.

It took a while to shake the dream off. Now, he sat at the kitchen table working on his second cup of coffee and marking the last of the book reviews on Winston Groom's *As Summers Die*. Groom was also the author of *Forrest Gump*, which came as a surprise to most of his students, who had no idea it was a book before it became a movie starring Tom Hanks. If they knew that, he'd reasoned, they might be more enthusiastic about the assignment, and he'd been right.

As Summers Die reminded him somewhat of Harper Lee's *To Kill A Mockingbird*. A few of the more avid readers in his class had also noted the comparison. There were some excellent book reports here, and others more than passable. All except for Derek Chesley's paper, which was blank. Disappointing, but not surprising.

The last report marked, he clipped the

205

pages together with a red plastic paperclip, set it on top of the others in his briefcase. Snapping the briefcase shut, he shrugged into his leather jacket. It was nearly eight-thirty.

As he passed the kitchen window, a goldfinch flashed at the corner of his eye. He stopped to watch it peck at the seeds in the birdfeeder. Mary Ellen had always made sure the feeder was well stocked when the cold months came, and Peter carried on in her honor.

The pancreatic cancer had slowly and cruelly stripped her of energy, of physical beauty, and finally, of life itself. She died at home, in his arms. A small breath expelled, then nothing. He'd waited for the next breath to come as it always had before, even with the long seconds between. But it never came. Though he'd known she was dying, it was a shock to feel her body cooling even as he held her. To see that eternal stillness on her pale lips.

There'd been no other woman in his life since her passing. He'd had no interest in dating. But he knew that was no longer true. From the moment he'd removed the splinter of glass from Rachael Warren's cheek, he hadn't been able to get her out of his mind.

Maybe that was why Tommy's comment about his lack of personal life had rattled him so. Sighing, Peter bid the finch good morning, picked up his briefcase and headed off to school.

★　★　★

As soon as he walked into his classroom, he spotted Chesley at the back of the class, a defiant smirk on his face and he wanted to smack it off. Some you couldn't reach; they already had all the answers.

Unlike Tommy's father, Derek's dad was a prominent lawyer who thrust out his hand and pulled his son up every time he fell into crap, while Nate Prichard was more apt to make a fist of his.

His classroom had grown quieter since Heather's murder. Some of the students were still having nightmares, and required counseling, which the school was providing. This tragedy involving one of their own had hit them hard, made them feel unsafe in their world. Thinking it might be helpful he suggested they write about what they were feeling, about how Heather's death had affected them.

Mary Brewer, a tall, studious girl, raised her hand. 'The psychologist already asked us to do that, Mr. Gardner.'

'Oh, of course. Well, those of you who

aren't seeing a counselor might want to take this opportunity to explore your own feelings. It's not compulsory. The rest of you can work on a short story of your choosing.'

A few groans went up around the room. Mary raised her hand. 'Everyone is saying Tommy Prichard killed Heather, Mr. Gardner,' she said, dark eyes solemn. 'Do you think he did it?'

'No. No, I don't think so, Mary.'

'Then who . . . ?'

A few more hands shot up.

'I don't know. Please . . . ' He smiled weakly. 'Just get on with your assignment.'

A whisper of doubt in his mind. Was it possible he was wrong about Tommy and the others were right?

No. He didn't believe that. Deep down he was certain that the man who went to Heather's room that night, posing as a doctor, had murdered her. And even though she didn't want to admit it, Nurse Janet Lewis believed it too.

22

Rachael ventured farther along the beach that morning than she had in years, scaling the same mossy, slippery rocks she had climbed as a girl. Along the stretches of hard sand, her long legs took on a rhythmic stride that gave her a pleasant sensation of flying.

She was growing stronger every day, both in body and mind. She could feel it. Although there were times when it was all she could do to put one foot ahead of the other, she'd learned that if she pushed herself through those times, the darkness would lift.

As it did now. The cry of gulls, the occasional call of a loon accompanied her on her journey. Tension soon ebbed from her body as if borne away on the waves that rushed the shore.

She'd been running for a good half-hour when she spotted a brown harbor seal — seadogs they called them when she was a kid — lounging on the beach in the morning sun. She slowed her pace, then stopped.

She approached the seal cautiously, not wanting to frighten it. Looking into those moist black eyes, the seal looking into hers, she felt a profound connection with the creature. A brief connection, but one as real as the salty breezes that now cooled her skin. A primal communion, ancient as the earth itself.

The connection broke as the seal turned away. Pushing itself forward on its flippers, the animal waddled into the bay where it became as liquid as the sea, pure grace in motion. She watched until it was a black dot on the deep blue water, and understood that she had been given a rare and special gift.

I am coming back to myself. I really am going to make it through this.

★   ★   ★

A slender figure in a dark green running suit, white sneakers flashing in the sun, she ran with the grace of a deer. As if it were in her nature to run. Strange, he did not recall her as being particularly athletic.

He kept her in his line of vision until she disappeared behind an outcropping of jagged rock. Then he lowered the binoculars and slipped his hand into his pants' pocket, fondled the key there. Useless since she'd had her locks changed. Not that it mattered. Soon, he would need neither key nor guise. Soon she would come to him of her own free will, her eyes all soft and loving just for him. He would forgive her transgressions.

★   ★   ★

Had Rachael run another quarter of a mile that morning, she might have been the one to find the body washed up on the rocks. As it was, a teenage boy scanning the shore with his metal detector for hidden treasures, came across it. Rachael had been headed back to the house when she heard the sirens. Within minutes, the ambulance and the police car came into view, followed by a train of traffic, including a van from the local TV station. People were running behind the cars. It seemed half the town was streaming in her direction. Rachael fell in with the curiosity seekers.

'I thought at first it was some kind of mutant starfish,' the boy was telling the reporter who was holding a microphone up to the boy's mouth.

Noticeably shaken, he was talking fast, hands gesturing wildly. Rachael could see he was also somewhat taken with being something of a celebrity. 'Then I realized it was a hand wedged in some rocks. And then I saw the body. His hair looked like seaweed. The smell was gross.' He glanced around at the crowd hanging on every word. 'Somethin' ate most of his face. His eyes were gone. Only hollow sockets left.'

The interviewer kept her face solemn, but her eyes held a spark of glee at these lovely graphic details. Rachael got a whiff of the odor the boy was talking about and backed away, stomach churning.

The beach swarmed with people as if this were a favorite tourist spot. Necks craned, onlookers hoped to see something, at the same time afraid they might. Whispers rose up around her. Questions, speculations, as men wearing plastic gloves worked quietly to disengage the body from the rocks.

Cars snaked back along the road as far as she could see. As the coroner and police zipped the corpse into a body bag, a hush fell over the scene.

The three boys she and Betty had had the run-in with in town were standing beside the black sports car watching the proceedings. As if sensing her looking at him, the one named Derek turned his head in her direction and made an obscene gesture with his hand that set her face aflame. Little creep.

Did Derek have the spare key to her house? Is he the one making the phone calls?

Similar thoughts plagued her that night as she tried to fall asleep. Not the least of which was the boy's explicit description of the corpse. So when the phone rang, Greg's voice was the last one she'd expected to hear. At first, hearing it, this voice from the past, she felt only a strange detachment.

'You're the best, Rach. I think I made a helluva mistake. Goddamn Lisa. She left me. I don't know where the hell she is . . . ' He broke into sobs. He was drunk.

She slowly, disbelievingly, hung up the phone.

'You bastard,' she said in the quiet of the room. 'How dare you?'

He called again the next night to apologize. She hung up again. The phone rang immediately, persistent. Sighing, she picked it up. Greg wasn't a drinker; he must be in a bad way.

'Rach. Are you there?'

She closed her eyes, receiver pressed to her ear. You could not spend half your life with a man, bear his children and feel nothing about him. At least she couldn't. Or maybe it was just that old habits died hard. She could only imagine what Betty would say to that bit of rationalization.

'Yes, Greg. I'm here.'

'Damn, it's good to hear your voice. I miss you, Ray-shul.' Either drunk again, or still drunk. 'I just — Lisa left me, you know. That bitch, Betty, prob'ly told you. Jeez, Halston and his big family image. It's okay as long as it's one of them. Lisa's a slut. You're the best, Rach. I want you to come home. I'll make it up to you. I will — '

'No,' she said quietly. 'This is my home now, Greg.' And finally, she knew it was true. 'I'm going to hang up now. You'll be okay. Just . . . ' Lord, was she about to give him advice? Pick him up when he fell down, like in the old days? Well, what the hell . . .

'You know you're the best salesman in the business, Greg. You need to stop drinking now and show them — show them you can rise from this. Halston needs you — '

'Goddamn Lisa, she's driving me nuts,' he said, and began to cry, fat, wet sobs that seeped through the line. Over Lisa. She held the receiver away from her as if it were not a receiver at all — but a teddy bear turned snake. If the whole damn thing were not so sad, she might have laughed. *You deserve this, Rachael.*

For a long time she lay staring at the ceiling and thinking about those first nights in this house, curled in a fetal position, crying herself to sleep. Sometimes she dreamed Greg had come to take her home. She would see his Mustang in the drive, and before he had time to park it she would run to him, throw herself into his arms. He would beg her to come back to him. Lisa was a mistake, he would say, a terrible mistake that it was Rachael he loved. In her dreams, she always forgave him.

That dream ending was no longer possible, if indeed it ever had been. Not for her anyway. Tout fini, as the French say. Thank you, Greg.

The phone rang again. She snapped up the receiver. 'Greg, go to bed and sleep it off. Please don't call here ag — '

Not Greg. Her words fell away as the familiar breathing slid over her skin like damp ooze.

★　★　★

She couldn't get to her pottery lesson fast enough the next day. To top off a very pleasant hour, Peter dropped by as she was getting ready to leave. She realized she'd been unconsciously looking for him.

I like him. I like being around him. He makes me laugh. Something she hadn't done in a long time. He was also damn good looking, but in a different way from Greg. His appeal grew out of a deeper, more solid place. And when he left a room, it seemed to pale in personality. Oh, yes, no question she was attracted to Peter Gardner and it scared the hell out of her.

* ★ ★

That night Betty phoned to tell her that Lisa had dumped Greg and moved on to bigger fish in the firm.

Rachael had been about to tell Betty that Greg had called, but for some reason changed her mind. When Rachel didn't reply right away, Betty went on to explain that one of her customers was a secretary at Halston's.

'She says Lisa's new interest is someone high on the ladder, big enough so that no one dares comment. Married, of course. Talk is that Greg is screwing up big time at work. Anyway, thought you'd like to know he's getting back a little of his own.'

'I don't wish Greg ill,' she said. Though, in fact, she'd wished him dead.

A pause. Then, 'He called, didn't he? I knew you were keeping something from me. He wants you back. I knew it.'

She sounded at once triumphant and disdainful. She actually thinks I'd go back with him. Doesn't she know I'm not the same person who sat across from her in the eatery pushing a piece of lettuce around on my paper plate? Lettuce as limp as my own backbone. Maybe she doesn't want to know.

23

Hartley enjoyed walking in the woods, especially in the early hush of morning, with Luke padding along beside him. It helped him to think clearly, like being on the water did.

Beneath his olive green boots, the forest floor was spongy, his steps all but silent, but for the occasional branch snapping. Snow had fallen overnight, dusting the ground. The autumn sun filtered through the trees, and the air smelled fresh.

The kind of morning that could clear a man's head of rotting corpses washed up on a beach. Hartley had the poor timing to come along only minutes after the boy came across it. Seeing half the town headed for a look-see, he didn't hang around.

Noticing the stack of cut wood piled up against the cabin, he turned his thoughts to more practical matters. Oughta gather that wood up before it rots and take it over to Ms. Warren's for her fireplace.

He wondered if she found her key okay. He'd felt bad her thinking he hadn't returned it. But he shouldn't have taken it personally.

Rachael Warren was a lady on her own after all and right to be on her guard. Lotsa nuts out there. Maybe he'd take her a couple of nice flounder as a peace offering.

Hartley uprighted a red wheelbarrow lying on its side. It was missing its wheel, beginning to rust. As he straightened, sharp pain shot through his shoulder. Damned arthritis was getting worse. He supposed he'd have to give in soon and start motoring like some tourist. He and Luke had trekked the distance this morning, taken the route through the woods, around the cove.

He spotted a moldy case of beer bottles setting by the back door, nearly hidden in the thick brush. George's little secret from Ethel, which Hartley suspected was really no secret at all. Couldn't blame a man for wanting to get off by himself now and then. Ethel would have understood. She was a lot like his Margaret in that way.

Hartley ran a hand fondly along the rough bottom of George's old boat. Right here where George left it upturned on two sawhorses. Splotches of green paint were still evident here and there along the sides. George had been intending on doing some work on her, but never got around to it.

A short bark from Luke drew Hartley's attention to the grimy cabin window.

'What is it, boy? You see something? Or are your old eyes playing tricks on you, too?'

It startled him to see the cabin door open and a stranger standing in the doorway. 'Morning. Nice day for a walk in the woods.'

"Tis that,' Hartley said. 'Didn't know anyone was staying here.' Hartley took him in — average height, stocky through the chest and arms. He'd seen him around somewhere.

'Just for a few days.'

'Don't say. Ms. Warren know you're here? This is her property in case you didn't know. And her cabin.'

'Oh, sure. We're old friends from college days. I'm doing a bit of fixing up inside in exchange for some retreat time.'

Despite his misgivings, Hartley's interest was stirred. 'That right?'

'Sure is. Look, uh — I was just about to have some coffee. Will you join me? Nice dog you got there, but I'm afraid I can't invite him in. Unless you want to see me break out in hives,' he chuckled. 'Sorry.'

'I've already had my mornin' coffee,' Hartley said. 'Thank ya, just the same. I'll be headin' . . . '

'You look like a man who knows his way around a hammer and saw,' he grinned. 'I could use your advice. Won't take but a few minutes of your time.'

For several long seconds Hartley said nothing. There was a gnawing deep in his gut — something not quite right. The hunter in him might have termed it 'the patch of brown among the green.' But Hartley was not the hunter here. He allowed himself to be flattered. For the first time in his life, the old man's pride at being asked to share his knowledge of work he'd been doing most of his life, caused him to turn his back on old, reliable instincts.

'Well, maybe for a minute or two. Sit, Luke.'

The dog whined fretfully as his master moved toward the cabin. His warning going unheeded, his tail sagged and he barked again. He fretted and whined. He growled at the man in the doorway.

'Good watchdog.'

'That he is. Getting on though. Sit, boy!'

Luke reluctantly obeyed, his eyes steady on the man. The stranger held the door open, and Hartley stepped across the threshold ahead of him. Luke's odd behavior sat uneasily within him, but like the gnawing in his gut, he paid it no serious mind. 'What is it exactly I can help you with, Mr . . . ?'

Hartley didn't hear the metallic clank of the shovel against the pot-bellied stove. Never saw its blade bearing down on him until it was too late.

The first blow stunned him, sent him reeling backwards, though he remained on his feet. His hands flew to protect his head. But the blood was already streaming through his splayed fingers. The shovel came down three more times before the old man finally fell, sprawling face down on the cabin floor.

★   ★   ★

Tough old coot, the man thought, grunting as he dragged the dead weight of the old man into the closet.

Whistling softly to himself, he set about opening a can of chicken from the stash on the shelf, thumbed back the jagged lid. Picking up the shovel, he propped it in the corner by the back door, within easy reach. He eased the door open.

Luke was already on his feet, a deep growl issuing from his belly.

'Hey, easy fella. Look what I got here.' He kept his voice kindly, unthreatening.

Luke's growl softened, confusion in his eyes as he tried to see past the man into the cabin, where he'd seen his master enter. He sniffed the air, growled again.

The man set the can before the animal and stepped back. 'Go ahead, boy. It's good. Eat up.'

Luke hesitated, then, tail wagging tentatively, inched toward the food. Abruptly, his tail stilled. Now he backed away, whining mournfully, for he had smelled death.

'C'mon, fella,' he said again, reaching behind him for the shovel. He gripped its wooden handle. Catching the subtle change of tone in his voice, the stealthy movement, Luke jumped to one side just as the shovel came down causing him to miss his target. Luke lunged at him, sank his teeth into his left leg just above the knee.

Stifling a howl of pain, he tried to shake him off, but the animal's hold only became more tenacious. He tried for better leverage with the shovel, but it was impossible with the dog so close. But he was a strong man, and dealt a powerful blow to the side of the animal's head. The dog let go and fled yelping into the thick woods.

To his relief, the bite wasn't serious; lucky the mutt was old. He'd pick up some antibiotic ointment at the drugstore tomorrow.

That night under cold, starry skies, he buried Hartley McLeod's body in a shallow grave and covered it over with brush and leaves. Scooping up handfuls of new snow, he sprinkled them over the top. Icing on the cake, he said aloud, and laughed at his own perceived wit.

He was ten when he did his first killing. A stray cat in the neighborhood. At first, he couldn't believe what he had done. But his shock and fear were quickly replaced with fascination as, lying on the ground on his stomach, chin propped in his hands, he watched the light go out in those clear green eyes — slowly, like they were attached to those dimmer switches they have nowadays.

It had been like that with his mother. Maybe especially with her. She had once seemed all-powerful, invincible. Even terrifying to the small boy he had been. It was purely satisfying to see her own terror reflected in her eyes as recognition of him dawned. To see the smile on her old face crumble. Before she could cry out, he clamped a hand over her mouth, silencing her cries. He could feel her loose dentures against his palm, the disgusting warm drool as she tried to call out for help. Hatred of him had blazed in her eyes even as they began to glaze over. Only when they remained fixed and dilated, and her hands fell limply to her sides, did he remove his own hand from her mouth.

A light going out. That always fascinated him. How a life could go out like that. So easy. So final.

24

On Saturday morning Rachael returned from her run to find Peter's Marquis parked in her drive, Peter sitting on her porch step. He stood as she approached.

'Hi.'

'Hi, yourself,' she said, breathless, and not entirely from the workout. 'What are you doing here?'

'Waiting for you,' he smiled, a trace of uncertainty in the smile. 'Hope you don't mind.

She didn't. 'Do the police have any new leads?'

'No. Then they haven't looked any farther than Tommy Prichard. But that's not why I'm here. There's something I've been wanting to ask you. It — uh, has to do with Iris.'

'Oh,' she said, her curiosity stirred. 'Well, sure, Peter. Would you like to come inside?' Slipping the knit band off her head, she absently finger-combed her hair. 'I'll make coffee.'

'Actually, I thought we might go out for coffee if that's okay with you. How about *Kathy's?*'

'Sounds fine. Give me a few minutes to change. On second thought, how about I meet you there? I have some errands I want to run afterward.'

Peter was already seated at a back table when she arrived. He waved, stood and pulled out a chair for her. As she approached the table, he sensed a certain aloofness he hadn't noticed at the house, and her smile was not quite as open. Sure. *She's had time to think*.

He wondered if Rachael knew anything about the Ouija board Helen had been cramming into a canvas sack when he walked in the room last week. Or the candles Iris had been nonchalantly blowing out. Somehow he doubted it. He'd known better than to question his aunt about what was going on, but one didn't have to be a rocket scientist to figure it out. He'd hoped to find Rachael still there, was as crestfallen as a kid to learn she'd already left.

Before he could say anything, the owner, Kathy Burgess, approached their table. She smiled warmly at Rachael, then, tucking a strand of hair behind her ear, turned a more serious expression on him. 'Peter, I don't suppose you've seen Hartley in your travels.'

'No, not lately, Kath. Why?'

'Well, he hasn't been around the past

couple of days. Had to buy my fish from another fella this mornin'. S'pose he's okay?'

'I'm sure he's fine. Probably a flu or something. I'll drop by and see him later. Thanks for letting me know, Kathy.'

When she left them, Rachael said, 'I hope it's nothing serious. He's a nice man.'

'Yes, the last of a rare breed. A man whose handshake is as good as a signature on a document.'

Rachael smiled. 'You said this had something to do with Iris.'

You wouldn't be here otherwise, Peter thought. So much sadness in those lovely grey eyes. A man could get lost in them. He wanted to drive away the sadness. He was dreaming.

'The St. Clair Arts Council is honoring Aunt Iris with a special dinner for her lifelong contribution to the arts community. I know it would mean a lot to her, Rachael, to have you there. She's become very fond of you. And I'd be lying if I didn't tell you I'd be delighted if you would come as my guest.'

'That's wonderful. I mean . . . '

'I should tell you I'm not usually big on these affairs,' he said, guessing that perhaps she wasn't either. 'But this is special, don't you think?'

'Incredibly special. Does Iris know?'

'No. I've been sworn to secrecy. Which is not going to be easy knowing my aunt. Rachael, I don't want you to feel any pressure about this, though. I know you're going through a rough time right now. Let's just think of it as — an unofficial date.'

She smiled, perceptively let her guard down. 'Unofficial sounds fine to me. I'd be honored to go with you, Peter. I'm thrilled for Iris. There's no one more deserving.'

Despite everything, Rachael found herself looking forward to the dinner. Peter had guessed right; she'd never been comfortable at large gatherings. Especially those cocktail parties Greg used to drag her to because Halston's thought it important to have a spouse on your arm. She'd always felt so out of place at those things.

Maybe that she could always count on seeing Greg in a corner of the room, flirting with some girl young enough to be his daughter, played a part in that. 'It's business, Rach,' he'd always say. 'I'm expected to mingle.'

Past history, Rachael. And you were wrong to put up with it.

At the hardware store, she took advantage of a sale on paint. She also found some pretty paper edged with marigolds for the pantry shelves. The kids were talking about coming for a visit at Christmas, and she wanted the place to look nice. Remembering how the windows rattled in that last storm, she tossed a package of putty into her cart.

She'd re-puttied windows when Greg was away on his business trips, even replaced one or two. She'd changed fuses, repaired the washing machine and once put a new chain on Jeff's bike. No, she wasn't quite as helpless as she'd thought.

Stowing her parcels in the trunk, Rachael drove a block farther to the little dress boutique she passed to and from her lessons with Iris. No markdowns here. But she wanted something special to wear for the occasion. It was Iris' night, after all.

The store smelled pleasantly of potpourri and designer clothes. Glass cases and brass adornments gleamed beneath a crystal chandelier.

In the tiny, plush dressing room, she tried on several dresses, finally settling on a winter-white, floor-length wool and silk blend, straight cut, a modest slit up one side. With its high neck and three-quarter sleeves, her gold rope chain and the earrings Betty had given her, would go perfectly.

'Absolutely elegant,' the elderly woman with the coifed platinum hair smiled, looking her over. 'It's so nice when a dress looks as the designer intended it to.'

Ordinarily, she wouldn't have lapped up a salesperson's flattery so readily, but she had to admit, turning slightly in the full-length mirror, all her running had paid off. In more ways than one.

God, she was behaving like a teenager on her first date. And forgetting that this wasn't really to be a date at all, except unofficially. He'd said as much. And she certainly had no desire to make it anything more than that.

So why are you going to so much trouble to impress him?

It's not for Peter; it's for Iris.

Right.

Impulsively, she also treated herself to a new winter coat. Even on sale, it was more than she had ever paid for a coat in her life. Seal black with a hood, double-pleat in back, half-belt. She felt wonderful in it. She ran her hand down the silky wool fabric as if it were an exotic pet. Beautiful detail, the woman said. She wore the coat home, refusing to let herself dwell on her dwindling bank balance.

She was watching a rerun of *Seinfeld*, enjoying a cup of lemon tea, when the phone rang. It was just past ten, not late. She heard a new brightness in her 'hello.'

As the silence met her ear, her smile of greeting faded, the fragile good feelings

229

drained away. And then came the whispered words that crept over her flesh like a thousand spiders.

'Nice coat. You always did look sexy in black.'

25

At the police station next morning, Rachael spied Detective Chuck Mason, the older of the two detectives who'd come to the house the night her windows were broken. He was across the room talking to a middle-aged woman with frowsy blonde hair, in a red mini skirt. Although it was as hot as a sauna in here, the woman was hugging herself as if she were cold. Her mascara had run, giving her face a sad, raccoonish look. Rachael felt sorry for her.

Seeing Rachel, he passed the woman on to a colleague, and came toward her. 'Nice to see you again, Ms. Warren. What can I do for you?'

She told him about the phone calls. 'I didn't report them before because I really didn't think there was anything the police could do about them.'

'Well, you're right on that count. There's isn't much we can do about anonymous phone calls. But it's always a good idea to have the report on file just in case something . . . you might want to consider having your number changed. Or get caller ID. That way we'll know where the calls are originating from.'

'I thought at first it was just a wrong number. But I've gotten a dozen calls now. Daytime. Middle of the night. Mostly hang-ups. Except for the last two.' She repeated the caller's comments about her new coat.

'He's stalking you.'

The very word stalking sent a thrill of fear through her.

Rachael felt the detective assessing her, deciding how much of her story was concoction. Was she just another lonely woman, hungry for attention?

There was something about Detective Mason that made her know she wouldn't want to be pulled over on a dark street by him. She'd seen the way he'd looked at the blonde woman. He didn't like women much. Maybe he thinks we're all whores. Up this close, she detected signs of the drinker in him — broken capillaries around the nose, hard eyes. Or maybe she wasn't being fair and it was just job burnout she saw.

'Did he make any direct threats? Sit down, please — I'll file a report.'

'No, not in so many words. But dammit, I felt — feel threatened.' She sat in the chair he indicated. The woman with the sad eyes was no longer in sight.

'You're divorced?' Seeing her expression, he added, 'Not idle curiosity, I promise. Just for the record.'

'In the process,' she said. She hated the half-smile that crossed his face. He was congratulating himself on correctly guessing her marital status.

'Maybe hubby's not too happy about the way things are turning out. Maybe he wants to scare you into co — '

'No, that's not Greg's style. And there's something else. I think someone has been in my house when I'm not at home. Things — figurines, candles — appear to be moved around. And one day last week I came home to find the TV turned up full blast, every light in the house on.'

'Are you sure you didn't . . . ?'

'I'm not senile, Detective Mason. Of course I'm sure.' She tried to soften her sharp reply with a smile that felt more like a grimace. 'We had that bad storm, and I did wonder if maybe a sudden surge of power could cause appliances and lights to come on.'

'Don't know. Can't say as I ever heard of it.'

She paused. Then, 'And my spare house-key went missing.'

'Missing?' He jotted the information down. 'You're sure you didn't give it to anyone.'

Why did everything he said sound like an insult?

'Actually, I did. I gave it to Peter Gardner who in turn gave it to Hartley McLeod. It was Mr. McLeod who replaced my broken windows.' She spoke slowly, as if speaking to a less than bright child. 'When I called him he told me he put the key on the ledge over the door. It wasn't there when I looked. I've been hoping he would come across the key in his overalls' pocket or in his toolbox, but that hasn't happened. Or maybe someone watched where he put the key, and simply took it.'

'The Prichard kid, maybe? He's practically your neighbor.'

'No. I — I don't think so.' She couldn't have said why not.

He raised an eyebrow, but didn't press it. 'I assume you've had your locks changed.'

'Yes.'

'Good. Anyway, it's my guess he'll tire of the game and move on to someone else. If he's not rewarded.'

'Rewarded?' she bristled.

'Don't get your panties in a knot, me darlin'. All I'm saying is don't make it interesting for him. Hang up the second you know it's him. And keep on hanging up. As far as those night calls, you could always unplug your phone.'

Did he imagine she hadn't thought of that? Or that I get some pleasure from some sicko's phone calls.

'I have two grown children. I'm expecting a grandchild. The call could be important.'

'If it is, they'll call back in the morning. It's been my experience that no one calls in the wee hours with good news. And bad news ain't goin' anywhere.'

He walked her outside. As she started down the steps, he called after her, 'And by the way, Ms. Warren — don't be too sure about your husband's style. Style's change.'

Feeling less than comforted by her talk with the detective, Rachael hurried along the snow-dusted sidewalk, gloveless hands buried deep in her pockets, November's icy fingers reaching inside her thin coat. She would have been warmer in the new coat, but she had not been able bring herself to wear it. Not today. He had spoiled her enjoyment of it.

Damn! She'd forgotten to tell the detective about the howling she'd heard outside her window last night. Like an animal in distress. Perhaps wounded? Had she dreamed it? She wasn't sure. Just as well she hadn't mentioned it. He probably would have sloughed her off as a head case.

The bare branches of trees lining the street clicked together like old bones as Rachael hurried to her car. The small parking area attached to the police station had been full, and she'd parked half a block away.

The metal sign over the door of the dry-cleaning shop swayed precariously in the wind, creaking above her head as she walked beneath it. Out on the street, a teenager executed some fancy moves on his skateboard.

That increasingly familiar feeling of eyes on the back of her head made her look around. But there was only the boy on the skateboard behind her, presently performing an impressive three hundred and sixty-degree twirl in mid-air. Once inside her car, she locked the doors.

★ ★ ★

Even in Iris' studio, working with the clay, she was unable to dismiss the dark thoughts from her mind. How could she? After all, it was Iris who had first warned her that she was in danger? For the first time, the work wasn't having its usual calming effect.

From time to time, she sensed Iris looking

at her. She was glad when the lesson ended.

That night, Rachael tossed and turned in the bed while sleep eluded her. She tried to read, but the words ran together in a meaningless jumble. When she did finally drift off, she dreamed of bloated corpses, disembodied voices whispering her name. Hands resembling starfish reached out for her, and when she tried to escape them, her legs would not move.

★   ★   ★

He called her at midnight, then again at one. Her phone rang and rang in his ear. She's there! I know she's there. The bitch has unplugged the phone. He slammed the receiver down, furious.

She shouldn't ignore him. That was a big mistake. As he turned to leave the phone booth, he came face to face with a hulk in overalls and a soiled checkered shirt, a wide grin on his bulldog face.

'Don't break it, okay, buddy,' Nate said, brushing past him, giving off a stench of body odor and booze that made him want to heave his guts. 'This is my office since the lightning knocked hell out of the phone. Been more'n a month now and they ain't fixed it yet. Working late. Promised a guy I'd finish up a welding job on his snowmobile. Nate Prichard, by the way.'

'Sorry, Nate. Didn't mean to hold you up. Just calling to let the little woman know not to wait up. I'm working a little late myself tonight.' He winked conspiratorially, an afterthought. Nate responded as he'd anticipated. With a crude knowing laugh, the man waved him off.

The two men had recognized each other. Brothers under the skin.

26

Despite the bad dreams and lack of sleep, Rachael rose next morning in a good mood and more determined than ever not to let some sick jerk destroy her new-found serenity, the independence for which she'd worked so hard. Sitting on the edge of the bed tying her sneakers, she decided to simply ignore the whole *stalker* business. If she got any more calls, she'd just hang up, as Detective Mason had suggested.

In spite of her resolve, she didn't get very far on her morning run when she felt someone watching her. Darting a look over her shoulder, she lost her rhythm, stumbled and nearly fell.

No one there. Just the trail of her own footprints reaching back along the stretch of beach. Other footprints pushed to the forefront of her mind. Those she had seen on the beach that first day. A man's.

Forget it, Rachael. Let it go. And on this perfect fall morning, with brilliant blue skies overhead, sun sparkling on the water, she managed to do just that.

★ ★ ★

When she was gone from his view, he lowered the binoculars, picked up the squirming canvas bag at his feet and headed for her house.

★ ★ ★

Iris sat in Doc Stetson's office thumbing through a recent copy of *Newsday* waiting for the vet to finish checking Cleo over, and give her a booster shot. She absently turned a page, and suddenly, shockingly, there she was — the girl who had appeared to her during the seance, or whatever you wanted to call it, with Helen. For a moment she could not believe her own eyes. It can't be the same girl, she told herself. But it was. Definitely her, absolutely no doubt about it in Iris' mind.

The headline screamed out at her: HIGH SCHOOL PROM ENDS IN MURDER.

Against every instinct in her, Iris had given in to Helen's pleadings. She knew how it was supposed to work. Her mother had owned an Ouija board that she and her friends sometimes used to scare themselves with, while Iris' grandmother would sit in her chair, in a shadowy corner of the room, rocking, looking on in bemused detachment. A mother watching her children at play, her

240

wrinkled old face bathed in mystery.

Everyone always said *she* was the one with the *sight*. But to Iris' recollection, she took no part in these games.

Iris could guess why not.

At Helen's urgings, she had asked the Ouija: 'Is anyone here?' At first, as she'd expected, nothing happened. She'd hoped the effort alone would satisfy Helen.

Iris asked the question a second time. Suddenly, beneath her fingertips, the planchette began to move. Iris clutched at the obvious explanation. It was Helen. Helen was making the pointer move with the pressure of her fingers. Unconsciously, no doubt, but still doing it.

Then Iris had felt a change in the air around them and knew they were no longer alone in the room. Someone — something — had joined them.

The feverish light in Helen's eyes was brighter still, her face cast in an evangelical glow bordering on madness. 'It says 'yes',' she whispered.

Cleo meowed fretfully. She too had sensed the presence.

'It says 'yes',' Helen repeated. 'I knew she'd come. I knew.'

But it wasn't Heather who had entered their midst.

The flame from the candle nearest them on the coffee table blew sideways, all but went out. Iris felt the coolness against her heart. Had a door opened somewhere in the house, letting in a draft? But she knew better.

'Iris, ask her — ' She clamped a hand over her mouth, cutting off the question, making a choking sound in her throat. Tears seeped through closed lids, even as she replaced her fingers on the planchette. 'Ask her if she — suffered. I need to know.'

Iris had done as Helen asked. At once, the pointer began to move in a diagonal line toward the upper right corner of the board. Iris' disbelieving eyes tracked its brief journey.

It stopped at *Yes*. She knew then that it was not Helen causing the planchette to move. What mother would want the burden of knowing that her child died in a desperate fight for her life? Cruelly. Wasn't it the first question people always asked after an unexpected death? Did my loved one suffer? All the while praying to hear the word *No*. Never felt a thing.

'It's not Heather,' Iris said, but Helen was beyond reason. A righteous fury had filled her eyes. 'Ask her who murdered her.'

Knowing it was futile to try to convince her it wasn't Heather, she asked the question. At once the air at her back had turned cold. Candles flickered and Iris felt an overwhelming urge to send the Ouija Board flying across the room, to end this dangerous game she had so foolishly agreed to play.

Once more, the pointer began to move. Slowly at first, then faster and faster, dispelling any remaining thought of Helen's influence. Darting like a live thing from letter to letter, Iris could scarcely keep her fingers on its smooth, warm surface, or follow its path with her eyes. An unpleasant prickling had started up in her hands, and she was about to follow her initial inclination to send the thing flying, when it stopped abruptly.

Then, as though a movie screen had unrolled before her eyes, Iris found herself watching a scene in which a young woman in a strapless dress was walking along a narrow path toward a house glimpsed through trees. Swept-up dark hair, wispy curls fallen down past her ears, a dreamy smile on her face. She appeared to be almost floating.

As a cloud passed beneath the moon, the girl's smile disappeared. She stumbled on the walkway. Something had startled her. Yes, someone else in the picture now, face hidden in darkness. The vision ended as quickly as it appeared. Iris blinked as one does when the lights came up in the theatre. But the vision of the girl remained imprinted behind her lids.

There'd been something familiar about the girl. *And* the faint scent of perfume in the air, mingling with the candle-wax smell. *Evening in Paris*. Iris recognized the fragrance easily because it was the first perfume she'd ever owned, a birthday gift from her dance teacher, Miss Dalling, when Iris was twelve. It had made her feel so grown up. She could still see the pretty cobalt blue bottle. Iris hadn't come across that particular perfume in years. Yet in life, this girl had worn *Evening in Paris*. At least on the night she was murdered.

By someone named Charlie.

A good thing I'm sitting down, she thought, as she scanned the lengthy article. Two paragraphs into it, she learned it was written by the reporter who had covered the murder trial seventeen years before. The reporter had apparently picked up on the victim's mother's recent passing in a nursing home, and parlayed it into a rehash of the murder.

The face now had a name — Marie Morley. Her older brother had raped, then drowned her in a ditch behind their house. He was sent to an institution for the criminally insane. As she read, a sense of foreboding spread in her breast like dark wings. She recalled the crow outside her store window that day. A harbinger of death. Lord, when had she become so superstitious? When had she become her mother?

Iris looked back at the photograph and knew now why the girl in the vision looked so familiar to her. She looked like a young Rachael.

Her dress was the same one she'd worn in Iris' vision. A prom dress. A pink corsage adorned her slim wrist. The caption beneath read: Photo of Marie Morley, taken earlier that evening by the victim's mother.

She was smiling in the photo, but Iris could see the deep sadness behind the smile. She read further. Her date for the prom that night had been a dentist's son named Harold Johnson, and a prime suspect in the case until Ruth Morley's own suspicions, and later indisputable forensic evidence, pointed to the adopted brother, Charlie Morley.

Neighbors were questioned. A Mr. Ralph Nealey was quoted as saying: 'Always was a mean bugger to the little girl. I was working in the yard one afternoon and I saw him whip a fistful of rocks at her because she was crying to go with him. She was crazy about her big brother. Damned if I know why. Pretty little tyke, she was.'

The article continued onto the next page.

Reading Ruth Morley's own words saddened Iris. The distraught woman had told the reporter, 'I only adopted him to please James. He'd always wanted a son. I thought I couldn't have children, until Marie. I always suspected there was bad blood in that boy.'

Why would anyone adopt a child to please someone else? But then Iris recalled reading about a case in which a woman, for reasons known only to herself, had singled out one of her biological children for horrendous abuse, while the rest she treated quite normally. Yet despite everything, the boy somehow managed to grow up and make something good of his life. He even wrote a couple of best selling books. Maybe it's in the arrangement of chromosomes, Iris thought. Not even the experts agreed on what went into the making of a killer.

Iris didn't know how this old murder case was connected to Rachael, but was quite certain that it was. *I was meant to find this article.* Not for a moment did she believe it was mere coincidence that she'd come here today, or that she'd picked up this particular magazine. The irony was that the magazines in this waiting room, but for this one, were always at least two years old.

The only other person waiting with her was a young man with a cage on his lap, an injured dove inside. He was making cooing noises at the agitated bird.

Iris rolled up the magazine and stuffed it into her bag. She didn't think Doc Stetson would mind. She knew she wouldn't be able to find an available copy on the stands.

At home, Iris reread the article until she could have recited it by heart. She studied the girl's face until it seemed the teenager might open her mouth and speak to her of the secret horrors she had suffered in her young life, even to the end.

But it was the killer's face she needed to get a better look at. In the photo shown on the page opposite the article, Charlie Morley, with his head down, might have been any young man being led away in handcuffs by police. He was thin, dark-haired. Face obscured in shadow.

There had to be other photographs taken during the time of the trial, didn't there? And those photographs would have appeared in magazines and newspapers, just as this one had.

★　★　★

The instant she opened the door Rachael sensed someone in the house. She stood unmoving. Then, slowly, reached behind her, closed her hand around the doorknob, ready to bolt if she needed to.

In the lengthening silence, a soft whimpering issued from the direction of the kitchen. It lasted only a moment then fell quiet. When the whimpering came again, she let her hand fall away from the doorknob, moved cautiously toward the sound. Halfway across the floor, she hesitated, looked around for something with which to defend herself. Spying the stove poker propped against the wall beside the fireplace, she picked it up. It would do. Gripping it by the handle, she took a few hesitant steps.

'Hello? Is someone here?'

Getting no answer, she hefted the poker as if it were a baseball bat.

Would she even be able to hit someone with it if it came to that? Yet she'd be damned if she'd let them take it and turn it on her.

The silence was more deafening then any explosion could be. Then she heard it again. Like the mewling of a cat.

Could a cat have gotten in here? Was it something as innocent as that? But she could feel the dark energy in the house, a lingering malevolence in the very air around her.

Making a conscious effort to breathe normally, Rachael took another step toward the kitchen, poker poised for swinging.

In the doorway, she froze, staring in horror and disbelief at the grotesque and pitiful sight before her. Snap . . . snap . . . snap went the shutter of her brain as it took its pictures — hideous pictures that would remain forever etched in her memory.

The impaled bird was flapping feebly on her cutting board, spattering specks of blood on the walls and floor, the handle of her butcher's knife and part of the blade protruded from its tiny body. The kitchen smelled of its terror, and blood.

'Who did this to you?' she whispered.

The little seagull grew very still, its black eyes watching her, seeming to plead for her help. She could feel the creature's panic, its helplessness.

I have to do something. I can't just leave it there. I have to pull the knife out. It will die if I do. Doesn't matter. It will die anyway. I still must remove the knife, set the poor thing free.

As she took a small step toward the impaled bird it began to flap its wings in a frantic attempt to fly away. She remembered a boy in school once who had pinned a yellow butterfly to a board. The butterfly too, had tried to fly.

Now more blood spattered. Several drops struck her arm; it was warm. A wave of nausea washed over her and she grabbed onto the counter. *No, damn you. Don't you dare wimp out like some weak-kneed damsel-in-distress.*

A feather floated to the floor at her feet as the terrible squealing filled the kitchen. Rachael was crying too, hands clamped over her ears. Then, forcing herself to approach the seagull, she laid a hand on its body and, closing her eyes, pulled out the knife. The bird lay quiet. She didn't know if it was dead.

Only then did it occur to her that the sadistic monster that did this might still be in the house. But she didn't really believe that. Whoever performed this cruel, cowardly act was long gone. He had accomplished what he came for.

Dropping the bloody knife in the sink, she walked on trembling legs into the living room and called the police.

'St. Clair Police Department.'

It took all her effort to speak calmly. 'This is Rachael Warren. I'm calling to report . . . '

'St. Clair Police Department,' the male voice repeated. 'How may I help you?'

After a couple more failed attempts to make herself heard, she hung up. Something was wrong with the phone. She'd been able to hear the person on the other end but they couldn't hear her.

Not quite ready to accept that explanation, she tried again, but the results were the same. She was getting her coat from the closet, intending to drive into town, when someone knocked on the door. She practically ran to answer, grateful to whoever it was.

'I'm sorry to bother you. I was wondering — ' Her caller's friendly smile turned to concern. 'Ms. Warren, is something wrong? You seem upset.'

'Mr. Dunn, I'm so pleased to see you. Please, come in.'

She didn't know the man well. They had merely waved in passing, spoken briefly. She knew only that his name was Martin Dunn and that he was a photographer writing a book about well-known eastern coastal areas. But right then he might have been her best friend.

'It's easier if I just show you,' she said, her voice barely audible. She ushered him out to the kitchen. 'I just got back from my run and it — I tried to call the police but the phone isn't working.'

The gull was still. Mercifully dead? Please let it be so. She hugged herself against the cold that had settled into her very bone marrow and tried to shop shaking. 'Who would do this?' she asked of no one in particular. 'Why?'

Martin Dunn just shook his head and laid a sympathetic hand on her arm. 'Who knows? Why don't you go inside and sit down, Ms. Warren. Try to calm yourself. I'll take care of things here.'

Glad to escape the carnage, she did as he suggested. But she couldn't just sit and do nothing. She tried the phone again, but again it proved futile.

She heard him moving about in her kitchen, the tap . . . tap . . . tapping of his cane on the floor. She heard the back door opening and closing, water running in the kitchen sink.

Then he was back in the living room, assuring her that everything was okay. As if it could be. Nonetheless, she was grateful to him for his help.

His expression thoughtful, he said, 'You know, I think I just may have seen the culprits responsible on my way here. A black sports car sped past me, wheels spraying dirt and rocks. One hit the roof of my car, dented it. I wouldn't swear to it in a court of law, but I think they were the same boys you and your friend ran into in town that day. They were moving pretty fast, but it sure looked like them.'

'But why would they . . . ?'

'Kids don't need much of a reason for

violence these days. I suspect they didn't like being interfered with. Especially by two women. They're out to prove something.'

'*Catch you later, lady.*'

Rachael sighed, feeling defeated. 'Could you use a cup of coffee, Mr. Dunn? I know I could.'

'Thanks. That would be great if it's not too much trouble.' He glanced toward the kitchen. 'Unless you — if you'll tell me where things are, I'd be glad to . . . '

'No, it's okay. I have to go into my kitchen sooner or later. Might as well be sooner. Cream? Sugar?'

'Yes. Thanks.'

Though all physical trace of the atrocity was gone from her kitchen, the seagull remained fixed in her mind's eye. She knew she wouldn't be using that particular cutting board again.

Ten minutes later, she was back in the living room. She handed him his mug of coffee. She had stopped shaking at least. 'Those boys aren't the reason you're here, Mr. Dunn,' she said.

'No. To be honest, I've been waiting for you.'

'Oh?'

'Yes. I've been looking for a place to rent around here, and someone said you had a cabin on your property. I was hoping you might consider renting it to me. I think I mentioned to you that I'm working on a book — well, I'm also working against a deadline and it would be a big help if I could be right on the site instead of having to drive back and forth from town.'

'That's only a few minutes drive.'

'You're right, of course. I suppose it's more the psychological advantage. It's just for a couple of weeks or so.'

Rachael recalled the real estate woman telling her about a cabin on the property, saying she thought it should probably be torn down. Rachael hadn't thought about it again.

'I haven't even looked at the cabin yet,' she said. 'But I don't think you could stay there. I doubt it's habitable. I'm sure there's no insulation or plumbing.' It was difficult to focus on anything else with the image of the little seagull so vivid in her mind. Anger at such senseless cruelty churned within her.

'My intention was to have it torn down,' she said, 'Before it falls down. Or those kids set fire to it.' A chilly afterthought that now seemed entirely possible.

She would go into town tomorrow and ferret out this boy named Derek, who wore a tee shirt boasting a madman's face on the front. A boy who drove a black sports car.

This was a small town. He shouldn't be too hard to find.

'The cabin is in pretty decent shape, actually,' Martin Dunn was saying, as he set his mug carefully on the coaster on the coffee table. 'I hope you don't mind, but I took the liberty of having a look inside while I was waiting. The door was unlocked. The facilities are crude, but functional. And there's hand pump for water. I — uh, from what you've said, assume you're not aware that someone has already been staying in the cabin.'

The statement got her full attention, striking her heart like an anvil. 'What?'

'I don't mean to upset you further, but it's true. The floor was littered with cigarette butts, along with some empty bean and soup cans. The stove was still warm when I went in.'

As Rachael's head spun with this unnerving revelation, Martin Dunn talked on about his plans for the cabin.

'The place needs a few repairs, but I'm a pretty handy fellow. Built my own place before my fiancée . . . ' He looked quickly toward the window. Back to Rachael. Clearing his throat, he said, 'Sorry. It's been a little rough.' He gestured to the cane propped against his chair. 'Car accident. It's been a year now since she's gone. I sold the place.'

'I'm sorry,' she said, trying to summon her natural compassion, but her brain felt like a computer on overload, about to crash. She was glad he didn't seem to notice.

Smiling thinly, running a hand through his hair, he said, 'I'm still trying to come to terms with it. At least I'm out of the wheelchair. Work helps. So, what do you say, Ms. Warren. Will you have me for a tenant?'

Rachael caught herself picking at the dried blood spots on her bare arm, abruptly dropped her hand.

'I promise, no wild parties,' he joked.

When he was gone, she went upstairs and stood under the shower for a long time.

27

Rachael drove the car into the space between a blue van and a motorcycle, and got out. Three yellow school buses were lined up in front of the double doors, spilling out throngs of students — noisy, high-energy, rambunctious teenagers. Normal kids. Unlike the one she was looking for.

A studious looking girl, arms laden with books, was walking in her direction. She cast Rachael a curious look as she passed.

'Excuse me,' Rachael called after her. 'I wonder if you can help me?'

The girl turned, shifted the books in her arms.

'I'm looking for someone.' She went on to describe the boy called Derek. 'He drives a black Corvette. Do you know if he goes to school here?'

'Oh, sure, when he decides to show up. Everyone knows Derek.' She gestured with her small dimpled chin. 'There he is now, just driving in.' Rachael saw a certain grudging admiration on her face.

The mere sight of the black Corvette pulling into the parking area was enough to send Rachael's blood pressure into orbit. Thanking the girl, she took off in the direction of the Corvette, anger fueled by the tormenting vision of the little seagull.

She reached him just as he was getting out of the car. 'I'd like a word with you, Derek.'

His expression conveyed surprise. Then fear flickered across his arrogant good looks. He slammed the car door shut, shrugged. All defiance now. 'What's your problem?'

'Why did you do it? That's all I want to know. Why?' Her entire body felt taut as a guy wire.

He looked blankly at her. 'Do what?'

'Don't play games with me, Derek. I'm not in the mood. You know perfectly well what I'm talking about.'

Mumbling something she couldn't quite discern, he tried to shoulder his way past her, but despite his being several inches taller, she blocked his way. He was big and muscular, but she was too angry to be afraid. As far as Rachael was concerned, he was a sadistic little boy who mistook himself for a man.

'I want an answer, damn you, and I don't intend to leave until I get one. I want to know why you would do such a cruel thing to a helpless seagull. Were you that angry at having your bullying tactics interrupted by two women? Is that it?'

He actually blinked. 'Seagull? What seagull? I don't know what the hell you're talking about, lady.'

Why did he look relieved? It was as if he'd been expecting her to accuse him of something quite different. His obscene gesture to her on the beach? And now he was off the hook. 'Lady, you're nuts. I don't know nothin' 'bout no seagull.'

'I don't believe you. I — '

'What seems to be the trouble?' said a familiar voice at her side.

Rachael was taken aback to see Peter Gardner standing beside her. But of course, if she'd been thinking at all, she would have remembered that he was a high school teacher, and that St. Clair had only one high school. In her single-mindedness, she'd forgotten that little fact. It had not entered her mind that she would run into Peter.

'This student has been terrorizing me,' she said, her gaze returning to the boy's smirking face. 'I believe he and his friends broke into a cabin on my property. He may also be responsible for making anonymous phone calls to me. Yesterday . . . he . . . impaled a seagull on my cutting board.'

A few 'eeoohs' and 'yucks' went up from the girls, nervous laughter from the boys. She had to admit, hearing herself say it aloud it did sound insane, like some gruesome fantasy heralded from a deranged mind. She could feel her face burning. The tears were right there, hot and threatening, just behind her lids. That's all I need, to start bawling in front of this audience.

It must have been Derek. Hadn't Martin said someone had been staying in the cabin, that the stove was still warm when he went inside? If not this boy and his friends, then who? And Martin had seen their car. *No, Rachael, he said it might have been their car. He wasn't sure.*

Standing there, with half the school in attendance, Rachael felt like a complete fool. The epitome of the hysterical female, hurling wild accusations with no proof to back them up. She was no longer sure of anything.

'Jesus, she's a basket case,' Derek Chesley said, now on full performance mode. Crude and crafty, but not insensitive, he'd immediately honed in on Rachael's uncertainty, the wavering in her conviction. 'It wasn't me. No way. I didn't knife no seagull. Maybe she did it herself.' He turned to her. 'And I sure as hell didn't phone you. I don't even know you. Not that you're hard to look at, lady, but I ain't big on older women.'

This earned him a chorus of laughter from the boys. Derek was lapping up the attention.

A girl's voice said quietly, 'He's such a jerk,' and Rachael could have hugged her.

Anger flashed in his eyes at the remark, but then he shrugged it off, refusing to let it ruin his big moment. Making an abrupt switch to self-righteous indignation, he said, 'I could have you up on false accusations, you know.'

'That's enough, Chesley,' Peter said, freezing him with a look of pure disdain. He turned a wry smile on Rachael. 'Sorry. He comes by it honestly. Mr. Chesley's father is a lawyer. He's big on litigation. All right, all of you. Go to your class.'

A reluctant shuffling of feet.

Peter's face turned to granite. 'Now. Go!'

Amidst a chorus of mumblings and excited twitter, the lone word 'seagull' met her ears, followed by a guffaw, bringing another rush of heat to her face. *They don't know. They didn't see it.*

'The seagull incident, Rachael,' Peter said. 'What time did this happen?'

'Around ten o'clock, I guess. I'd just come back from my run. I heard it before I saw it. It sounded like a kitten.'

Another dream? Was she going crazy? The thought had visited her on more than one occasion since she arrived in Jenny's Cove, perching there on her shoulder like a waiting vulture.

Peter seemed almost disappointed as he said, 'I'm afraid this fellow was in school yesterday morning. All day in fact.' The blue eyes looking into hers were sympathetic. They seemed to say, 'I wish I could hand you his head on a silver platter, but I'm afraid you're way out in left field on this one.'

Rachael watched a yellow balloon skimming across the ball field. Beyond it, the school banner with its blue and gold colors flapped gaily in the wind. The colors melded in her vision, their lines of distinction blurred. She forced back the tears.

'I'm sorry,' Peter said, beside her. 'Ordinarily Chesley would be a good bet for any manner of misdeed, but in this case . . . ' He shrugged helplessly.

'I feel like such a fool. Coming here like this. But I was so sure. I thought if I met him face to face, he would have to own up to . . . '

His hand was strong and steadying at her back as he walked her back to her car. 'I'd like to hear more about . . . what's been going on, Rachael. I had no idea. Maybe I can help. At the very least I can listen. I've been told I'm a pretty good listener. How about I come by your place after school? Damn, I forgot. I've called a rehearsal this afternoon for the Christmas play, but after that . . . ?'

'No, it's okay.' She noticed for the first time

that he wasn't wearing a jacket. His white shirt billowed in the chill wind. His hair blew too, exposing a hairline just beginning to recede. A nice face. Kind. Thoughtful. Strong. He was also very good looking, she noted again, a detail not lost on his female students.

'You must be freezing. I'm sorry, Peter,' she repeated, getting into the driver's seat. She switched on the ignition, wanting nothing more than to be away from here, away from the scene of her self-inflicted public humiliation. 'Have a good rehearsal.' She tried on a smile that didn't fit.

'Here's my phone number,' he said, scribbling it on a piece of paper and passed it to her through her open window. 'Call me anytime.'

Driving out of the parking lot, she could see him in her rearview mirror looking after her, hands in his pockets, fair hair tousled by the wind. He must think I'm mad. She wondered if he might be having second thoughts at having invited a mad woman to be his guest at Iris' dinner.

Rachael opened the car door to the echoing ring of an axe, marring the late afternoon quiet. She followed the sounds around to the back of the house.

Martin straightened, wiped a slick of sweat

from his brow with the back of his hand and smiled. 'Afternoon. Just cutting up a couple of the trees downed in the storm. I thought you could probably use the wood for your fireplace. No point in letting good wood go to waste.'

'This is very kind of you. But there's no need — '

'To show my appreciation? Of course there is. Being on the site will make the book move a lot faster. Anyway, this is good physical therapy for me.'

'Well, then, I'm glad. Can't very well stand in the way of art, can we?' she teased lightly. She hesitated, then, 'Would you like to come in for coffee, Mr. Dunn?'

'Thanks. Another time. I'll just stack this wood here and get on back. I've another chapter I want to finish up while there's still light. The kerosene lamp is fine, but natural light is better. Of course, being an artist yourself, you know that.'

She smiled. 'My grandmother was an artist. I'm just a dabbler.'

'Oh, I doubt that. Well, I just wanted you to know I'm indebted to you for renting the cabin to me.'

'Don't be silly. I'm actually glad to have you there. Certainly better you than . . . well, I'm just pleased it's working out for you.'

28

'I'm delighted you're going to be at the dinner, Rachael,' Iris smiled, pouring the tea into the china teacups, a ritual before every lesson. 'It means a lot to me.'

'I wouldn't have missed it for the world. I'm surprised you know about it, though. I thought it was supposed to be a secret.'

'Oh, I knew Peter was hiding something from me,' she grinned mischievously. 'He cracked under my third-degree.' She laughed. 'Always works.'

Rachael reached for one of Iris' bakery sugar cookies. 'I bought a new dress for the occasion.'

'New hair-do, too, I see. Very nice. You look like the girl in the shampoo commercial.'

Rachael had to admit she also liked it. Since leaving Deering, and Greg, she'd done little with her hair except to run a brush through it, or pin it back to go running, or pull a headband over it. Now her hair was cut in a sleek new style, parted on the side, ending just below her ears. It was silky and sort of swung when she turned her head quickly.

Iris said, 'I haven't seen Peter this happy for a long time.'

'He's proud of you, and with good reason.'

She gave Rachael her 'Mona Lisa' smile. 'Oh, I don't think that's the only reason.'

Rachael had needed Iris' company today like a man wandering in the desert needed water. She wondered if Iris knew about her little trip to the school. But she would have said something, wouldn't she? Maybe. More likely not.

Refilling their cups, Iris said, 'You seem distracted, Rachael. I noticed you were the last time you were here, too. Is anything wrong? Something you want to talk about.'

'No. Not really.'

'Are you sure? I'm a pretty good listener.'

The very words Peter had spoken to her.

'I'm sure. And I know you're a good listener. But I don't want to talk about me. I want to talk about this wonderful honor you're receiving. And no one deserves it more than you. You are a wonderful artist, but more than that, you so generously share your gift with others. Me, for instance.'

'Well, that's very sweet of you to say, Rachael. But I think this recognition is because I've reached that time in my life when dear friends feel the need to give you a pleasant send-off. But it is a lovely gesture, just the same, and I do feel honored. By the way,' she said secretively, 'you're not the only one who's been shopping. Would you like to see my new dress?'

'I'd love to.'

'Then you shall. But first, there's something else I need you to see.' Her tone was darker now. 'Come into the living room.'

Rachael followed, curious as she watched Iris take a file folder from the sideboard drawer. From it she removed a sheaf of papers, fanned them across the coffee table. 'These articles appeared in the papers seventeen years ago.'

At the bewilderment on Rachael's face, Iris said, 'Let me go back a bit.'

Rachael listened as Iris told her about her vision of the girl on the day Helen Myers came to the house. 'I believe the reason this girl appeared rather than Heather,' she said, 'is that she'd been waiting for justice for a very long time. I opened a door, and she was simply there. There's no other way to explain it.

'Last week I took Cleo for her check-up and picked up this magazine. It had this article in it. I was meant to find it, Rachael.'

'I'm not sure what you're getting at, Iris.'

'You will in a minute. Believe me, Rachael, I'm no medium. Certainly, not willingly. It was only at Helen's insistence that I agreed to hold a séance, or whatever — well, that doesn't matter now. I only hope I didn't do her further harm. The point is, this is the young woman who appeared to me in the vision.' She handed Rachael a magazine, pages folded back to the story. 'Look familiar?'

Rachael looked at it, shrugged. 'No, not really?'

'Are you saying you don't see the resemblance to yourself?'

Giving the photo closer scrutiny, she said, 'Well, I suppose if you want to go back a hundred years . . . '

'Rachael, she could be you at that age.'

'I'm still not — '

'Look, I'm not sure I understand it myself. But take a look at these. I dug them up at the library and made photocopies. This is Charlie Morley, the man who murdered Marie Morley. He was her adopted brother.'

Rachael picked up the pages and, one by one, studied them. But the man in the photo was no one she knew. Looking at the photos, he might have been any college student struggling to make passing grades and drinking beer with his buddies on a Friday night.

Iris seemed so distraught Rachael almost

268

wished she did recognize him. It was strange, though, the longer she looked at the person in the photo the more menacing he looked. Something in the eyes. Or perhaps more a lack of something. But of course she knew that he was a vicious killer — that he had raped and murdered his little sister. Because the article said so. And because Iris told her. Would she have seen those same dark qualities if she had not known? She wasn't sure.

'Are you certain, Rachael?' Iris asked hopefully. 'You might have glimpsed him behind you — in a shop — on the street. He would look different now — older.'

To please her, Rachael continued to look over the photos. As her gaze moved from one to the other, she felt some tiny niggling of recognition. But she knew that what she was experiencing was a bogus sense of déjà vu, the result of her brain's already having snapped pictures and stored them in her memory bank. Then, when she looked at them again they played back to her, as memories. At least that was how she understood the theory presented in a recent television documentary she'd watched.

'Something else,' Iris said. 'This will probably sound crazy to you. God knows it does to me. When I asked her who murdered her — the Ouija spelled out — Charlie.'

While agreeing that the whole thing was pretty creepy, Rachael assured Iris that other than the mailman back in Deering, a jolly fellow with seven kids, she personally knew no one named Charlie.

Visibly disappointed, perplexed with all this evidence that apparently connected to nothing, Iris slipped the articles back into the folder, and returned it to the drawer. They went into the studio.

Over the next hour, Iris said little. It was her turn to be distracted. Not because she was lost in her work this time, though she was idly sketching in her sketchpad, but rather lost in some dark, disturbing place.

It didn't help knowing that Iris was convinced that all these happenings had something to do with Rachael. She wished she could share with Iris all that had been happening lately. But Iris would only worry more, and she should be enjoying this lovely time in her life. She'd earned it. Anyway, I feel safer with Martin Dunn staying at the cabin even if it is only for a couple of weeks.

With more enthusiasm than she felt, smiling, Rachael said, 'Oh, Iris, you forgot; you promised you'd show me your new dress.'

Iris smiled back at her. A thin, knowing

smile. 'That I did.' She understood the ploy well enough, seemed not to mind. She closed her sketchpad. 'I hope you like it.'

As Rachael preceded Iris into the bedroom, she could literally see the heaviness slipping from her friend's shoulders, a lightness come into her step. For a fleeting moment, despite the difference in their ages, she let herself imagine that they were teenagers about to share a delicious secret.

★ ★ ★

Finding the door locked, Peter entered Hartley's cabin through a window. It had seemed strange, even eerie, that Luke hadn't come bounding over to greet him when he got out of his car. And now, inside the house, Peter felt the silence even more profoundly. The place felt abandoned, as if no one had lived here for a long time. Unless you counted the plate, fork and knife, and a mug left on the brown and white checked plastic tablecloth. Grease from fried eggs had hardened on the plate.

Coffee dregs had congealed like tar at the bottom of his coffee mug. Evidence that Hartley hadn't been here in a while. Peter wandered through the rooms, checked out the bathroom, thinking his old friend might have taken sick and passed out on the floor, but the cabin was quite deserted. Anyway, that wouldn't have explained Luke's not being around, would it? Luke would never have left Hartley's side of his own accord.

He walked outside and looked around. The rowboat was in its place, tied to the tree. Beyond it, the bay was dark blue, silent.

Keeping its secrets.

29

Early the next morning as she was applying the last brush full of paint to the remaining patch of pantry ceiling, someone knocked on the door. It was her new tenant.

'I don't mean to disturb you, Ms. Warren, but I was just going into town and wondered if you needed anything. I'd be glad to . . . ' His eye flicked over the brush in her hand, the scarf tied about her hair. 'Ah, I thought I smelled paint.'

She'd left the kitchen window open a crack to let the fumes out. 'Just trying to brighten the place up a bit. The whole house needs redoing, but I'll get to it a little at a time. I guess that's part of the fun of owning an old house. Or so I've heard,' she smiled. 'It's nice of you to ask, but no, I don't need a thing.'

As she started to close the door, he said, 'I don't suppose you could use another hand. I mean, I'd be happy to help you — painting, papering — whatever. Anytime.'

'Thanks. But I'll be fine.'

'No charge of course. As I said, I'm an old hand at this sort of thing. And the physical work would be a welcome diversion from the book. Therapeutic.'

He was pressing her to accept his offer, and Rachael had to admit, it was tempting. 'Well, are you sure? I mean . . . '

'Oh, the leg,' he said. 'I manage okay.'

'I'm sorry. I didn't mean to imply that you're not capab — as a matter of fact,' she said, making her decision on the spot, 'I could use some help, Mr. Dunn. But I couldn't ask you to work without pay.'

'Martin, please. 'Mr. Dunn' makes me want to turn around to see if my father is standing behind me. But you're not asking. I'm offering. Please, Rachael — if I may call you Rachael . . . '

'Of course.'

'You'd be doing me a favor, Rachael.'

★ ★ ★

Martin was as adept at papering and painting as he'd said he was. 'I'm lucky to have discovered him,' she told Iris the following day.

Seeing the rooms in her home brighten and come alive under a fresh coat of paint and new wallpaper gave her a sense of permanence, as the sculpting gave her a sense of purpose.

At the far end of the table, Iris' deft hand

guided the fine, forest-green dipped bristles of her brush along the lip of her newest creation, a variation on the Grecian urn. Behind her, the late afternoon sun glinted against the window. Cleo was curled up asleep on the sill. Rachael felt peaceful inside herself.

This room was becoming more and more important in her life. But it was the moment when Rachael smoothed her hands over the moist lump of clay, not yet deciding what she wanted to make of it, that was most exciting. Possibilities seemed boundless then. Other times she was reluctant to begin, intimidated by her own limitations. She had told Martin she was a dabbler, but secretly she had come to want more from herself. Iris said she had natural ability. She wanted it to be true.

Iris looked up from her own work and smiled. 'So, where's this Martin Dowd from?'

'Dunn. Martin Dunn. I'm not sure if he said. I know he travels a lot in his work. Anyway, the arrangement seems to suit him, and it definitely suits me.'

'Well, that's wonderful.'

'Yes. Although I'd rather his misfortune wasn't my good luck. His girlfriend died in the car accident. He was driving. He's still recovering from his own injuries, both physically and emotionally.'

'How tragic,' Iris said. 'To lose someone you love like that.'

Rachael nodded, thinking how when she walked into the pantry this morning where he was painting the shelves, he smiled absently at her, as if his mind were elsewhere. It was not hard to guess where. If not for the accident that robbed him of the woman he loved, he would most likely be spending his labors on their own home right now instead of a stranger's. Nonetheless, Rachael was grateful for his help.

Rachael had considered going to the police over the seagull horror regardless of the evidence having been literally washed away, and taking Martin with her as proof that it happened. But she couldn't very well repay his kindness by taking him away from his book, could she?

The question of who her stalker was, however, remained unanswered. Derek and his friends had alibis. Both Peter and Iris seemed to be in Tommy Prichard's corner, and believed in his innocence. And strangely enough, so did she. And she barely knew the boy.

But what about his father, Nate? Iris had said he was the meanest son-of-a-bitch she'd ever meet. Was it possible he was doing all this, that he killed Heather Myers? She rolled the theory around in her mind. Had the man with the small, mean eyes secretly lusted after his son's girlfriend? Such a thing was not unheard of. Heather would certainly have been repulsed by him. Did she threaten to go to the police? To tell Tommy?

Iris had told Rachael that Nate's wife ran away when Tommy was only seven years old, apparently so desperate to escape her husband she abandoned her child to a man she loathed and feared. Whatever her reasons, it was a safe bet her running off hadn't endeared Nate Prichard to women in general. Rachael recalled his ravings that day in the parking lot of Iris' store.

Iris' voice broke through her thoughts. 'Nate's capable of meanness, Rachael,' she said. 'Make no mistake about that. But he's too dull-witted to be purely devious.'

Iris' powers of sensory perception never ceased to amaze her.

★　★　★

That night Rachael was wakened by a blood-curdling howl outside her window. She sat up in the bed, heart racing. No way was she dreaming this time. 'Luke?' she whispered.

She slid the piece of paper from under the

phone, dialed the number Peter had written on it.

His deep voice mumbled a sleepy hello.

'It's Rachael, Peter. I'm sorry for calling so late. I just heard howling outside my window. It woke me. Iris told me Mr. McLeod and Luke are missing. I wondered if it might be Luke?'

'Maybe. Could be just a coyote.' The sleepiness in his voice was gone now, replaced with the same sense of urgency that Rachael felt. 'I'm on my way. Don't open the door until I get there.'

As she replaced the receiver, the animal howled again, a mournful sound that reached out to her, and touched her heart with pity. She couldn't wait for Peter. She had to do something. Now. Donning robe and slippers, she hurried down the stairs.

Retrieving the flashlight from the kitchen drawer, she unlocked the front door and stepped out onto the porch. Moving the flashlight in a low, slow arc, she shone its beam over the grounds, let it penetrate the darkness beyond where the porch night-light did not reach. She guided it over stump and rock and tree, and along the length of deserted road going past to her house. And toward the bay, now silvery black in the moonlight. Moving, murmuring water. Restless tonight.

Padding in slippers down the steps, the cold night air bit at her bare ankles, crept inside her robe. She drew up the collar, tightened the robe around her.

'Luke?' she called softly. It had to be Hartley McLeod's dog she heard. She prayed she was right. 'It's okay, boy. Where are you?'

A soft whine issued from the crawl space under the porch. Rachael knelt down on the ground. Directing the light into the narrow well of darkness, she was suddenly peering into two amber eyes that stared warily into hers. 'It's okay, Luke,' she coaxed softly. 'You can come on out now.'

But Luke refused to move. Rachael kept coaxing, trying to gain the animal's trust. At last, he began to inch toward her on its belly. 'That's a good, boy,' she said. 'No one's going to hurt you.'

Suddenly, the dog froze in its movement and let out a growl that grew from its belly. But it wasn't Rachael he was growling at; Luke's eyes were looking to one side of her, just over her shoulder. The hairs lifting on the back of her neck, Rachael aimed the light behind her. But she couldn't see anyone. Luke began to whine again. She turned back to him. 'What is it, Luke?'

At the sound of a car motor, relief washed through her. Seconds later Peter was kneeling beside her, calling softly to the dog.

Recognizing Peter's voice, Luke wriggled the rest of the way out of his hiding place, tail in a listless wag. He licked Peter's hand in friendship.

'Hey, fella? What happened to you? Where's your master?'

Luke only whimpered. Then he gave a short bark.

'Too bad he can't talk.'

'He can. We just don't understand the language.' Peter checked him over for injuries, was alarmed to feel the sharp outline of Luke's ribs beneath his hand. He gently moved his fingers over the animal's head, feeling for any damage. When he touched a spot above his right eye, Luke jerked back, yelped in pain. 'Sorry, boy.'

Taking the flashlight from Rachael, he focused the beam on the wound. The fur around the cut was dark with dried blood, matted. 'It could use a couple of stitches,' he said, 'but it doesn't look deep. You never know, though.'

'And there's always the risk of infection,' Rachael said.

'What happened to you, Luke?' he repeated. 'Where is Hartley?'

'He needs medical attention, Peter. He's shivering. I think he's in shock. God knows what he's been through.'

Giving the dog a gentle pat, Peter then rose to his feet. 'You're right. I'll get him over to Doc Stetson's. There's a blanket in the car. I'll wrap him in it, help to keep in some body warmth.'

'I'll get dressed and come with you.'

'No. You go back inside and lock the door. Try to get some rest. I'll phone you first thing in the morning.'

Peter lifted Luke in his arms, cradling the dog as if it were a hurt child. She was moved at his gentleness. Peter Gardner was a good man. He was a man who moved easy inside his own skin. She found herself wondering what it would be like to be made love to by such a man.

But that wasn't going to happen. Her plan was to carve out a nice, safe niche for herself, and be content with that. As her grandmother had. As Iris did. One could live quite contently without emotional entanglements.

Yet, she could not deny her growing attraction to him.

'You sure did come to the right house, fella,' she heard him say to Luke, and it pleased her out of all proportion.

Careful, girl.

A poem by Emily Dickinson came into her mind:

He fumbles at your spirit
As players at the keys
Before they drop full music on;
He stuns you by degrees . . .

Rachael went inside and locked the door, the image of the tall man cradling the dog in his arms, still with her. Knowing she would get no further sleep tonight, she put on water for tea. Waiting for it to boil, she said a silent prayer for Luke. And for Mr. McLeod. A kind, hard-working man who had once hung a swing for her out by the old elm tree.

Where was he? What happened to him?

30

'It really does look wonderful, Martin,' Rachael said, as he was stepping down from the ladder. 'You could have done this for a living.'

Painted white, the kitchen looked larger and flooded with light. She'd found some pretty country curtains with yellow polka-dot tiebacks. They worked fine with the green tile floor. A matching valance for the window over the sink completed the effect.

Other than the ceiling, which Martin painted, she did the living room herself. She'd chosen gold leafy wallpaper for the wall behind the sofa, painted the other three walls in soft eggshell, carrying the color into the hallway.

There was no way she wasn't going to pay Martin for his work, she thought, reaching into her purse.

'Actually, I did do this for a living for a while,' Martin said. 'And put the checkbook away, Rachael. Please. We had a deal, remember? I'm enjoying the work. Like I said, good therapy. It keeps my mind off . . . other things.'

She felt a rush of compassion for this man who had suffered so much, and was now trying to rise above the tragedy. To carry on as best he could. He was an inspiration. 'Are you sure, Martin?'

'Positive.' With that, he went to the sink and began washing the roller under the tap.

To his back, Rachael said, 'I expect you'll be moving on soon. You won't want to stay in that cabin much longer. It's getting so cold now, especially at night.'

'It's not so bad. You've got a good little woodstove there.'

He was holding the roller under the running water, squeezing out the paint that ran watery-white into the sink, swirled noisily down the drain. With each action, the muscles in his arms and shoulders flexed and unflexed. With his jacket on, Rachael hadn't realized he was so muscular. Muscles developed, no doubt, from all those months of pushing himself around in a wheelchair.

His sleeves were rolled up, and Rachael could see part of the snake tattooed on his upper right arm. It surprised her; he didn't seem the type. Probably did it on a whim. A wild and crazy moment in his younger days.

'But you're right,' he said. 'The book is just about finished, so my time in Jenny's Cove *is* coming to an end.'

She had a thought, went with it. 'Martin, if you won't take any pay for your very good work, at least let me thank you by making you dinner tonight.'

He turned to face her, drying his hands on a rag he'd taken from his back pocket. 'That's not necessary, Rachael. You don't have to — '

'I know. But I want to. A hot meal will be a nice change for me, too. I've been existing on sandwiches and salads for months. I insist.'

'Well . . . '

'Six o'clock, then,' she smiled. 'And no work tomorrow. I'm calling a holiday.' The truth was, tomorrow night was Iris' big night, and Rachael had no intention of showing up with paint spatters in her hair, worn out from working. On the contrary, she intended to pamper herself with a long, hot bubble bath, do her nails, the works.

He returned her smile. 'Okay. That'd be nice.'

'Fine. It's settled, then.'

★   ★   ★

Peter phoned as she was putting the meatloaf in the oven. The news about Luke wasn't good. Though his wound wasn't all that serious, he showed no interest in food or drink.

'The vet says he seems to have lost the will to live. And he's pretty old. But he's doing everything he can to help him. There's nothing to do but wait and see.

'In the meantime, I've spoken to Derek again. He still denies everything, but it's possible he put some of his pals up to breaking into your house and leaving the atrocity there for you to find.'

'He must have great friends.'

'Yeah. He's one of those people with the dubious gift for attracting hangers-on. The sort who would do just about anything to gain favor with him.'

Iris was right about one thing: a strange darkness had entered all their lives. Heather murdered, a body washed up on the rocks. Mr. McLeod going missing, Luke maybe dying. She thought of that old Ray Bradbury title, *Something Wicked This Way Comes*.

'I think it's already here,' she said to the empty house.

Lord, she was starting to sound like Iris.

✶ ✶ ✶

Martin arrived promptly at six. Seeing him standing in her doorway, bearing flowers and wine, she knew at once she'd made a mistake. Dressed in a blue suit, shirt and tie, he looked spiffy as a boy on his first day at school. No! Boy, he was not. More like a man on a date that was important to him, she thought uneasily.

She didn't miss the disappointment on his face at her own informal, to put it mildly, attire. Ah, yes, big mistake.

'Whoa, enough, thank you,' Rachael said, shielding her glass with her hand, as Martin attempted to pour her more wine. It would not have occurred to her to serve wine with this dinner, but since he'd brought it with him, what could she do?

'I feel like maybe I should have served something more exotic than meatloaf,' she joked feebly.

'No, it's great. Really. You make great meatloaf, Rachael. Don't you like the wine?' he said anxiously. 'You've hardly touched yours. I guess I should have consulted you about — '

'The wine is perfect, Martin,' she said, taking a sip to prove it. It was too heavy for her taste, too sweet. 'Very good, in fact. I'm just not much of a drinker.'

And definitely less so at this moment, she thought, annoyed with herself for not seeing how he might have taken her offer of dinner to mean something more than a simple thank you.

He'd lost someone dear to him, was still going through recovery himself. Of course he was vulnerable right now. She, of all people, should have understood that. How could she have been so unthinking? So insensitive?

His shaving lotion wafted across the table to her, something flowery, cloying. Or maybe it was the carnations. The meal was decent enough, but she had no appetite for it. Nor for Martin Dunn. Damn, I need this like the proverbial hole in the head.

Spearing a baby carrot onto her fork, she paused before putting it in her mouth. It wasn't that she didn't like Martin; she did. She liked his soft-spoken way, his generosity, his determination to move on with his life. But he did not appeal to her romantically in the least. She would have to make that clear to him, without hurting his feelings. Not an easy task, she thought again. Probably impossible.

'So Martin,' she said, breaking off a section of her shamrock roll, 'when do you think you'll be shipping the book off? Or is that a question one shouldn't ask of an author?'

'I don't mind. Except when it's my publisher asking.' He was smiling at her, reaching again for the bottle of wine. Rachael watched with growing discomfort as he refilled his glass. She couldn't very well forbid him to drink his own wine, could she?

'A few days at most. You'll celebrate with me. My treat this time.'

Not a question, but a decision.

'I'll meet my deadline, and it's all because of you.' He downed half the wine in the glass, set it down and looked deeply into her eyes. Against her will, he held her gaze; she could not look away.

'You know — even in jeans and a sweatshirt, you are a beautiful woman. Though, if you don't mind my saying so, I did like your hair longer.'

'Well, thank you — I think.' She gave an uneasy laugh. Presumptuous of him. Assuming an intimacy between them that didn't exist. *You're not a child, Rachael. You can handle this. And you better handle it right now, before it goes any further.*

'Have you always been interested in photography, Martin?' *What was she waiting for?*

'Ever since I got my first camera,' he said, picking up his wineglass again. 'I'd like to photograph you some time, Rachael. Will you let me?'

'Sorry, I'm not much for having my picture taken. I — '

'Yes, I remember.'

She knew he was referring to the morning

she'd met him while out on her run. He'd pointed his camera at her and she'd put up a hand to cover her face.

'You're a wonderful cook,' he said, apparently having decided to set the subject of her posing for him aside, at least for the moment. 'What is this sauce?'

On just the right beat, playing stand-up to his straight man, she said, 'Tomato soup.' She had hoped for at least a chuckle to break the tension, but he didn't so much as grin. She was clearly not taking him as seriously as he wanted to be taken. Sighing, she poured their coffees, served Martin a slice of store-bought apple pie with cheddar. Then she discreetly watched him eat it, silently hurrying each forkful into his mouth as she drank her own coffee.

He'd barely set the fork down when she stood up and began clearing away the dishes. 'You go ahead and finish your coffee, Martin. I'll just put these in the s — '

'I'll help,' he said, leaping to his feet, nearly knocking the chair over in his eagerness.

'No, please. Sit. I'm just putting them in the sink for now. They'll wait until morning. If you don't mind, Martin, I don't want to rush you, but I am pretty tired.' At the stunned look on his face, she added off-handedly, 'I think I'll turn in early.'

Something one would say to any good friend, wasn't it? She made herself smile at him. 'And you can get some more work done on the book, too. In fact, why don't I just put the rest of the coffee in a thermos? You can take it with you.'

Smooth move, Rachael. 'Here's your hat; what's your hurry?'

'It's not . . . ' He looked at his watch, ' . . . even eight o'clock yet.'

'Yes, well, you know what they say about being healthy and wise.' *Dumb. Really dumb.* She was not handling this well at all.

'Martin, I know this — is entirely my fault. I . . . '

Very softly, he asked, 'Are you laughing at me, Rachael?'

Her fingers tightened on the plate in her hand. 'Oh, no. No, of course not.'

At last she was holding the door for him, more than a little relieved at having the evening done with. It would not be repeated, that was for sure. He seemed to be taking forever getting into his jacket.

How well did she really know him? Other than what he deigned to tell her. Not well at all. She hadn't even bothered to check his references. What if he decides he doesn't want to leave? She could scream her lungs out and no one would hear, only the birds and the squirrels, and they weren't coming to her rescue.

The thought was barely complete when he was upon her, pinning her against the doorframe with his body, his mouth seeking hers. It happened so fast that for a moment she felt only surprise. But surprise quickly gave way to panic as she twisted her head away, trying to avoid his mouth. His breath was moist against her face, smelling of the heavy wine. She pushed at his chest, but it was like trying to move a tank.

'Stop it, Martin,' she gasped. 'Don't — '

She felt his hesitation. Then he let her go. 'I'm sorry.' He was breathing hard. 'I swear I've never done anything like that before in my life. It's just that you looked so beautiful standing there. I couldn't help myself. I know that's no excuse. I promise you, Rachael, it will never happen again.'

'No, it won't. I was trying to show my appreciation for all your help, that's all. You took it to be something more, and it wasn't. Could never be.' No holds barred now. 'I'm sorry if I did anything to make you think otherwise. I hope I've made myself clear.'

'Yes. And you did nothing. This is all my fault. I acted like a jerk. Can you forgive me?' He put out a hand to her, and she backed away from his touch. 'Please, just go now,

Martin.' She heard the trembling in her voice. 'Please.'

He was about to say something else then changed his mind. His hand dropped to his side. Nodding, he left without another word.

She locked the door after him.

A few more days, he'd said. She supposed she could wait it out as long as he kept his distance. She was furious at him, but more so at herself for being so naive.

Upstairs in the bathroom, she splashed her burning face with cold water from the tap. She was still shaking from what she could only call an attack. His strength had been terrifying. If he hadn't released her of his own accord, she would have been at his mercy. She would have been no match for him.

One thing was certain; he would not be stepping foot inside this house again. Maybe I won't wait for him to leave on his own. Maybe I'll tell him tomorrow that I want him gone.

Later, still upset over the *episode* with Martin and trying not to dwell on it, Rachael curled up on the sofa, wrapped snugly in her robe, watching television. She'd only been half watching the news when Hartley McLeod's picture flashed on the screen. His twinkling eyes seemed to look right at her.

'In spite of waning optimism, and as

temperatures drop, the search for a local man continues. Seventy-five-year old Hartley McLeod has not been seen since . . . '

Rachael leaned forward on the sofa, hoping for some clue into the disappearance of Mr. McLeod. Sadly, there was none. Rachael did not believe he would be found alive.

If he was found at all.

If only you could tell us what happened, Luke.

* * *

At five minutes to nine the following morning there was a knock on her door. Knowing intuitively that it was Martin, her stomach clenched. She'd told him they wouldn't be working today. Why was he here?

Look at the bright side. Now you won't have to go up to the cabin to tell him you want him out, which probably wasn't the best idea anyway. She had his check made out. She signed it.

She opened the door, smiled coolly. Best not to appear hostile. Just get this over with as fast as possible. 'Martin. I guess you forgot we weren't working today.'

She saw his eye flicker uncertainly over the check she held in her hand. He tried to ignore it. 'You go ahead with your day, Rachael. I just thought I would paint — '

'But I'm glad you're here,' she interrupted. 'I hope you'll consider this fair pay for all the work you've done, Martin.' She handed him the check. 'If not, just make out a bill for the balance and I'll take care of it.'

'Rachael, there's no need for this. If it's about last night, and I know it is, I told you, I'm so very sorry that happened. I promise — '

'And I accept your apology. Please, take the check. It's only right that you should be paid for your work. I insist on it.'

She saw him about to argue further, think better of it. He must have seen in her eyes that there was no changing her mind, no talking her out of it, because he took the check from her hand and slipped it into his billfold. 'All right. Thanks. You're dressed for your run. You go ahead and I'll get started on the — '

'I've changed my mind, Martin. I'm going to leave the rest for now.'

His face darkened. 'But you said you wanted — '

She kept her voice calm. 'Martin, you're not hearing me. I said that's it for now. The downstairs was my main concern. I do appreciate all your good work, though, I want you to know that.'

He looked at her, said nothing.

'Anyway, not being tied up here, you'll be able to finish your book that much quicker.'

Why am I not telling him I want him out of the cabin?

Because you're hoping he'll get the message and you won't have to. Because you hate confrontation. Because you feel sorry for him. And because you're just a little bit afraid of this man. All of the above.

Please let him be gone when I get home tonight.

31

The meeting with Mike Bennings had gone sour for Greg Timmins. Like everything else in his life, unraveling like an old sweater in the first five minutes. The guy just didn't like him and now his competition had snapped up one of the few accounts Greg still handled himself.

And the hospital account was too damn big to lose.

He wanted his wife back.

Greg set his rum and coke on the dresser, the top already covered with overlapping rings, sticky from other drinks. He picked up his blue and grey silk tie from the unmade bed. Just the thought of all those dirty dishes in the sink downstairs made him nauseous. It felt like the whole stinking mess was coming to life, overwhelming him, crowding him out.

He wouldn't ask her to come back to this, though. He'd check out a maid service in the morning, he promised himself as he adjusted his tie in the mirror. He ran a comb through his hair, noticed the grey was returning. Rachael hadn't minded the grey. She always said it made him look distinguished.

To hell with Lisa. She was a nut case anyway.

He'd messed up big-time and he knew it. But Greg Timmins was like a cat, always landed on his feet. No sense in trying to hard-sell Rachael, though. He should have known it wouldn't work with her. Sincerity was his best bet. Yeah, he'd go with sincerity.

Goddamn Lisa was head of public relations now, up on the eighth floor, while he was swimming in crap. He never saw her now, except for that one time in the elevator. As she pressed the button to her floor, he'd caught the hint of a mocking smile on that sexy mouth and he'd wanted to slap it off. Whatever happened to Halston family values, he wondered self-righteously.

It had been a mistake telling Lisa she should look for another job. Like a concerned father, he'd explained that Halston's frowned on employees fraternizing. He'd even offered to write her a glowing letter of recommendation. Well, she'd gotten another job all right, but not exactly what he had in mind.

To add to that humiliation, the new boyfriend, who also happened to be the boss' nephew, was on Greg's back like a stinking blanket. *He wants me gone. He can't stand looking at me, knowing I slept with Lisa. I'm a thorn in his side. How long will I be able to take his garbage? It isn't fair, dammit. Forty-eight is too old to start over.*

I miss Rachael, he thought, picking up his drink and taking a swig. Just one to bolster the old courage. She'd sounded so final on the phone. So strong. Why did her strength seem to weaken him?

But she loved him. He'd always known that Rachael loved him. She would come back. He just had to play his cards right.

32

Rachael stepped back from the mirror to get the full effect of her efforts. The gold chain and earrings went perfect with the dress as she'd known they would. She'd taken time with her make-up, with everything, even to giving herself a pedicure. For the first time ever she'd painted her toenails, choosing an almost clear polish, with just a hint of peach to match her fingernails. Though it wasn't likely anyone would see her feet. Still, they felt lovely inside her new ivory shoes with the narrow strap across the ankle. She'd have to wear boots, though, carry the shoes in a bag. No matter.

'You look marvelous, darling,' she told her reflection in a bad imitation of Billy Crystal, and had to laugh at herself.

Leaving the mirror, she rifled in the dresser drawer for her good black gloves. Susan had bought them for her two Christmases ago. They were expensive, butter-soft, came up high on her wrists. Because she had a tendency to lose one glove, she wore them only for special occasions. Not here. She sifted through the other drawers, but they were not there either.

How could that be? She distinctly remembered putting them in that drawer. She was standing in the middle of the floor puzzling over the mystery of the missing gloves when the doorbell rang, shooing all thought of missing gloves from her mind. *Peter.*

Settling for her old black wool gloves, she changed into her boots, slipped into her new coat, grabbed up her evening bag. Forcing herself to walk, not run, she went to answer.

On opening the door, her smile of greeting wavered, her stomach dropping into no-man's land. 'Martin. What are — ?'

'Hi. I — I've been feeling pretty crummy about — well, I just wanted to tell you again how sorry I am for what happened.' He shifted his feet on the porch floor. 'I was hoping you might let me try to make it up to you. I thought maybe you'd let me take you out for . . . '

He stopped, his eyes taking her in, realization dawning. Apparently, he'd had his little speech ready and went straight into it before gauging the situation. She felt sorry for him.

'Guess someone else beat me to it,' he smiled ruefully. 'Lousy timing on my part. You were just on your way out.'

'Yes.'

His eyes swept over her a second time, more thoroughly. She felt uncomfortable beneath his gaze. Never mind that he nodded his approval. 'You look real nice, Rachael. Real nice. He's a lucky guy.'

'Thank you, Martin. I'm sorry I — '

'Think nothing of it.'

Why did she get the feeling he was remembering the jeans and tee-shirt she'd worn last night, resenting that she'd thought him so unworthy of any effort on her part. Well, tough. If she'd worn something more presentable, it would only have further encouraged him. Someone else would have to make Martin Dunn feel like Mr. Wonderful. It wouldn't be her. And she was sure that in time, someone would. Martin wasn't hard to look at, and he wasn't a bad person.

She considered telling him right then and there that she thought it best if he vacated the cabin as soon as possible, but Peter drove into the yard. The headlights of the Grand Marquis swept the front of the house like sunshine breaking through a dark cloud.

Why start the night off with unpleasantness? So Martin had tried to kiss her. Big deal. Hardly the end of the world, was it? She'd get over it.

Watching Peter get out of the car and stride up the path toward them, she couldn't help thinking how incredibly handsome he looked in formal dress. He carried himself with the same ease in black tie as he did in jeans. Neither could she deny the girlish thrill that made her heart sing.

'Your date has arrived. Another time, perhaps,' Martin said.

She didn't reply. None was necessary. She knew the answer was in her eyes, and that Martin had read it. Because he stopped smiling.

★　★　★

'Aunt Iris mentioned you'd rented the cabin,' Peter said, searching the stations on the car radio until he found one playing rhythm and blues. 'How's that working out for you?'

'He's leaving tomorrow,' she said, resolved to make that a reality. One way or the other. She'd brought this on herself and she would take care of it. As Betty would say, 'Ain't no such thing as a free lunch.' She should have known better, she berated herself again.

Sensing her reluctance to discuss her tenant, Peter moved on to a new topic, for which she was grateful. She soon found herself relaxing in the plush seat of the Grand

Marquis discreetly tracing Peter's profile with her eyes, thinking again how handsome he was. She wanted to touch his face. He smelled wonderful, too. Slightly woodsy, subtle.

'Iris must be excited about tonight,' she said. 'I'm so happy for her.'

He grinned proudly. 'Yeah, me too.'

Neither Rachael nor Peter spoke again until they were driving along the main street, heading into St. Clair. Snow fluttered past the windshield. Only a few flurries, the weatherman said.

At a stoplight, Peter turned and gave her a slow admiring gaze she felt all the way down to her pedicured toenails.

'May I say, Ms. Warren, you look absolutely fetching this evening.'

Fetching. Such an old-fashioned word, it made her smile.

'Thank you, Mr. Gardner. And may I say you look rather dashing yourself.'

★ ★ ★

He took a quick look around to make sure he wasn't observed, then, producing a jackknife from his pants pocket, slipped the blade under the sash of her kitchen window. At a sharp nudge upward, the lock gave.

304

The window slid up easily with barely a whisper.

He climbed inside, heard the floorboard creak softly as he stepped one foot onto the kitchen floor.

33

The dinner was held at the *Rankin*, St. Clair's only hotel. Although built in the mid-1800's, it remained as elegant as a grand duchess in her prime.

The tables had been arranged strategically around the large room, to allow room for dancing later. Every attention to detail had been paid. Blue patterned china and crystal graced snow-white tablecloths, glittered beneath a chandelier befitting a production of *Phantom of the Opera*.

After a half-hour of mingling, guests were summoned to dinner. After numerous heartfelt toasts to Iris, the meal, which began with a consommé and green salad, was served in spectacular fashion.

The main dish was breast of chicken broiled in a special sauce, definitely not tomato soup, Rachael mused, with lemon-parsleyed potatoes. There were side dishes of baby peas, glazed carrots, beets, and baskets of warm crusty rolls, along with an assortment of pickles and relishes set out on each table in cut-glass serving dishes.

A banquet fit for a queen, Rachael thought,

glancing affectionately at Iris who looked positively regal in the sapphire taffeta gown and the single strand of pearls Peter had given her to mark the occasion. At the moment, she was deep in conversation with the woman seated to her right who Rachael knew to be Hedda Neilson, President of the Arts Council.

Rachael was quietly enjoying the last crumb of her strawberry cheesecake, and the witty conversation and laughter that drifted around the table. Earlier, there'd been a few hushed comments and speculations about the body having washed up on the rocks, and Hartley McLeod's disappearance, but each time Peter deftly steered the topic onto more pleasant paths, clearly determined that nothing was going to spoil the mood of the evening. But Rachael didn't miss the distress that came into his eyes at the mention of his old friend.

She was happy to follow his lead.

Up on the small dais, a five-piece band, its members looking splendid in maroon jackets and white pants, had launched into a rendition of *Deep Purple*. Above the music, Iris was saying, 'You know, Hedda, Rachael is becoming quite a fine sculptor. You should see her latest creation. A work reminiscent of Rodin, if he'd been a

307

woman, and lived in this time. He worked mainly in clay and wax, you know,' she said to the table at large.

The outlandish praise both warmed and embarrassed Rachael. Iris was smiling at her with the pride of a teacher for her favorite student. The flame from the glassed-in candle danced in Iris' blue eyes.

'Yes, I do believe you mentioned it once or twice, Iris,' Hedda Neilson said in a teasing tone. She was a tall, handsome woman in a shimmering burgundy dress. Her smile showed off large, perfect teeth. 'Perhaps, Rachael, you'll let us arrange a showing of some of your pieces, come spring.'

Rachael had to tamp down the rush of excitement at her words. Don't let it go to your head. An idle comment made at a dinner party. No doubt to please Iris.

'That's very kind of you, but I'm really just a beginn — '

'Posh,' Iris broke in, waving off her protest. 'You're far too modest, Rachael. She has her grandmother's genes, you know. You can't escape your destiny, dear,' she said, reaching over and patting Rachael's hand. 'You have the soul of an artist.'

The soul maybe. Talent was something else. Rodin, indeed. She couldn't deny, though, the buzz of warmth that flowed through her body. Or maybe it was just the wine.

'I was so delighted, Rachael, when I learned your grandmother was Emily Warren,' said Irene Lord, the gamin-faced woman with silvery hair and little girl voice, seated across from her. Peter told her earlier that Ms. Lord had been a fixture at the town library practically from the day of its inception. 'We have two of Emily's paintings hanging in the gallery. She was a fine artist,' Ms. Lord said. 'Underrated, unfortunately. But then so was Van Gogh in his lifetime. The only painting he sold was to his brother.'

'If Iris says you're ready, my dear,' Mrs. Neilson of the Arts Council said, 'then you are. You mustn't hide your light under a bushel, Rachael. When one has been given a gift, there is a duty.' Her tone was at once warm and mildly chastising.

'Yes,' Peter said, as he refilled those wineglasses nearest him, hers included. 'My aunt is a fine judge of talent and I learned long ago that it does no good to argue with her once she gets that determined look in her eye.' His smile included both Rachael and Iris.

Rachael graciously thanked them for their vote of confidence then subtly brought the attention back to Iris, where it belonged. Nonetheless, the seed had taken root. Was it possible that someone would actually pay her for her work? Work that had begun as therapy, and was now a passion? It seemed like a dream, too good to be true.

And probably, despite all the good hearts here, it was. Still, what harm to fantasize? At least for a few hours. Who would have thought that at her age, she could become someone's protégé? Especially someone as well-respected in her craft as Iris. *Dream on.*

She sipped the wine. Neither too sweet nor too dry. Perfect. Everything was perfect. She felt Peter watching her, was acutely aware of his physical presence beside her. Easy, Rachael, she told herself, feeling just a tad light-headed, and pretty sure it was not all due to the wine.

Deep Purple glided smoothly into another old standard — *September Song*, music chosen especially for Iris, but that were among Rachael's own favorites. Swaying inwardly to the music, she hadn't realized she'd closed her eyes until Peter spoke to her.

'May I have the pleasure of this dance, Ms. Warren?'

He was smiling down at her, his hand outstretched in invitation. Looking past him, satisfying herself that a few couples were already up dancing, she slipped her hand into his and let herself be led out onto the dance floor.

At first, she felt awkward, like she was made out of wood. It had been so long since she'd danced with anyone. But then, with the warm pressure of his hand on her back, guiding her about the floor, she began to relax. Soon, she was following his rhythm until their bodies were moving as one. As if they had always danced together.

'Enjoying yourself?' he said into her hair, drawing her closer to him.

'Oh, yes. It's a wonderful evening.'

Her senses were intoxicated with the touch and smell of him — the velvety feel of the fabric of his jacket against her cheek. The strong beat of his heart against hers. The way his arms felt around her, the warmth and strength that flowed from them, into her, into every fiber of her being. Like being submerged in a warm bath. Like coming home. Yes, that was what she felt. That she had come home.

'Careful,' the warning voice said again, pricking at the lovely bubble she was moving inside. Absolutely, she thought vaguely. But she did not open her eyes.

'The food was heavenly,' Mrs. Neilson was saying when they returned to the table. 'I'll have to fast for the next two weeks to make up for tonight.'

Peter held out Rachael's chair and she was grateful to sit down. Her breathing was feathery in her chest. Her head still in the dance.

'Oh, listen,' Iris cried, clapping her hands in child-like delight, 'they're playing *La Vie en Rose*. I haven't danced to that since I was a girl.'

The words had barely left her lips when Peter whirled his aunt onto the dance floor. Rachael smiled after them, sipped more wine, chatted with Mrs. Neilson who wanted to know more about her. So hard to believe that only a few months ago she had found herself wandering among the ruins of her life. Dazed. Detached from all but her pain.

But it was more than that. Always before she had felt like an alien in social gatherings. But tonight — tonight she belonged — she was with friends.

All at once Rachael was gripped by a certainty that just beyond the periphery of laughter and good spirits, something hovered. Something dark. Like a black, malignant cloud.

Waiting to descend.

The room faded from her, voices growing fainter. She became aware of a faraway buzzing in her head. Her hand was shaking. Realizing she was still holding her glass of wine, she set it down. What was wrong with her? Why was she thinking like this? Couldn't she let herself enjoy one pleasant evening without . . . ?

She looked up to see Iris watching her. When had the dance ended?

34

Captain Elton Sorrel was in his den, nursing a beer and watching some rookie trying to snap the puck past the goalie and pull one out of the fire for the Rangers, when the phone rang. A collective groan went up in the stadium. Close, but no cigar. Where was Gretsky when you needed him? The Great One would be missed.

His eyes riveted on the game, he picked up the receiver. 'Sorrel.'

'Captain Sorrel?'

'One and the same.'

'I'm Doctor Alan Whittaker.' Without waiting for a reply, he went on to explain that he was the retired head of the state mental hospital. Listening to that deep, hypnotic voice, Sorrel wasn't at all surprised to find himself talking to a shrink.

'Yes, Doctor.' He turned down the volume on the TV. 'What can I do for you?' *Whittaker.* Where had he heard that name before? Recently too.

'Perhaps it's more what I can do for you, Captain. I just minutes ago opened a package from a woman named Iris Brandt. She lives — '

314

'In my neck of the woods,' Sorrel finished. 'I know Ms. Brandt.' He'd read the article in the local paper about her receiving some artsy honor tonight over at the hotel. Sorrel didn't know or care much about art.

'I see. Well, as I said, I'm in possession of this package. Came by courier. There are copies of several articles here, written some years ago. One recent. My name appears in one of the later articles. She circled it in red pen or I might not have noticed. At any rate, Captain, Ms. Brandt seems very concerned about a friend of hers — a woman, who, by the photograph I'm looking at right now, looks uncannily like Marie Morley. Or how she might look if she were alive today. Not that that would make an appreciable difference. Morley will project onto his victims whatever qualities he needs them to have for his dark purpose. A curve of cheek, a tapered back, a walk, even a smile could be enough to trigger the psychosis. But that Rachael Warren actually does look like his sister certainly adds another dimension.'

What the hell was he talking about?

'As I say, it's an old case. He was a boy then.'

'Who, Doctor Whittaker? Who was a boy?'

'Oh, sorry. Charlie. Charlie Morley, the brother. There's a certain irony that he would

315

use my name in connection — but, perhaps not so strange if you think about it. The bottom line is, Captain, I think you have a murderer in your midst.'

He knew that much. Sorrel switched off the game. 'I'm listening.' It hit him now — Whittaker. The phantom doctor.

'Divulging a patient's confidence is not something I do lightly, sir, but in this case I believe it's warranted. From what I've been reading in the papers, coupled with this correspondence from Ms. Brandt, I believe it's highly possible Charlie Morley is the man you're looking for in connection with the murder of Heather Myers. And possibly other young women whose untimely deaths have gone unsolved.'

'So how come he's out, Doctor? Why is this animal still walking the streets if you know he's a killer? If you don't mind my asking.'

He heard the quick intake of breath, followed by a sigh. 'Sometimes terrible mistakes are made.'

'Yeah,' the captain conceded, thinking of Tommy Prichard. 'I've been known to make a mistake or two myself.' Detective Mason had recovered Iris Brandt's radio in a pawnshop today. The owner identified Derek Chesley and two of his toadies as the ones who'd brought it in. The stolen radio had netted them all of three bucks. 'You mentioned, Doctor, that the killer and the victim had the same last name — Morley?'

'Well, I don't know for a fact that he's your killer. I'm suggesting it's possible. But that was observant of you, Captain. Yes. She was his sister, though not his blood-sister. Charlie was adopted, you see. You've heard of the love/hate syndrome, I'm sure, pop psychiatry being what it is. Well, this relationship was far more complex then simply perversion.'

'How so?'

'It's a long, sad story, Captain.'

'His momma didn't like him, right?'

'Something like that.'

★   ★   ★

He huddled on the closet floor in the darkness, surrounded by her scent, breathing it in like life-sustaining air. A different perfume from that which she'd worn on the night of the prom. That perfume had come from a blue bottle that always sat on Ruth's dresser. Ruth had dabbed it on Marie's inner wrists and behind her ears, the two of them laughing, close, loving, shutting him out like always. The door was open a crack and he could see them.

A lighter scent, this perfume. Like shampoo. If he turned his head just so, her clothes would brush against his face. Soft as a caress, making his head swim.

Waiting there for her return, Charlie's eyes began to grow heavy, as if weights were attached to his eyelids. In a little while, his eyes closed and he was soon asleep.

The old dream that was not a dream at all, came rushing in, an old enemy skilled at catching him off-guard.

His father standing in the doorway holding the pink bundle in his arms, smiling, bending low so that Charlie could better see his new little sister. 'Her name is Marie,' he said. A tiny hand emerged from the pink cocoon. He glimpsed a thatch of black hair, a doll-like face, and something like joy and wonder rose in his chest like a balloon lifting into the sky.

His own thin arms reached out to her. Suddenly, his mother's hand came out of nowhere, striking him across the face, snapping his head back. He staggered backwards and fell, cracking his head against the edge of baseboard. 'Don't you ever touch her,' she shrieked at him. 'Don't you ever let me catch you touching her again.'

He woke with a start, hands covering his face as though to ward off the next blow. He was sweating, his eyes wet with tears.

Suddenly, Charlie's head jerked up at a sound. His body tensed with animal alertness. The dream faded, as it always did.

Someone was out there. *Not part of the dream, Charlie.* He rose awkwardly to his feet, legs stiff and cramped from sitting so long, and listened. What had he heard? Had she come home? What time was it? He couldn't have slept all that time, could he?

The sound came again — like sleet pelting against a window. Charlie opened the closet door. When he was satisfied that he was alone, he crossed the room. He reached the window just as the rattling came again.

Not sleet at all. Someone was throwing handfuls of pebbles up at the window.

Keeping back so as not to be seen, he observed a man in a dark overcoat standing down below. Collar upturned, he was stomping his feet on the ground for warmth. His breath was visible in the cold, night air. Charlie felt confused at first. Surely not a salesman at this time of night. Then, he saw that the stranger had come bearing flowers. Another rival? Someone else come to court his fair lady, who, as it turned out, was not so fair after all? Unknowingly, he cradled his throbbing hand against his chest. Earlier, in a rage, he'd struck his fist against a tree, blood still seeped from his wounded knuckles.

319

Charlie watched him walk up the porch steps and disappear onto the porch. His eye moved to the Mustang parked behind Rachael's car. Then the doorbell rang, echoed throughout the house, jangling his nerves. Getting no answer, the stranger came back into view. He was looking up at the window again. Then searching on the ground for more stones. Straightening, he tossed these too up at the window.

Charlie settled into an icy calm. He watched the man stomp around for another five minutes or so before getting back into his car. He didn't appear to be leaving though. After a pause, a cigarette winked at Charlie from behind the windshield.

He's decided to wait for her.

The darkness was all around him now, and in him. He turned from the window.

Her nightgown lay folded at the foot of the bed. He gathered it in his hands, pressed the silky fabric to his face, breathing in her essence, understanding at some level that this was a kind of ritual he was performing. At last he let the nightie fall away and stood up. The void of aloneness opened inside him like a huge maw that threatened to consume him. As he had always done before, he filled it now with the comfort of his hatred, and descended the stairs.

In the kitchen, he retrieved the butcher's knife — the one he'd used to impale the seagull on her cutting board, from the back of the drawer; he'd put it there himself after washing the blood off.

Quietly, he slipped the bolt on the back door and went outside.

★ ★ ★

Why doesn't she answer the door? Greg wondered. I know she's home. Her car is here. Then Greg remembered that the old Cavalier had been falling apart for years. Probably broke down, and she probably took a cab wherever she went. He'd buy her a new car. Even let her pick it out herself.

He glanced at the roses lying across the passenger seat. Maybe she knows I'm out here and is deliberately ignoring me. Hoping I'll go away? No. That wasn't like Rachael. Rachael wouldn't do that to him.

He needed her. He always had. He just didn't know how much. He'd got bored sitting behind a desk, that was all. And Lisa became a fever in him. A fever broken, thank God. He was used to the road, to the freedom. So he'd picked up a few women in the towns he'd traveled through; he'd handled it, hadn't he? He never brought trouble home. It was all innocent. Didn't mean anything.

I'll beg her on my hands and knees if I have to. And maybe my kids will start speaking to me again.

Especially Susan. He and Jeff didn't hit it off that great, anyway. *Seeing you coming out of that hotel in Dayton with the blonde, whose name Greg couldn't even remember, if he ever knew it, didn't help.* Lousy timing, he thought, crushing his cigarette out in the ashtray. He shivered inside the overcoat; the car was cooling.

How was I to know Jeff was in Dayton on a computer course? He'd felt hot shame looking into his son's eyes that morning. No point in trying to bluff it out, either. Jeff knew. He'd kept on walking, pretending not to know his father. At home, he never spoke about it, but it was always there, between them.

And now he's going to make me a grandfather. Great. Knowing Rachael, she probably thinks it's cool. Maybe the idea would grow on him. Never mind that she had told him on the phone not to come here, or even call her again. It didn't matter. He'd make her change her mind. Wasn't he the best-damned salesman in town? She'd said so herself. Yeah, his wife was a class act.

322

From the moment he laid eyes on her, sitting behind the typewriter, long dark hair fallen forward as she typed a mile a minute — he knew she was special. The new girl. She didn't come on to him like the others. Always helpful, though. Sweet. A little on the shy side. He liked that about her.

A light tapping at his window scattered his reveries like a flock of sparrows from a gunshot. He turned to see a stranger's face smiling in at him, motioning him to open the window. Curious, apprehensive, Greg pressed the button. The window sighed open. *Did she send him out here to give me the bum's rush?*

'Greg Timmins,' he said in his best salesman's voice. 'I'm here to see my wife.' *She's still legally married to me. The divorce isn't final yet. Is she living with this guy?* Jealousy twisted hot in his gut. *But he wouldn't be smiling, would he, if that was the deal? He'd be ticked that I was here.* No, Rachael wouldn't shack up with anyone. She had principle. His wife believed in the sanctity of marriage.

Catching a sudden, horrifying glimpse of shiny, moving metal, Greg's heart lurched, as if trying to escape his body in pursuit of the sparrows that had taken flight.

Adrenaline flooding his veins, he dove away from the blade thrust through the open window. But he could only go so far in the front seat of the car, and the knife's blade, though intended for his throat, slipped between his ribs instead, with the ease of a knife through cheese.

At first, Greg felt nothing at all, and then a slow, sharp burning started in his side, quickly escalating into a scalding pain that spread and deepened. Warm blood spilled from his wound, soaking his new shirt and jacket.

He must be more ticked off than I figured, was his final thought before darkness enveloped him.

Scurrying around to the other side of the car, Charlie dragged the dead weight of his newest victim into the passenger seat. He propped him up then fastened the seat-belt around him. Breathing hard from the exertion, he slid into Greg Timmins' place behind the wheel.

The key was in the ignition; Charlie turned it. The engine revved to life.

As he drove with his mute passenger beside him, Charlie thought, for some reason, of Ruth. How he'd gone back and smoothed down the wisps of hair so that her death would not look suspicious, only a heart attack, not unexpected. He'd been about to leave again when he noticed that *Bewitched* was on, credits still rolling. He knew it was one of her favorite sitcoms. He liked the rightness of that; the way events had come full circle. Sort of like in those Greek tragedies Doctor Whittaker used to tell him about. He'd likened Charlie's own life to a Greek tragedy. Charlie couldn't recall which one.

'When did you first begin to look at Marie in a sexual way, Charlie?'

Twelve. Around twelve when he began to notice her small round breasts under the pajama tops when she came down to breakfast. And her child-woman shape in the leotards and short skirts she wore to her dance class.

'But she became happy again, didn't she, Charlie. Like a puppy starved for her big brother's attentions. She adored you, Charlie. Until you . . . '

'Shut up,' Charlie shouted, twisting around in the seat as if expecting to see the doctor sitting in the back. But only the man beside him, whose head lolled to one side, shared the space with him.

No Doctor Whittaker with his mild, interested eyes, his hand holding the yellow pencil, tap, tap, tapping on his green blotter. Just the tires humming softly over the snow-covered pavement.

35

Charlie banged the receiver into its cradle, checked his watch in the light of the phone booth. After midnight and she still wasn't home. He waited another ten minutes then tried again, letting the phone ring a dozen times before hanging up.

His heart was a block of concrete in his chest. He'd go back to the house and wait for her. She had to come home sooner or later. And when she did . . . He turned to leave and there stood the grinning fool who could easily have been cast in a key role in *Deliverance*. The guy who owned the welding shop. He'd been hitting the sauce, stank of it.

'We gotta stop meetin' like this,' Nate laughed, a phlegmy, disgusting sound that made Charlie want to puke. 'Someone else gettin' it on with the little piece tonight, ol' pal?' He grinned drunkenly.

Too bleary-eyed to see the danger that surfaced in Charlie's eyes, Nate slapped him good-old-boy like on the back. 'The hell with her. They're all tramps, ya know. Can't trust 'em far as you can throw 'em.' He gave

Charlie a sly wink, which seemed to suggest he knew things.

What? What did he know?

'Don't know what you're up to, exactly, buddy, and don't much care either. Ain't no skin off my hide what you do. But I do know that guy you left in the car back there ain't goin' to be doing no blabbing, either. If you get my drift.'

'Not sure I do,' Charlie said softly, having to work hard at keeping his voice even.

'Hey, don't try to con a con, pal. I passed you in my truck not five, ten minutes ago.' Nate's voice grew quieter now, steady, almost sober. 'You was headed in this direction, walking. I knew I seen you before. Thought you was a gimp. You ain't though, are you? Yeah, I knew you looked familiar. It was right after I passed that Mustang parked on the shoulder of the road.' He grinned, licked wet lips, as if already tasting the spoils of his victory.

Charlie knew now where this was going.

'I says to myself, 'Now what's that fellow doin' walking along this road at night, without even a flashlight? Gonna get hisself killed.' Then I see your face, and I remember. But I don't see no cane, no limp. Something not right here, says I. So I do a u-ee, go back to check out the car. Just a hunch, you know?

Just a funny feeling I had. I kept telling myself on the way there that I was prob'ly way off base and the driver just pulled off the road for a little shut-eye. That's until I look in and see all that blood. And the friggin' knife-handle sticking out of him.'

He was clearly enjoying himself. Charlie let him rave. Charlie was thinking.

'Now, Nate Prichard ain't a greedy man, but maybe we can do each other a favor, you and me, work something out.'

'Maybe. What have you got in mind, Nate?'

'Look, maybe the guy was hittin' on your woman, and you did him. Good riddance as far as I'm concerned. And I sure as hell ain't got no love for the cops. So why don't you and me head on over to the shop for a few drinks and a little dealin'. I got me some real good whiskey stashed.'

'Sounds fair enough,' Charlie smiled. He draped an arm around his newfound friend's shoulders. 'Lead the way.'

★ ★ ★

Rachael and Peter had been sitting in her drive for the past ten minutes, talking and enjoying one another's company, reluctant to end what had been a perfect evening.

'I want you to know,' Peter said, 'that I had

a terrific time tonight, Rachael. And it's because of you. It's been a while since I've danced or — well . . . '

'I know,' she said softly. 'Me too.' Despite his losses Peter Gardner exuded life. She knew that his mother, Iris' sister, and father were killed in a tour bus crash when he was twelve, which was when he'd come to live with Iris. And then to lose his young wife from cancer. Yet there seemed no bitterness in him. Or at least it didn't show. 'It must have been very hard for you after your wife died.'

'To put it mildly. But, as the old saying goes, 'Life goes on.' Even when you wish to hell it wouldn't.' His face took on a boyish, hopeful expression that touched her heart. 'And then, sometimes life surprises you.'

Yes. She knew what he meant. She had felt the same way tonight. Carefree. Young. But she was not ready for a new relationship. For a while, she had thought she never would be again. Her divorce wasn't even final. But she also knew that she'd given Peter every reason tonight to believe she was ready to hop into bed with him.

But it wasn't going to happen. Not tonight anyway. It was the wine and the night itself that had intoxicated her. Had made her lose her inhibitions for a time, she told herself. But she knew better. It was far more than that. You're falling in love with him. No doubt about it. Still, time to take a few steps back. Think with her head instead of her heart. She was just beginning to find out who she was without a man in her life. Who she was, all on her own.

She reached over and brushed the curve of his cheek with her fingertips. She smiled. God, he was so beautiful. 'Friends first. Okay?'

He covered her hand with his own, squeezed gently. His touch was electric, made her secretly catch her breath. She longed to move into his arms, let his touch, his mouth, his passion fill all the neglected, hurt places. But she remained where she was.

'That's going to be rough,' he said, kissing her briefly on the mouth. A mere peck. But enough to turn her knees to water and make her rethink her decision. 'Could we start Monday?' he asked softly.

'Yeah, I'd like that.' And then she was in his arms, and he was kissing her, and it was sort of like before when they were dancing. Like coming home. Then his hands were moving up through her hair, his mouth kissing the hollow of her throat. He moaned softly against her skin. It took every shred of willpower she possessed to move out of his embrace and get out of the car.

She floated up the porch steps, her head still in the clouds, and saw the note pinned to her door. Removing it, already knowing whom it was from, she slipped it into her pocket. Behind her, Peter was backing out of the drive. He gave a short blat on the horn. She smiled and waved.

Inside, she turned on a light and read the note.

Dear Rachael,
Just wanted to thank you for everything and to tell you that I've moved out of the cabin. You know, the nights are getting a little cold at that. Anyway, finished the book on time, thanks to you. Count on an acknowledgement; you deserve it. Hope you had a nice time tonight, and that we'll meet again sometime. I left your check in the cabin, on the table. My pleasure to help out, honest. Thanks again. And please forgive my clumsiness.

All the best,
Martin.

Hallelujah! It seemed to be her night all around. Head still woozy from the wine, and the evening, feeling like she was sixteen, she took off her boots and left them by the door, dropped the crumpled note on the end table on her way upstairs.

She hung her new dress in the closet and slipped into her nightie, not noticing that it was not folded as she had left it, or that there was a smear of blood on the hem, and crept into bed. For a little while, Rachael lay reliving the events of the evening, replaying Peter's words in her mind, seeing his changing expressions as he talked. She drifted off feeling his arms about her, the two of them floating about the dance floor to the music. She fell asleep with a smile on her lips.

At 3:00 a.m. the wailing of sirens wakened her. Ignoring her wine-induced headache, and a mouth tasting like cotton-balls, she stepped into her slippers, donned her robe and hurried to the window.

Horror filled her to see the night sky alight with a rosy glow. To her left, flames leapt higher than the tallest trees, sparks exploding into the sky like Fourth of July fireworks.

Behind her, the phone rang chorusing with the wailing outside her window.

'I figured the sirens would wake you,' Peter said. 'I didn't want you to worry that your own place might be in any danger. It's not. Nate Prichard's Welding Shop burned down. With Nate inside, unfortunately.'

'Oh, Peter . . . '

'I know. I'm going over there now to see how Tommy's doing.' Rachel said she'd see him later.

Downstairs in the kitchen, she made herself a strong cup of black coffee, her eye passing absently over the small puddle of melted snow on the floor near the window. Taking her coffee into the living room, she switched on the local news channel.

TV cameras were on the scene of the fire.

Rachael felt sick about Nate Prichard, unpleasant a man as he might have been.

He wasn't last night's only victim. In other news, an unidentified man was found in his car, unconscious and bleeding, by a passing motorist. The knife used on him was still buried in his side. The man who found him blurted this latter chilling detail to the reporter interviewing him.

The policeman standing nearby looked visibly annoyed at the release of information that was probably important to the investigation. The victim was in critical condition, the reporter said.

At least he was still alive. Poor Nate Prichard. Such a horrible way to die. She hoped he'd died of smoke inhalation before the flames could reach him.

★   ★   ★

It was dawn when Rachael dressed and left the house. Smoke drifted above the trees, grey smudges against the lighter grey of the morning sky. Stepping off the porch step, her eye caught bits of red on the ground. Petals. Like drops of blood on snow. She picked them up. And stood in the quiet of this Sunday morning, with its tragic message written in the smell of smoke, puzzling over the three rose petals curled in the palm of her hand.

Shrugging, she set them down almost reverently on the bottom step. Minutes later, she drew up in front of what used to be Nate Prichard's Welding Shop, but was now smoldering ruins. The branches of nearby trees were blackened, their stark, tortured limbs seeming to claw at the sky.

Aside from the dozen or so firefighters still on the scene, their faces solemn, exhausted, blackened with soot, only a handful of people were milling about. The TV people had gone. Two police cars were parked near the rubble, lights flashing, implying urgency where there was none.

She spotted Peter just inside the charred structure, standing with his arm around Tommy's shoulders. As if sensing her there, Peter turned around. Saying something to

Tommy, to which the boy nodded dispirit-
edly, he came over to the car. He leaned in
her open window. She noticed the smear of
soot on his forehead. The network of fine
lines at the corners of his eyes seemed more
deeply etched this morning. Not so surprising.

'Hi.'

'Hi, yourself. Thanks for calling me, Peter.
How is he?'

'Pretty shaken up. Bad enough about Nate,
it's a hell of a way to go. But maybe it's ironic
justice. Not ten minutes before you got here,
they found the skeletal remains of a woman
buried under the broken cement floor.
Tommy recognizes the pale blue coat with
pearl buttons as belonging to his mother, Rita
Prichard.'

'Oh, Peter.'

'I don't know why any of us is surprised.
Nate must have discovered she was planning
to leave him, and followed her that day. And
killed her.'

*Nate Prichard apparently had a more
devious mind than Iris had imagined.*

'I'm going to take Tommy back to the
apartment, put him to bed.'

'Good,' Rachael said. 'You try to get some
sleep, too. You look beat. You've been here all
night, haven't you?'

'We both have. They just took Nate out a little while ago. What there was of him.' He sighed heavily, massaged the bridge of his nose with thumb and forefinger. 'You know, I think I will take your advice and hit the sack. I'll call you later if that's okay.'

It was more than okay.

On the drive back Rachael thought of the check Martin said he'd left on the table in the cabin. Remembering that Martin wasn't the only one who'd spent time in the cabin, she decided she'd better pick up the check before someone else did. She didn't let herself think too hard on the fact that she also wanted to get a look inside.

The path leading up to the cabin was narrow. As she walked, the smell of smoke mingled with the scent of pine. Strangely, it made her think of her living room that night after the second rock came crashing through the window, landing in the fireplace. Of the cold rain coming in the window. The newspaper hanging there limp and sodden. Of Betty stomping out the live sparks on the carpet.

The woods were cool and silent. Eerily silent, she thought, and unconsciously hugged herself in her jacket. Odd that Martin didn't just tack the check to the note. As she approached the cabin, she grew more acutely aware of the deepening silence around her. A hush. No birdsong here. No rustle of undergrowth or snap of a twig caused by some scurrying creature.

Rachael turned the knob. The door swung open. She hesitated then stepped across the threshold into the room. The first thing that struck her was how clean and neat everything was, though sparsely furnished. A small-unpainted table stood in the middle of the floor flanked by two hard-backed chairs. Against the left wall, the cot was made up, covered with a grey army blanket, drawn taut, smoothed. Her eye went to the pot-bellied stove in the corner. To the round-nose shovel leaning against the unfinished wall. To the shoeprints on the floor.

His parka hung on a nail, on the wall, his camera slung over it. She frowned. Why would he leave these things behind? Some bit of important information tugged at her consciousness. She looked back at the table. No check. She looked more closely at the shoeprints, at their distinctive pattern of circles and half-moons. She had seen them before. Where? Of course — embedded in wet sand, leading out of the water.

Something else caught her attention then. Something black peeking out from beneath the pillow on the cot. Her heart skipped in her chest like a stone tossed into a pond, sending ripples of shock through her body. Barely conscious of moving, she crossed the room and slid the missing gloves from beneath the pillow. The gloves Susan had given her.

Holding them in her hands, she stared at them. Felt their butter softness, like silk, against her palms. How did they get here?

How do you think? He let himself into your home when you were out, went into your bedroom and took the gloves from your drawer.

But why? What would Martin want with her gloves? An obscene thought struck her and she dropped the gloves as if they'd suddenly turned into slithery vermin. Repulsed, she absently wiped her hands on her jacket. *He didn't forget his things. He's still here. He hasn't left at all. Get out! Get out now! Run!*

Rachael tried not to hear the voice as she looked around, so stunned at the revelations of the last few minutes she could not quite process all the information. But it didn't surprise her to see no typewriter or battery-operated laptop, no pencil or notebooks to show that a writer/photographer lived and worked here.

Again, she looked at the camera hanging

over his parka on the wall, and guessed that if she were to open it she would find no film inside. She would have been right.

She moved robot-like to the window. From here she could see her own house through the now leafless trees. Had he watched her comings and goings from here? Her every move? Why?

Because he's sick, that's why. Sicker than you know, Rachael.

There were three more doors in the room. One leading out back, a window beside it. She opened the door to her right, which revealed a washroom, consisting of a toilet and small, chipped sink with an attached hand pump. The third door opened into a broom closet. About to close it, to heed the voice inside her head telling her to flee this place, she spied a single, high, green rubber-boot lying on its side on the floor — the kind of boot Mr. McLeod wore.

The voice was shrieking at her now, 'Get out . . . go . . . run . . . ' Thoughts tumbled about in her mind like a foul-smelling avalanche. Thoughts of Mr. McLeod and what had happened to him. And the seagull, and Martin showing up at the door at exactly the right moment. The phone suddenly not working, then fine after he left. All coincidence?

Other darker possibilities rushed to the forefront of her mind. While those boys were less than model teenagers, she doubted they ever saw the inside of this cabin, let alone stayed here. Derek Chesley had been telling the truth.

The roaring in her ears was not so loud she didn't hear the soft creak of the door opening behind her. Terror seized her, clawed at her throat. And for an instant blinded her.

He had lured her here. And she had taken the bait. She should have listened to the voice.

Too late.

Too late now.

36

'I've been waiting for you, Marie.'

Easy. Stay calm. Don't let him see your fear. She turned slowly, heart pounding so hard she was sure he could hear it. She tried to smile as if being here was the most natural thing in the world. Why shouldn't she be here? She had every right. This was her cabin, on her own property.

'Martin, you frightened me. I didn't expect you to be here. Your note said you'd gone. You also said the check was on the table, but I don't see . . . '

Marie. He had called her Marie. As Rachael continued to study his face, the contours and angles, coarsened by time and circumstance, her eye, like a sculptor's tool, chiseled away the hint of jowl, exposing the more refined face of the younger man in the photograph that Iris had shown her. His hair was longer now, lighter in color, his brow and jaw heavier, body muscles he hadn't possessed as a young man. But it was the same man. Why hadn't she seen it before?

His gaze flicked indifferently from her to the gloves, no longer beneath the pillow, but on the floor. 'You betrayed me Marie,' he said simply.

He spoke softly and Rachael thought of how she had rather liked his soft-spokenness. Now his voice coiled serpent-like around her throat, squeezing ever so gently. It was hard to breathe. Looking into his eyes, she could see darkness at their depths. Danger. She had seen the danger once before, just a glimpse when she rebuffed his attentions. He had wanted to hurt her then. She had felt the hatred coming off him like heat waves off a furnace. For an instant, his mask had slipped away. So fleeting she told herself she had imagined it. Had she been going around in a daze? She, who had always told her kids to listen to their own inner voice.

The awful silence compelled her to fill it with words. 'You — you're right, Martin, it really is quite comfortable here.' She made a silly gesture with her hand as though to compliment a girlfriend on the décor of her apartment. 'It's — rustic. I'm glad you decided to keep the check, Martin. You certainly earned it. Well, I'll just get out of here and let you pack up your things.' She literally had to clamp her lips shut to halt the babbling coming out of her mouth. She made a move toward the door and he stepped in front of her. *You are in big trouble here, Rachael.*

He was not an exceptionally large man, but she had already born witness to his frightening strength. He had seemed such a pleasant, gentle man. *You really are a lousy judge of character, Rachael.* Or maybe she was being too hard on herself. Maybe he was just a very good actor. No. There'd been signs along the way that should have alerted her. The way his limp came and went, especially if he thought he wasn't being observed. Those innocent brushes against her when they passed in the hallway — weren't so innocent. An accident, she'd told herself. But she knew now that Martin — Charlie wasn't innocent. He didn't have accidents. His every move was carefully calculated.

'You wanted me gone,' he said. 'Just like mother wanted me gone, like I was a bad smell she couldn't get rid of. Flaunting yourself, then pushing me away. 'Stop it, Charlie. Don't Charlie',' he whined in girlish falsetto, mocking what she knew was his dead sister's voice. A chilling sound. 'You always thought you were too good for me. Thought I was scum, just like she did. I thought you'd changed. I wanted us to have another chance. Wasn't I respectful enough? Didn't I bring you wine and flowers, Marie?'

She spoke calmly through her fear. 'I'm not Marie. My name is Rachael.' *In some part of himself he knows I'm not her.*

'Believe me this is not how I planned for things to end, Marie,' he said, as if she had not spoken. 'You brought it on yourself.'

She could sense the animal tension in him, smell it as if she'd stumbled unwittingly into the lair of a beast. Well, hadn't she? But she also sensed he was in no big hurry to go in for the kill. His prey cornered, he was savoring the moment of triumph, his time of vengeance against some long ago injustice, as he perceived it.

It was hard to think above the drumming of her heart, the wild din of panic in her mind. It was his eyes that frightened her most — not what she saw in them, but what she didn't see — the abyss within. If he ever had a soul, it had long since withered and died. But maybe not. Maybe there was some semblance of good in him, of reason, that she could still reach.

'Mart — ' Her mouth and throat were dry as dust. 'Charlie, you have me confused with someone else. I told you, my name is not Marie. It's Rachael. It's always been Rachael.'

'Let it go,' he said quietly, almost regretfully. 'There is no point in your carrying on with your charade. I gave you every chance and you failed. Again, you failed. How do you think I felt watching you drive away with him last night? Seeing you smile at him?' Not one of those stingy, guarded smiles she reserved for him, but warm, inviting. He'd felt her coldness when she opened the door to him yesterday morning, had braced himself for what he knew was coming. His services were no longer needed. He was no longer needed. When she gave him that check he'd wanted to make her eat it. Maybe he still would. 'No answer to that, have you?'

'I'm — I'm sorry. I didn't . . . '

I have to make him understand that I am not Marie. Iris had seen the resemblance. Why didn't I? Keep him talking. Hadn't she seen the ploy used in any number of TV shows? Read it in novels? Did it ever work? She couldn't remember.

'Someone must have hurt you very much, M — Charlie. Maybe I can help . . . '

His mouth twisted in amused contempt. 'You're wasting your time. You must know that I've been psychoanalyzed by the best of them.'

Yes, of course you have.

'Look, maybe you feel I haven't paid you enough for your work. And you're probably right. Whatever you think I owe you, I'd be glad to . . . ' She stopped abruptly, not quite believing the drivel that insisted on coming out of her mouth. Fear must be scrambling her brain cells.

He cocked his head like a dog tuned to a sound only it can hear. 'Owe me?' he repeated, incredulously. 'Owe me? How much do you think fifteen years living in a cage might be worth, Marie?'

'I am not your sister returned from the grave, dammit!' she cried.

Rage flashed in his eyes.

Oh, God. She couldn't have said that. The cabin was growing smaller, the walls closing in on her. Her own primal senses seemed to heighten her terror. She could detect the smell of blood. The dark energy that lingered in the room. She thought of the seagull. What manner of violence had occurred here? She remembered the boot in the closet. Willed herself to breathe normally. 'I'm sorry that bad things have happened in your life, but it was nothing to do with me. My name is Rachael Warren. I don't even know anyone named Marie.' Like I didn't know anyone named Charlie, except for the mailman back in Deering.

For a moment, she saw confusion in his eyes, uncertainty, and dared to hope. Had she pushed a button of sanity in some corner of his mind? However tenuous her advantage might be, she snatched at it. Willing firm resolve into her next words, she said, 'I have to go now, Charlie.' She dared a step toward him, was surprised when he moved aside to let her pass.

But when she tried the door, it wouldn't give. It was locked. Of course. What a fool she was to think she would get away so easily. Once more she turned to face him, her mind working feverishly for a way out of his nightmare. 'I'm not your sister,' she repeated emphatically. 'I may bear some resemblance to her when I was her age, people often do resemble one another. It's not that uncommon. But I am not her.'

He was watching her the way a callous hunter might watch a rabbit in a trap struggling to free itself. Which was exactly what she felt like. She steeled herself for the aftermath of what she was about to say, knowing that she was facing a massive pit bull on a very short chain. It wouldn't take much for the beast to snap it. Yet he was also a man in control of that leash, at least for the moment.

'Your sister is dead, Charlie. She's been dead for seventeen years. I read the newspaper clippings. You remember, don't you? It was the night of her prom. You waited for her to come home. You were very angry with her — '

'Shut up!' he bellowed, freezing her to silence. A dark flush had risen in his face. 'You think I'm some damn pervert to have sex with my own sister. I was adopted. We were not blood-related.'

My God! He's more concerned with people thinking him guilty of incest than he is about being a murderer. *He spoke in the past tense. He knows you are not Marie.*

'But you know that,' he said, chuckling as though she had tried to play a joke on him, one that almost worked. 'Yes, you do. You're lying. She — you were the one who told me, Marie. I remember your words exactly. 'I hate you, Charlie,' you said,' he mimicked his sister, but in a child's voice this time. The sound was chilling. ' 'Mommy and Daddy hate you, too. I heard them talking, Charlie, and they said the only reason they 'dopted you was because they thought they couldn't have their own little baby.' '

'I'm sorry,' she breathed, remembering having read the mother's cruel words in the article, knowing what he said was true.

'Oh, you were mad at me when you told me, you even tried to take it back. And I admit it knocked the ground from under me at first. But then it all began to make sense. I understood everything then. You told me the truth, Marie. Maybe that's part of why I have always loved you.'

And hated you, Rachael thought.

He smiled tenderly and touched a hand to her face. She recoiled instinctively and he withdrew his hand, hurt coming into his eyes. He searched her face. 'You really are not her, are you?'

'Oh, please. No, I've been trying to tell you. I'm Rachael. I — '

'You're lying,' he cut in calmly, extinguishing any hope that this might be over.

In some compartment of his mind he knows I am not Marie. Yet he needs me to be her so that he can play out this dark obsession in his mind, bring it to its final conclusion.

She didn't have to think too hard to know what that final conclusion would be. Fear clamped a vice-grip around her heart and lungs. She fought back the panic. There had to be some way out of this.

The back door. Unwittingly, she darted a look behind her to gauge the distance, foolishly tipping her hand even with cards not all that promising to begin with.

Charlie grinned. 'You might make it. You're a pretty good runner.' But she knew she wouldn't. No matter how fast she was, he would be on her in an instant.

He had madness on his side.

37

He was watching her, alert to any sudden movement she might make. Rachael knew that on one level, this was a game to him. A game of cat and mouse.

'I wasn't going to run,' she said reasonably. 'I thought I heard something outside.'

'Not even a good try. You disappoint me.'

She forced herself to meet those chilling eyes squarely. 'What happened — after she told you that you were adopted?'

The flicker of uncertainty again. 'Why?'

'I just wondered . . . '

'You're all the same,' he said, his voice much softer now, far more terrifying to her than his blatant anger. 'You tease, you run away. You're all whores — flirting, smiling, promising. Well, there are some who aren't smiling anymore. And soon, neither will you be.'

He moved so fast there was no time to react other than to cry out as he gripped a handful of her hair, twisting it until she was sure it would rip from her scalp. He slammed her down into a chair so hard it nearly toppled with her in it. She shot back up, tried to run but he caught her in his powerful arms. She struggled to free herself, but she might have been a child trying to fight him.

Suddenly, Rachael sensed something change within the struggle, a shift of focus. He was breathing hard and pressed her against him, his mouth open on hers, crushing. His thick tongue forced her lips apart, thrust into her mouth, triggering a gag reflex. She jerked her head to one side. 'Don't . . . please . . . '

'You want me. I know you want me.' His eyes were glazed with lust as his mouth tried to find hers again. His rough hand moved under her sweatshirt, squeezing her breast. She cried out in pain.

Pulling one of her hands free, she raked his face with her nails. He let out a curse and slammed her back into the chair. She was still struggling to get away when suddenly the point of the blade was pressing against the soft flesh of her throat, its sharp, cold sting, paralyzing.

'Be still. Or I will make you still.'

Taking a roll of duct tape from his back pocket, he bound her wrists. He worked fast and sure, knotting, yanking, sometimes gentle when she whimpered, as if he had not really meant to hurt her. Merely an accident, unavoidable, his expression told her. And as he himself had said, sometimes her own doing.

Blood trickled from the deep scratches on his cheek, giving her a semblance of satisfaction. He wiped at the blood with the back of his hand, succeeding only in smearing it across his face. She would pay for doing that. As she would pay for every injustice he had suffered in his life, real or imagined.

He shoved a fist in her face, and she cowered in the chair, braced herself for the blow.

'Don't be silly. I'm not going to hit you. I just want you to see what you made me do last night when you drove off with your new boyfriend.'

She'd seen that his knuckles were bloody, beginning to scab over. She hadn't known from what.

'I punched a tree. Childish of me, wasn't it? Though I don't want to mislead you about the fate of the one who called himself your husband. A man can only stand so much, Marie. Let's just say, I don't think he'll be bringing you any more flowers.'

The rose petals in the snow. Oh, Greg.

Now that she was tied and bound, he knelt before her like an adoring suitor. With the back of his index finger he stroked the curve of her breast through her jacket and sweatshirt. The very pores of her skin closed in revulsion. His tenderness was almost harder to bear than his rage. She quivered in fear and revulsion as his fingers traced the line of her chin, like a blind man intent on memorizing every feature through touch. Tears streamed down her face. She could taste their hot saltiness.

He stopped, smiled. 'Are you afraid of me?'

'Yes,' she whispered.

'Yes, I can see that you are. I really do love you, Marie. It could have been so wonderful.'

Charlie carried her, chair and all, to the broom closet. Ignoring her pleas, he closed the door, abandoning her to total darkness. He would have to wait until night to carry out his plan. But then he was well schooled in the art of patience.

Fishing his pack of cigarettes from his jacket pocket, he half-laid on the cot. It groaned under his weight. Stretching out his legs, he leaned his back against the rough wall, soundlessly tearing a spider web that spanned two studs. He lit a cigarette and sucked the smoke deep into his lungs. His mouth formed an 0 and he blew a slow, perfect ring at the rafters, watched it floating there, expanding, dispersing into the shadows.

Each time Charlie brought the cigarette to

his lips, smoke curling up past his slitted eyes, the fanged, hooded cobra tattooed on his upper right arm bulged like a thing alive.

Charlie butted his cigarette into the overflowing sardine can, with its jagged lid pulled back. In the gathering darkness that entered the cabin, he was all but oblivious to the thumping noises inside the closet. He was instead imagining her face — those eyes looking at him as if he were something vile. Just as they always had.

No, not always, Charlie. Remember. Once she followed you around like a puppy, looking at you with adoring eyes whenever you came into a room where she was. No matter how much you ignored her.

She'd been running after him that day, calling his name, dark curls bouncing in a frenzied dance about her sweet face as she tried to catch up with him. 'Wait for me, Chowie. Wait for me. Mawie come wiff you.'

He had yelled at her to go home, called her a nuisance, but she just kept coming. So he picked up a handful of rocks and whipped them at her. One struck her face. And his heart. He turned away. When he looked back, she was still standing there looking after him, crying. She looked so small and forlorn in that pink frilly dress, the kind Ruth always made her wear, that he'd wanted to wail in shame, to run to her and beg her forgiveness. But he did none of these things. And, as he stood there something that had been metamorphosing within him for a long time completed its process, all in an instant. Not that that was the moment when the beast gasped its first breath. But it was the moment when he began to give it its head.

'You've got to control that beast inside you, Charlie,' Doctor Whittaker had told him.

Last night, he'd stood at the edge of the woods watching them drive away, the nerve in his jaw twitching and jumping, hands clenching and unclenching at his sides. His fury too great to contain, he'd let out a primal wail that ripped the dusky silence, sent a rabbit scurrying into the underbrush, and slammed his fist into the tree. Lightning fire had flashed the length of his arm into his shoulder.

He'd sucked at his torn, bloodied knuckles, almost welcoming the distraction of physical pain. Why was she doing this to him?

Just like before. Stomping on his love. Painted up like a whore — for someone else. Always for someone else. Hadn't he been patient? Hadn't he waited for her?

Outside the cabin window, the light of day was fast fading.

Sitting in the palpable darkness, bound and gagged, her tongue probed the raw place inside her mouth where her teeth had cut into the soft tissue when he'd gripped her jaw and squeezed. Her head hurt where he had grabbed her hair. Her backed ached and her legs were prickly from lack of circulation. To add to that, she had to pee. Badly. Hitching the chair toward the door, she bumped it with her shoulder. And again. Oh, God, someone help me. He's crazy.

★ ★ ★

. . . thump . . . thump . . .

She wanted out. Yes, he thought. It was time. Getting up off the cot, he pulled the cardboard box from beneath it and took out the blanket. He thought about how he'd damned near frozen to death his first night in this cabin. He'd considered lighting a fire in the stove, but decided it was too risky. Someone might have seen the smoke. Instead, he had settled for this blanket. Threadbare and stinking as it was, it had been warm enough to let him sleep.

They'd come across from Harding in a rowboat Jimmy Ray had stolen from some old fisherman he knew.

'You're sure that's the house?' Charlie asked as they drew nearer the beach.

'Sure I'm sure. Jeez, man I used to live there, didn't I? I oughta know, huh?' Jimmy had shivered in the faded denim jacket, hugging it to his bony frame. 'You won't be sorry, Charlie. Didn't I say I'd make it worth your while? I wouldn't screw you around, man.'

'I surely hope not, Jimmy boy. I surely do.'

Jimmy had tried to smile. 'Hey, I told you that old bastard kept money in the house, and a helluva lot of it too. I just couldn't ever find the real mother lode, that's all.'

'So what makes you think you'll find it this time?' Charlie had asked, resting the oars in their locks, fishing his cigarettes from his jacket pocket.

''Cause I got my good buddy with me, that's why. We'll find it together and do an even split just like I promised. Uh, don't think you should light up.'

Charlie returned the pack to his pocket. 'Not as stupid as you look are you, Jimmy boy?'

Jimmy smiled that shit-eating grin of his. 'Jeez, Charlie, I'm freezing,' he whined, hugging himself tighter against the biting wind. 'Let's go man.'

When Charlie didn't answer, the weasel tried to seduce him with talk of his Aunt Ethel's good cooking, coffee that burned your mouth, steaks smothered in onions and beds with sweet-smelling sheets. His aunt would take care of them. A God-fearing woman, she would have forgiven Jimmy Ray by now. She'd be glad to see them, he said.

There was only mild puzzlement in Jimmy Ray's eyes when Charlie drew only one oar from its oarlock and stood up in the boat, careful to plant his feet firmly to keep the boat from rocking too much.

Jimmy opened his mouth probably to ask him what the hell he was doing, but the oar was already arcing through the air. It connected with the side of his head in a dull *thunck* Jimmy never heard, leaving a deep dent in his skull, just above his left ear. He had slid bonelessly over in his seat, mouth still open in protest, blood streaming blackly down the side of his face.

Charlie picked him up in his arms and dropped him over the side. Barely made a splash.

But Jimmy Ray didn't sink right away, instead floated just beneath the surface of the water, the moonlight catching his pale eyes, making them seem alive, giving Charlie a creepy feeling. *Son-of-a-bitch can't even die right.*

Using both hands, he'd measured the oar carefully against Jimmy's midsection then gave it a hard thrust. He watched with satisfaction as Jimmy Ray sank out of sight, the water closing over him like a black-silver curtain, just as if Jimmy never was.

Nothing personal, Jimmy old boy. I just like to travel alone.

He was a loner, he thought now as he spread the blanket on the floor for what would be its final purpose. In fact loner was one of the words the media used to describe him. He liked the term; it made him sound special, above needing anyone else. Don't know how he got hooked up with the weasel in the first place. *Downtime, you might say.*

The thumping against the closet door grew more insistent. Regret was heavy in him. She had betrayed him again. This was her own doing.

You're mistaken, Charlie. Just as you were mistaken about the others. She's not Marie. Marie is dead.

'No, you lie,' he railed at the voice inside his head.

★ ★ ★

Hearing his cry, Rachael's skin crawled with fear and dread. Why hadn't he killed her before now? What was he waiting for? She wasn't sure she wanted to know. In fact, she was quite sure she didn't.

I have to get out of here. I have to!

She cried out, a muffled sound through the tape covering her mouth. Her breathing had become shallow, rapid. She was starting to hyperventilate. *Get it together, Rachael.* She concentrated on breathing through her nose, letting it out slowly. She began to feel calmer. She'd been about to give the door another bump with her shoulder when it opened. He was looking down at her, face unreadable.

Then he said, 'I'm going to remove the tape from your mouth. Don't scream. Not that anyone will hear you. But don't.'

She shook her head to reassure him. Neither brutal nor gentle, he peeled off the tape. Her mouth stung briefly, but that was okay. She could breathe. 'Thank you,' she said, voice raspy, dry. 'I have to go to the bathroom.'

He paused then undid the tape from her wrists and ankles. He had to help her to her feet, but she managed to walk to the washroom on her own, albeit on shaky legs. She closed the door after her. Saw that there was no lock. Never mind. The important thing was that she was untied. This might be the last time she was, giving her a one and only chance to escape this madman.

But how?

After relieving herself, Rachael righted her clothes. As she did, her gaze darted around the small space for something to use as a weapon. She was about to give up hope when she spotted a can of Lysol on the floor, half-hidden behind the toilet. She picked it up as if it were a bar of gold. Thank you.

'Hurry up,' her captor said through the door.

'Just a minute.'

Grimly determined and at the same more terrified than she had ever been in her life, Rachael pointed the nozzle of the can at the door, hopefully in line with his eyes. Her finger poised on the button as if it were the trigger of a gun. She willed her hand steady. Even though she was expecting it, when he banged on the door with his fist, she jumped a foot, nearly dropping the can. Fear threatened to engulf her.

Focus, Rachael. Focus. He wouldn't wait long.

She was right about that. When he yanked the door open she depressed the button, aimed directly into his eyes.

Nothing happened.

38

Iris tried Rachael's number for the tenth time. Getting no answer, she replaced the receiver, took to wandering about the living room, trying to decide on the best place to hang the plaque she'd received last night. An activity designed to take her mind off Rachael. It wasn't working.

Iris had practically insisted that Rachael spend the night here last night, rather than going home. Not that it had done any good. Even Peter had raised an eyebrow at his aunt's adamancy. She supposed she could have told Rachael the real reason she didn't want her to be alone in that house — that the *bad feelings* were on full power. But it would only have frightened her and spoiled what had otherwise been a delightful evening.

There are worse things then a spoiled evening, Iris.

She'd heard nothing from Doctor Whittaker since sending him the package. Of course it was Sunday and perhaps he took his day of rest seriously. More likely though he thought she was some kind of crackpot and had tossed her package in the garbage. She prayed that at least he had looked at the photo of Rachael, compared it with the one in the article.

Last week while snapping a few photographs of Rachael's latest work to show Hedda, she'd impulsively snapped one of Rachael. In it, Rachael was wearing the apron, had clay on her hands and a dab on her forehead. But since that was the only photo she had of Rachael, it was the one she'd sent to Doctor Whittaker. Surely he would see the strong resemblance to Marie Morley even if Rachael couldn't.

Iris hung the brass and wood plaque on the wall above the sideboard. Straightening it, she wondered if displaying it on her wall would make her seem pretentious. Well, so be it.

It *had* been a wonderful evening. How elegant Rachael had looked in the winter-white dress, slim as a model, seeming to glow from within. Iris understood part of the reason for the glow, even if Rachael wasn't ready to admit it yet. She was a woman in love.

And what a lovely couple they made. Everyone had said so. Such a long time since she had seen Peter looking so happy, or so dapper. And Rachael had, over these past few months, become like a daughter to her.

Iris went to the window, parted the curtains enough to reveal a smattering of stars in the darkening sky.

Where could she be?

She could be anywhere, she answered her own question. Rachael was an adult, free to come and go as she pleased. True. But it did little to stop her worrying. Maybe she's not feeling well and isn't answering the phone. Or maybe she can't answer it . . .

Iris was getting into her coat when the phone rang. She snapped up the receiver before it could ring twice. But it wasn't Rachael as she'd hoped. It was Elton Sorrel on the phone, informing her that he'd had a call from a Doctor Alan Whittaker, and wanted to drop over and have a talk with her about her friend, Rachael Warren.

Doctor Whittaker must believe there is something to all this to have phoned the police, she thought. As relieved as she was that the doctor had taken the matter seriously, it also frightened her.

Waiting for Elton, she picked up yesterday's unread paper from the sofa, tried to find something interesting enough to distract her until he got here. Didn't find anything.

Iris checked her watch. Ten to seven.

Something is wrong at Rachael's. Something is definitely wrong.

The doorbell rang, and as Iris hurried to answer she detected, ever so faintly, the scent of *Evening in Paris* in the air.

39

From the look on Charlie's face, it was a toss-up which of them had been most surprised when the can of spray proved impotent. A myriad of emotions crossed his features — shock, amusement and finally anger as he snapped the can from her hand and tossed it across the floor

'Another good idea gone bad,' he said in mock sympathy.

The nozzle had been plugged. Why hadn't she had the sense to try it first? How could she have been so stupid? She might have succeeded in blinding him, at least long enough to allow her to escape.

'It's time,' he said. Over her futile struggles he easily lifted her in his arms and carried her to the cot where he slapped another length of tape over her mouth, shutting off her screams. 'Can't have you disturbing the neighbors, can I?' he smirked. 'You have to admit, Marie, I was quite brilliant in the execution of my plan, though in the end it failed. But you have only yourself to blame for that. You know, of course, that it was I who impaled the seagull to your cutting board. I who took the transmitter out of your phone. I put it back when you were in the kitchen making coffee. Just thought you'd like to know.'

The entire time he was retying her wrists and ankles he bragged about his cleverness, by turns cursing her betrayal of him. When he began to wrap her in the moldy-smelling blanket, covering her face with it, Rachael panicked. She struggled frantically to free herself, but it was no use. *Please, no, I don't want to die.*

Her silent pleas went unheard, as minutes later he lifted her in his arms and carried her across the floor, his boots making a hollow sound on the wood. She heard the click of the lock releasing. They were outside now; she could feel the cold night air through the thin blanket as he carried her down a hill. Toward the beach.

'The water in the ditch wasn't deep enough to keep you in the grave,' he said. 'The bay will be.' His mouth pressed against her ear as he whispered through the blanket, 'I love you, Marie.'

Seconds later, she felt herself being lowered, ever so gently, into what she guessed rightly was the bottom of a boat. As he laid her down, a sharp pain stabbed between her shoulder blades, lifted her bodily. Although the lifting was really only in her mind. She tried to cry out but managed only a faint moan through the tape and blanket. He had placed her directly on the point of a protruding nail, which dug savagely into her flesh. Rachael strained to arch herself off the nail, and succeeded to a small degree. She both felt and heard the boat being dragged over the sand, then sliding free into the water. It dipped and swayed as he got in.

They were moving now, boat slicing through the water, waves lapping against the sides. The blanket was rough and scratchy against her face, made worse from the salt of her tears. It was so hard to breathe, suffocating. But she knew that to panic would just make it worse. She must stay calm. There had to be a way to save herself. But how? She was bound hand and foot, wrapped like a mummy in this blanket. She knew that as soon as they were far enough out to suit him, he would simply toss her over the side.

How long did it take to drown? Would her body be found washed up on some rocks too? Or would she never be found, her children never to know what happened to her? This last thought filled her with new determination. She would not die without a fight.

Holding her body above the nail as much as was physically possible, at the same time straining against the tape that bound her wrists under her, she tried to claw at the tape with her fingers, stretching them as far as they would go, but it was no use. The harder she struggled the deeper the nail cut into her back. She tried to roll away from the searing pain, and found some relief in this way. Even in her misery it struck Rachael that if she could just get her wrists positioned over the point of the nail, then maybe she could tear the tape binding them.

She could try. She could at least try. Pushing past the pain, Rachael began inching herself backward, toward the stern. It was a slow and agonizing process, with the nail digging into her back, tearing her flesh in direct proportion to her progress. The tears came of their own accord and she tried to ignore them. She would wait for the fire in her back to subside to a steady flare then start the process again. Stop. Wait. Repeat. All the while praying that her efforts would not be in vain, and that she wouldn't pass out in the meantime. There were moments when the pain was so severe she thought she would go mad.

Inside the blanket, despite being drenched with sweat, every nerve and muscle in her body trembled with exertion.

But at last she was there. Her wrists poised

369

directly over the nail, she was able to force her hands apart just enough to bring the tape down on its point. She repeated this action again and again, each time having to lift herself bodily. Her arms and shoulders ached horribly from her efforts. Efforts that failed more times than they succeeded. Sometimes she missed the tape entirely and the nail would gouge her wrists. If the tape had not been across her mouth, she would not have been able to stop herself from screaming. And above all, she knew she must not alert him.

The boat must be leaking. She felt water seeping up through the blanket and her clothes, chill against her skin. But, intent on her mission, she was barely mindful of it. Once more, arching her back, Rachael brought the tape binding her wrists down on the nail. And again. Beyond thinking now, driven, the pulsing pain in her back distant from her, yet at the same time was a constant, familiar shrieking to which she had grown accustomed.

The realization that the boat had stopped moving came suddenly, jarring her into full awareness. She heard wood scraping against metal as he drew the oars up through their oarlocks. Terror made her light-headed, and she feared she was going to pass out after all. She breathed in, closed her eyes. *You are not going to pass out. Keep going. Don't stop now!*

Once more, she arched her back, brought the tape down on the nail. *Hurry! Oh, please, hurry!* Again. And at last, felt a small rip in the fabric, a loosening. Afraid to believe, for a moment she did not move. Then, with a single, outward jerk of her hands, her wrists parted from one another. Her hands were free.

Her back felt like it was being systematically scalded with hot pokers, but she could bear the pain. She had succeeded. Rachael tried to quiet her labored breathing as she heard him say, 'Far enough.' She fought back fresh panic. The boat began to rock, and she knew he had stood. And then, once more, she felt herself being lifted in his arms.

Heart thudding in her chest, Rachael steeled herself for the icy waters. She tried to gauge her chances of making it back to shore. How far out were they? Half a mile? Farther? She'd been so intent on freeing her hands that time was lost to her. It could have been an hour that she was in the boat, or fifteen minutes. But she was a good swimmer, or at least she used to be. And she was strong from all the running. She could make it. *I have to make it.* Time stood still. Why wasn't he throwing her in? What was he waiting for? In horrible answer, she felt herself being lowered back down onto the bottom of the boat. As he unwrapped the blanket from her, her heart sank like a rock into the sea. But still she kept her hands tight together behind her back, praying he wouldn't notice they were no longer bound. But when he turned her onto her stomach, she knew he had somehow guessed, and that she was going to die. Her last chance to escape this madman was gone.

'Clever,' he said softly. 'Almost fooled me.' He tore a strip from the blanket to retie her hands. 'This is your own doing, you know that, don't you?'

So you keep saying.

You're not tied yet, Rachael. If you let him succeed in doing that, it really will be over. There was still a chance. Slim, but a chance. Her timing would have to be perfect. Bracing herself in both mind and body, every nerve taut as a cat about to pounce, she focused on a single move, visualized it. As he reached for her hands, she executed it. With every ounce of strength she could summon, Rachael reared up hard and fast, catching him full in the chest. With a grunt of surprise, Charlie flew backward in the boat. Without hesitation, Rachael was over the side.

Nothing could have prepared her for the icy waters of the Bay as they closed over her, freezing the breath in her lungs, dragging her down into its green depths, thundering in her ears. Her clothes were weights that pulled her deeper. She kicked frantically to bring herself back up. As she broke the surface, gasped in air, something hard glanced off her shoulder, bringing a flash of pain. The oar slashed down again, missing her by inches, chopping the water beside her. She ducked under again, at the same time ripping the tape from her mouth. She swam hard away from the boat, resurfaced about twenty yards away, lungs bursting for air. She gulped it. Held the last breath. This time when she went under, she brought her legs up in a crunch and fumbled at the tape around her ankles, trying to remove it, but only managed to sink deeper. Her fingers were clumsy and stiff from the numbingly cold water. Twice more she resurfaced, coughing up salt water, gasping for air. But at last the tape was off, and floated away from her like some strange water snake.

The boat was maybe six yards from her. He wasn't rowing now, just sitting there, watching her, enjoying her helplessness. She used the moment's reprieve to rid herself of shoes and jacket.

Along the stretch of shoreline, an occasional light shone from a window, beckoning to her. Her own house was in darkness. She could just make out its shape against the darker woods, and the inky blue sky scattered with stars.

He was rowing after her. She swam, every stroke a reminder of where the oar had struck her shoulder. Thankfully, it had been a glancing blow, and wouldn't halt her progress significantly.

'You'll never make it back to shore, Marie,' he called out to her. 'Get back in the boat. I won't hurt you.' His insane laughter chilled her even more than the water. A little closer and he could finish her off with the oar if he chose to. She was swimming as fast as she could but she knew she was only buying time. Because the bottom line was, he could row faster than she could swim. Still, she swam.

★ ★ ★

He rested the oars. Charlie was taking his time. In no hurry. Even though the wind's blade cut through his clothes, the way it had the weasel's the night they rowed across from Harding. The night it all began. It had all led him here, to this moment. It was fated. Her death would free him.

She was about thirty yards from him now; he could just see her head above the dark

374

water, pale arms emerging alternately from the choppy waves. He smiled to himself and reached once more for the oars.

And then he saw something that filled him with stark terror.

★ ★ ★

Daring a look behind her, Rachael was surprised at how far away from the boat she had managed to swim. And even more surprised to see Charlie standing up in the boat. He appeared to be taking bows before an unseen audience, looking as absurd as a character in a cartoon. Up and down he went, up and down. *What is he doing?* And then she noticed how low the boat was in the water, and she knew.

Treading water, she continued to watch him bail water from the boat with what appeared to be only his cupped hands. From the frantic dipping and rising of his body, she could only assume the water was coming in faster than Charlie could scoop it out. Like viewing a surreal movie, she saw her tormentor shift his weight from one side of the boat to the other until suddenly, and predictably, it flipped over, sending Charlie into the bay, leaving her with a vague sense of astonishment. For several long seconds, she did not see him at all. Suddenly he reappeared, reaching for the upturned boat.

'Help me, Marie,' he cried out. 'Help me. I can't swim.'

She could not quite believe what she was hearing and seeing. This unexpected turn of events disoriented her. They did not seem real. None of it seemed real. Rachael looked back toward the shore. Strangely, it did not seem quite so far away as it had only moments ago. There was a faint throbbing in her shoulder, but nothing she couldn't handle. The cold water acted as a balm on her nail-torn flesh.

She resumed swimming, her strokes cutting strong and sure through the choppy waves, taking her farther and farther from him. When next she looked back she could no longer see him in the darkness. But his pitiful cries reached out to her. 'Please. Help me.'

She rested, moving her arms and legs just enough to stay afloat. Can this be happening? Is it possible? The questions came with something more akin to amazement than relief. But relief did come, in a rush, like a damn bursting inside her and she was laughing — a hysterical laugh that quickly turned to sobs, so violent they caused her to swallow water, sobering her. She turned her back to him and once more, directing all her attention on the shoreline and the faint outline of her house, she swam toward home and safety.

Behind her, Charlie's terrified cries pulled at her like hateful magnets. They wouldn't let her be. She tried not to hear them. *To hell with you. Die, you crazy bastard. Like you wanted me dead. Like you killed the others.* She swam hard, intent only on putting more distance between them, on reaching shore. Determined not to hear him.

But his cries, so like a child's in their terror had already crept inside her mind and set up a terrible din she could not ignore. They pulled at her conscience making her break her rhythm. She tried harder to block them out, to push on. But it was no use. Though she raged at him, the deeper part of her simply could not allow her to leave another human being to die and do nothing to help. Whether or not he deserved her help seemed to have little to do with it.

But what if it was a trick? What if he could swim, after all, and was just play-acting? But she didn't think so. Even so, he was crazy. He would drown them both. *You can't help him. You can't go back. You have to try to save yourself.*

She swam.

Soon, she could no longer hear his cries,

and sensed he was gone.

She kept on swimming. And swimming.

Then, exhausted, she treaded water. She looked toward shore and wondered how she could have made so little headway. She was shivering. She tried to estimate how long she had been out here. A half hour? Two hours? No, not that long. But she couldn't be sure. She did know that shivering meant her body was trying to keep itself warm; she remembered that from a first-aid course she'd taken in high school, a lifetime ago. And yet, only yesterday.

Buffeted by the icy waves, Rachael felt like so much flotsam in the black undulating water. A wave washed strands of hair into her eyes, stinging them with the salt water. She raked them away. But for the sound of the waves, and the keening of the wind, all else was silent. The world seemed far, far away. She might have been on another planet.

She was so very tired. Whatever strength she'd possessed was gone, siphoned away as surely as if a hose had been attached to her body, draining the life force from it. It shamed her to think that even for a moment, when her marriage crumbled, she had not wanted to live. For life had never seemed so precious as it did at this moment, nor so fragile. Soon, the sea would claim her too, as it had claimed Charlie.

Don't give up, Rachael. You can make it.

She looked around her to see who had spoken? It had sounded like her grandmother's voice. She listened, but there was only the grumblings of the bay, the wind and her own breathing. And then the voice spoke again. 'Swim,' it told her. But her grandmother's voice was not *out there;* it was inside her own head. Yet somehow not hers. Soft, insistent.

You must fight for your life as you have always done. Swim, Rachael.

She blinked water from her eyes, pushed away the sodden tendrils of hair plastered to her face.

Swim.

'I can't.'

You can. You must.

She heard herself whisper 'yes.' After maybe a dozen strokes, she knew it was no use. She had no strength in her arms. Nothing left.

Don't think. Push beyond the pain. You did before. Do it now.

Yes, I must try. Find the zone, stay in it. Like I do when I'm running.

And for a time it worked.

Grimly concentrating, Rachael swam, and kept swimming until her arms began to feel like slabs of concrete. Then she treaded water again.

The shore blurred in her vision, seemed a hundred miles away. Land glimpsed in the distance. So far from her reach. How could that be?

40

Captain Sorrel had scarcely brought the car to a stop when Iris bolted from the passenger seat, bounded up the porch steps. For an old gal, she's in damn good shape, he thought, a tad slower in getting out of the car himself.

Rachael's Cavalier was in the yard. There was no night-light on, and the house itself was in darkness. Iris felt an awful dread even as she rang the doorbell, already sensing there was no one in the house.

'Rachael,' she called out. But there was no answer; she hadn't really expected one. Still, she called out her name again, pounded on the door, a hollow demand for her to be all right.

Elton swept the powerful beam of his flashlight along the ground by the edge of the house. Minutes later he was standing beside Iris on the porch. 'There are fresh footprints under the kitchen window, Iris. The window's unlocked. Looks like someone got in that way,' he added unnecessarily.

'Oh, dear God . . .'

'I think this situation warrants the breaking of a rule or two,' the captain said. It took two hard kicks to the door before it flew open.

Inside, they were met with ominous silence. She followed Elton into the kitchen, where a telling puddle of water beneath the window confirmed Elton's suspicions of how the intruder had gained entry. They searched upstairs and down, but there was no sign of Rachael. Of anyone.

Where was she? What had he done to her? Iris looked around the kitchen as if the answer might be written on the walls, or on a refrigerator door magnet. Elton was talking into his cell phone, his back partly toward her to prevent her hearing. It didn't.

In the living room, Iris saw the crumpled up note on the end table. She unfolded it, read it and passed it to Elton with a hand not quite steady. After reading the note, the policeman slipped it into a plastic bag, sealed it. They went outside just in time to see Peter driving up. As he hurried toward them, Iris could see her own fear reflected in her nephew's eyes.

'Aunt Iris. Captain. What's going on? I've been trying to call Rach — '

'Something terrible has happened, Peter.' Iris tried to stop her voice from shaking. 'Martin Dunn, the man Rachael rented the cabin to is not a photographer at all, as he claimed. He's a murderer. He murdered his own sister. He also killed Heather.'

'What? What are you talking — '

'We don't know that for certain, Iris,' Captain Sorrel cut in. 'But — well, it does seem that Martin Dunn and Charlie Morley are one and the same person, Peter. But we're only guessing here.'

But Iris wasn't guessing. She knew. Everything added up to it. The vision she'd had of the girl, the article, Rachael resembling Marie Morley — everything.

'Martin Dunn is actually the name of Morley's biological father,' Elton said. 'He apparently saw his parents' names on some papers when he was a kid. He never searched for either of his birth parents as far as anyone knows, but he did remember the name. When he got out of the nuthouse, he used it for his own. A private joke, I suppose. At least, that's his shrink's story. And it's a long, involved one,' he said to the confused man before him. 'Enough to say he's a murderer.'

'And he has Rachael, Peter,' Iris said, her own voice breaking.

'No.' A single word of denial — denial of the unthinkable.

'Sorry,' Sorrel said. 'Wish I had more time for tact, folks. But your friend is in serious trouble. I'm going to check out the cabin. I've already called for backup.'

'I'm going with you,' Peter said.

'No, he could have a weapon. It's better if — '

'You've got a gun. Use it if you have to. I'm going, damn it, Elton.'

'Me too,' Iris said. 'I'll get another flashlight.'

'Great,' Sorrel muttered, but he didn't argue further.

As the three made their way up through the woods to the cabin, Peter and Iris walking behind Captain Sorrel, Iris recalled the words Rachael had used in describing her tenant: 'Too good to be true.' *Oh, dear Lord, why wasn't I listening?* Even at the dinner last night, the bad feelings had churned inside her like some foul witch's brew. A couple of times when someone spoke to her, it was as if the voice had come from far off, out of some other dark and alien dimension.

The cabin came into view. Elton moved toward it warily, gun drawn, his other hand waving them back, telling them to come no further.

But it was evident that no one was inside. The door to the cabin was wide open. The first thing Iris saw was the overturned chair on the floor, strips of tape still clinging to the arms and legs. The sight restricted her ability to take a complete breath.

As soon as they stepped inside, Iris saw what looked like a pair of women's gloves lying on the floor. Rachael's? Last night, Rachael had casually mentioned that her good leather gloves were missing. Her daughter had given them to her, she said. Iris' gaze shifted to the Lysol can on the floor, to the cigarette butts overflowing in the sardine can by the cot. The place reeked of stale cigarette smoke. She looked back at the gloves, took a step in their direction.

'Don't touch anything,' Elton ordered. He was down on one knee shining the flashlight over the blade of a shovel propped against the wall, behind the stove. 'Looks like blood,' he said to no one in particular.

'Oh, no . . . '

The note of horror in her whispered words made him look up. 'It's dried, Iris. Been there a while.' Leaving the shovel, he checked out the washroom and broom closet, retrieved an olive green boot from the closet floor. Holding it up gingerly by its top, he looked questioningly at them.

'Sure as hell looks like one of Hartley's,' Peter said hoarsely. 'Why did they let this bastard out if they knew he was a cold-blooded killer?'

He'd asked the same question himself. 'From my conversation with Whittaker, I gather Morley could be downright charming when it suited him. He was crazy, but apparently not stupid. He told them what they wanted to hear, so they figured he was better and let him go. Shrinks like to think they cured you. Makes them feel god-like.'

Peter shook his head at the comment and went outside, returning a few minutes later. 'George's boat's missing.'

'That right?' Sorrel said, frowning, but making no immediate connection between Peter's news and the missing woman.

'Just the two sawhorses left that it was sitting on.'

'Kids, you think?'

Peter shrugged. 'Who else would bother with that old siv?'

The singular thought struck the three of them simultaneously: Charlie Morley would have no way of knowing the condition of George's old boat.

41

Like a child learning to swim, Rachael splashed feebly at the water. Ineffective, clumsy efforts at best. She was so tired. She wanted only to sleep. Just close her eyes and sleep forever. So tired. So very tired.

Stop moving your arms and you'll just slip away. It will be over.

Just then a rogue wave crashed overhead, nearly taking her under. When it subsided, she gulped in precious air and knew how badly she wanted to live. *I want to get to know Peter better. To become a better artist. I want to hold my grandchildren.*

Yes. And you will. Her grandmother's voice again.

I'm not so sure, Emily.

She pushed on even though her efforts now were barely moving her forward. It was not long until her arms refused to lift out of the water at all, until she could not feel her legs. She floated on her back for a time, stared at the upside down bowl of stars, fragmented in her blurred vision. She was moving her arms just enough to keep her from drifting farther away from shore.

In her darkest moments when letting go seemed the easy choice, even the welcome choice, the voice would return to her, urging her on. Encouraging her. But the voice was growing fainter now and she had to strain to hear it. Her arms and legs kept moving as if with a will of their own. But barely. Now and then she would call for help, but she was no longer sure if she was making any sound. Thought and memory flitted through her mind like birds on the wing — like blue jays darting from tree to tree. Images of Peter laughing, of Iris brushing green paint onto the rim of a bowl. Of her children creating play dough creatures at the kitchen table back in Deering. She moved as if in a dream. Once, she even imagined she heard a siren.

Then, ever so faintly, she heard the drone of what sounded like an outboard motor. She must be hallucinating. Everything had an unreal quality about it, like in the grey zone between sleep and waking.

But the drone was louder now. In her dreamlike state, she turned her head in the direction of the sound, and saw a yellow light bobbing above the surface, speeding through the night toward her, growing larger and larger as it came closer, like a huge yellow sun. She blinked her eyes, expecting it to disappear again, merely a mirage to further torment her. But it didn't disappear. Rachael tried to raise an arm to signal where she was, but managed only to slip beneath the water. Resurfacing, coughing the salt water, she cried out weakly, 'I'm here. I'm here.'

Minutes later, familiar, gentle hands were lifting her from the water and helping her into a boat. As those same hands wrapped her in something warm, she heard Peter say, 'Hit it, Captain.' He held her close, murmuring 'You're safe now, Rachael. It's over.'

His reassuring words repeating themselves in her heart, and at last she gave herself over to the blessed oblivion of nothingness.

42

Rachael remained in hospital for four days recovering from severe hypothermia and exhaustion. Ironically, Greg was up on the next floor, in intensive care, following the removal of his spleen. She went to visit him two weeks later and was relieved to see that he was almost back to his old self, even to flirting with one of the young nurses. Clearly, there would be other Lisas.

He had wanted her back not because he loved her, though he insisted that he did, but because she represented safety to him. As Jenny's Cove had represented safety to her. But she knew now that the only real safety came from within.

Fingerprints lifted from the cabin proved beyond doubt that Martin Dunn and Charlie Morley were indeed one and the same person. Other connections were made, linking him to the murder of a number of women, Heather Myers among them.

The body that washed up on the beach turned out to be that of Jimmy Ray Dawson, the Bates' nephew. From the large gash in his head, it was clear he hadn't come to Jenny's

Cove alone. The general consensus was that he'd met up with Charlie Morley at some point. Iris thought Jimmy Ray might have lured him here with talk of his uncle's hidden stash. Maybe Morley decided he didn't want to share. Or maybe Jimmy Ray just knew too much about him.

Sadly, it was not to be the end of the horror.

Two weeks later police found the remains of Hartley McLeod buried in the woods. Almost within the hour of finding him, Luke died. As if he knew and passed on to serve his master on a different plane. Some people believed such things were possible. Rachael was one of them.

Epilogue

Snow was falling outside her living room window. A fire crackled and snapped in the fireplace. Carols played on the new stereo, a gift from her children.

'You always did have the best tree on the block, Mom,' Susan said. Jeff, his arm around a very pregnant Nancy, agreed a little too heartily over his mug of rum-laced eggnog. They were all coping as best they could with the divorce. It would take time. Jeff, Nancy and Susan would be spending New Years with Greg in his new condo. Greg's coming so close to death himself had softened his son's heart toward him, made forgiveness possible.

The new brown and white wriggly puppy she'd named Teddy, Peter's gift to her, was ecstatically wrestling with a piece of wrapping paper, delighting everyone with his antics.

Betty's poinsettia brightened the corner by the door. They didn't see much of one another now. Perhaps because Rachael was a different person from the one Betty knew, the dynamics of their relationship had changed. But the bond would always remain.

She was blessed. Even the nightmares were

coming less frequently. Now and then, Rachael wondered if it really was her grandmother's voice she heard out there on the water that night, or if she'd merely conjured it out of a sheer will to survive.

She would never know for sure. And somehow it didn't matter.

We do hope that you have enjoyed reading
this large print book.

Did you know that all of our titles
are available for purchase?

We publish a wide range of high quality
large print books including:
Romances, Mysteries, Classics
General Fiction
Non Fiction and Westerns

Special interest titles available in
large print are:
The Little Oxford Dictionary
Music Book
Song Book
Hymn Book
Service Book

Also available from us courtesy of Oxford
University Press:
Young Readers' Dictionary
(large print edition)
Young Readers' Thesaurus
(large print edition)

For further information or a free
brochure, please contact us at:
Ulverscroft Large Print Books Ltd.,
The Green, Bradgate Road, Anstey,
Leicester, LE7 7FU, England.
Tel: (00 44) 0116 236 4325
Fax: (00 44) 0116 234 0205

NOWHERE TO HIDE

Joan Hall Hovey

Rage at her younger sister's brutal murder has nearly consumed Ellen Harris. So when her work as a psychologist wins her an appearance on the evening news, Ellen seizes the moment. Staring straight into the camera, she challenges the killer to come out of hiding. Phone calls flood the station, but all leads go nowhere. Then it happens: a note, written in red ink, slipped under the windshield wipers of her car. 'YOU'RE IT.' Ellen has stirred the monster in his lair — and the hunter has become the hunted!

LISTEN TO THE SHADOWS

Joan Hall Hovey

When artist Katie Summers emerged from a four-day coma, she remembered vividly the horror of that night — the terrifying dead eyes that had stared back at her in the rear view mirror, causing her to crash her car. But no one believed her. Released from the hospital, Katie took a taxi to her remote farmhouse on Black Lake. Darkness had already fallen. There was only the wind in the trees to greet her — and the cold, empty house. But the house was not quite empty. Something awaited her, upstairs in her bedroom. Something with cold, dead eyes . . .

HALLOWED GROUND

Margaret James

In 1984, Alex Colborn and Helen Tremain were contemporaries: graduates from the same college course, and following a similar career. And Alex was also in love. Renting a decrepit, about-to-be demolished Jacobean townhouse, they intended to begin a new life together. What they hadn't bargained on, however, was the obsessive and violent jealousy of Helen's ex-boyfriend, Thomas Stenton. Now, years later, Alex and Helen have not spoken since they lost touch after the last time Thomas came to the house. But the consequences of Alex's past actions lie buried on a site of national heritage . . .

A VISIBLE DARKNESS

Jonathon King

Max Freeman is seeking refuge from the demons of his former life. But his self-imposed isolation in a shack deep in the Everglades is interrupted when he receives a desperate call from his best friend, attorney Billy Manchester. There has been a string of homicides — all elderly women from a poor neighbourhood, and all with sizable and recently sold-off insurance policies — which the police have been unable, or unwilling, to investigate. To help his friend, Max must reluctantly pry where he's not wanted, and act like the cop he's trying to forget he was. To discover an unseen killer, he will confront the dark corners of his own past.